LORIAL & NESTRAYA

AN ELVEN HEARTBOUND NOVEL

ELIZABETH ASH

This is a work of fiction. Names, characters, places, and incidents either are the product of the author's imagination or are used fictitiously. Any resemblance to actual persons, living or dead, events, or locales is entirely coincidental.

Copyright ©2021 by Elizabeth Ash

All rights reserved.

No portion of this book may be reproduced or used in any manner without written permission from the copyright owner, except for the use of quotations in a book review and as permitted by U.S. copyright law.

ISBN: 978-1-961510-01-2

Published by Beauty & Ashes Publishing

www.elizabethash.com

CONTENTS

Dedication		VII
Note to Readers		IX
The World of Elven Heartbound		X
1.	A Fallen King	1
2.	The Tree of Memories	7
3.	A Council of Kings	13
4.	Chosen Family	19
5.	The Barracks	25
6.	Council of Elders	31
7.	First Nestraya	37
8.	Emerald Eyes	45
9.	Meeting of the Seconds	51
10.	March Through the Woods	57
11.	Alone	65
12.	Stone Magic	71

13.	The King's Elite Warriors	77
14.	Ceasefire	83
15.	For Our King	89
16.	Heartlanding	97
17.	Distracted	103
18.	Warrior Leathers	111
19.	Flying Lessons	117
20.	Warrior Training	123
21.	I Am Who I Am	129
22.	Recharging	135
23.	To Climb a Tree	141
24.	You Belong to Me	147
25.	A Different Kind of Motivation	153
26.	Westaria	159
27.	Burning	165
28.	Standing on Air	171
29.	Sparks and Waterfalls	177
30.	Not Ashamed	183
31.	Starhaven	189
32.	Unwritten Rules	195
33.	Become the Wind	203
34.	Slay Your Demons	209

35. Magic and Promises	217
36. Life Magic	225
37. Queen of Lostariel	231
38. Practice Sessions	237
39. Approaching Magic	243
40. The Outerlanders	249
41. The Hope of Lostariel	257
42. A Formidable Force	263
43. For Restoval	269
44. How the Story Goes	275
45. Aftermath	281
46. Stardust	287
47. Sleep Well, My Love	293
48. Stronger Together	299
Epilogue	303
Elven Heartbound	309
My Time or Yours	310
A Dance of Sand and Magic	312
Did Someone Say Bonus Content?	313
Thank You!	314
About the Author	316

For Lucy
This one is mine
And you are beautiful and smart and amazing
You are enough

Note to Readers

Lorial & Nestraya is the standalone prequel novel to the bestselling *Elven Heartbound* serial. It's meant to be a complete story all on its own, so while the epilogue does lead into the premise for *Elven Heartbound*, you don't need to worry about a cliffhanger ending. Thanks for reading, and I'll see you in the heartlanding! -Elizabeth xoxo

1
A FALLEN KING

"It's time, Lorial."

Lorial looks up from the map on his father's desk. Mother stands in the doorway, and the pain in her eyes mirrors his own grief.

"You need to be strong now, my son. For our people. They will take their strength from you."

Lorial says nothing as he folds the map and replaces it in a drawer before following Mother from Father's study.

His study now.

As he passes through the doorway, Mother hands him a large earthen jar, and he clutches it to his chest.

"My king." Nestraya waits in the corridor, ready to guard Lorial as he visits the Tree of Memories, as all new Lostarien kings must do.

As the closest friend Lorial has ever known, Nestraya's presence is a comfort. She was brought into the king's family as an orphan when Lorial was only a child. Now they're both grown, and she stands guard over him as a Third among Father's warrior elves.

His warrior elves.

Her words land on him with an awkwardness borne of unfamiliarity. Newness. And a distancing between them that leaves Lorial unsettled.

My king.

The title should have belonged to Father far longer than it did.

"Thank you for doing this," Lorial says, and Nestraya nods.

"It is my honor to accompany you on this journey."

Lorial studies her. Her long black hair, plaited in a single braid, hangs just past her shoulders. It used to stretch nearly to her waist, but she cut the tail when her king fell, as they all did.

Lorial's own silver hair barely brushes his shoulders now.

Little does it matter. His hair will soon grow again as Lostariel moves on without her king. As will Nestraya's and that of all the elves who honored the ancient tradition.

The old generations give way to new ones, and time speeds on regardless.

"What is it, my king?" Nestraya asks.

Lorial turns his gaze back to the corridor in front of him. "Nothing. Shall we begin?"

With a nod, Nestraya follows Lorial and his mother as they make their way out of Windhaven House, the royal residence in Darlei, the elven city closest to the Nunian border.

Or what's left of Windhaven. Nunian soldiers burned part of the tree-grown residence to the ground before the elves fought them back to the border of the Wildthorne Woods.

Elves with plant magic have already begun repairs.

It was the same night Father's most elite band of elf warriors got cut off and cut down by the soldiers as they fled.

Did the humans know who it was they killed that night in their retreat? By the time Lorial and Nestraya found Father lying in a pool of his own crimson blood, not even a heartbinding could have saved him.

And as Father passed from the light while clutched to Lorial's chest, the elf prince became the elf king at the tender age of thirty-two.

That night, Father's sticky red blood seeped from the wound near his heart as Lorial pressed his hands over the gaping hole and begged Nestraya to save him. The memory assaults Lorial now as their boots clack on the floor with each heavy step. The smell—sweet and coppery—is still burned into his nose.

It took an hour for him to scrub the blood from his hands once Nestraya dragged him back to Windhaven, and Mother, always full of strength, looked him in the eyes and told him there would be time to mourn later.

For now, he must be strong. Their kingdom is depending on it.

The acrid odor of lingering smoke and ash assails them as they pass through the burned portion of Windhaven House on their way to the Tree of Memories.

Darlei. The City of Kings.

Normally, a new elf king would travel from the capital city of Celesta at the heart of the Wildthorne Woods to Darlei to lay his father's ashes at the base of the Tree of Memories and take his own place among the Kings of Lostariel.

Lorial need only travel the short path from Windhaven to the sacred tree.

A line of elves has already gathered on either side of the road he'll walk, and the sight slows his steps.

"Be strong, my son," Mother says, and Lorial pushes his feet forward again.

As they tread the path toward the Tree of Memories, Mother slows her own steps. This is not a journey she can make with Lorial. Lorial walks alone as his companions follow at a distance. The elves gathered along the path turn their palms skyward as he passes.

"Be at peace on this last journey." Over and over, the elves whisper the traditional words as Lorial walks among them, carrying his father's ashes. Their voices rise in a lilting chorus, and he clutches the urn more tightly to his chest as the elves of Lostariel pay their final respects to the king whose reign was far too brief.

Nestraya stays on high alert as she watches over Lorial. Her life magic traces the path around him, searching for anything or anyone out of place, but only the familiar essences of elves greet her. It's challenging to sense anything around Lorial's powerful air magic. No humans are nearby that she can detect, though she doesn't lower her defenses.

Something about Restoval's death still niggles at her—a sense that all is not as it seems. With little more than a vague feeling of unease to go by, though, she dares not say anything to Lorial. Not yet, anyway.

Tonight, she will simply keep him safe as he journeys into the Tree of Memories. Perhaps, somehow, he will receive a morsel of truth while entranced that will either confirm or allay her suspicions.

She was surprised at first when he chose her to hold the magic for him. She's merely a Third. Surely someone of higher rank would have been better suited for the role. Perhaps he wanted to do this with as few people as possible. Few elves bear dual affinities for plant and life magic, and both types are required to access the Tree of Memories.

Other than his mother, Nestraya is now the closest thing the young king has to family, and that likely influenced his choice as well.

Nestraya's parents struggled for hundreds of years to conceive, and they were already aged when she was born. Some elves speculated that her mother made a deal with the powerful Lothlesi people to open her barren womb, and that's why Nestraya was born with more magic at her command than any other elf alive today. Dual affinities are rare among low-born elves, like Nestraya's parents.

Nestraya wields the magic of three elements.

It was why she was brought to the king as a child when her parents died of old age. Because she was an anomaly.

And Restoval, the crown prince at the time, soon to become king, welcomed her into his home. Into his life.

Into his family.

The daughter he never had.

She received the best of everything. Training. Education. Opportunities to shine.

Losing him was like losing her own father all over again.

Perhaps that's why Lorial chose her to accompany him. Her grief mirrors his own, even if she can't claim the former king as her father.

She loved him like one.

As Lorial approaches the ancient willow, his skin blanches, though he gives no other outward sign of the struggle warring within him. His shortened hair still catches Nestraya off guard whenever she looks his way, as it has since he cut it two days ago. The same feeling overtakes her every time she looks at her own reflection in the mirror.

Lorial stops in front of the tree and turns to face his people. The youngest king in Lostarien history.

He looks strong. From the outside.

But to Nestraya's eyes, he seems lost.

Lorial searches her out, and she steps toward him and the willow tree that looms behind him, its drooping branches guarding the secrets it hides.

The Tree of Memories.

Nestraya reads the beckoning in Lorial's gaze, and she stops beside him. The branches won't part for her. Only for him. And when they do, his right to claim his father's throne will be established. His rule absolute. And the tree will respond to the magic of anyone the king grants entry to this sacred place. To Nestraya, as she temporarily joins Lorial's life force to that of the Tree of Memories using her life and plant magic.

What he will see there is a secret he can never share. Not in this world, at least. It is rumored that all secrets are laid bare in the heartlanding for those who are heartbound.

Hopefully, this new King of Lostariel will never face an injury grave enough to warrant a heartbinding.

As Nestraya stands at Lorial's side, she lays her hand on his arm so the willow will grant her entry as well. Together, they face the Tree of Memories. The air hangs thick around them, and Lorial's knuckles are white where he clutches the urn carrying his father's ashes. Gingerly, he releases his hold with one hand and reaches toward the willow.

Holding her breath, Nestraya waits for the branches to part. The chanting of their kin has ceased, and the distant sound of frogs croaking and crickets chirping is all that breaks the silence.

Then, slowly, with a soft creaking, the tree's branches open to receive her new king.

2
THE TREE OF MEMORIES

As the branches part, a soft gasp rises from the crowd behind Lorial and Nestraya. For a moment, Lorial stares into the misty underside of the sacred tree.

"We face this together, my king," Nestraya says softly.

Her words both soothe and rankle Lorial.

"With you, at least, may I simply be myself?" he whispers so no one else can hear.

Nestraya stiffens. "The gulf between us—"

"Is little more than a construct. Please, Nestraya. We are family, are we not?" He glances down at her where her lips press into a thin line, and he sighs.

Always so cognizant of her low birth, as if her adoption into the royal family meant nothing.

Father would have disagreed.

"Shall we?" Lorial asks when she doesn't respond.

She nods, and he steps forward while she clings to his arm. One step and then another as the mist floats around them. Then, with another soft creaking, the branches fall back into place, and Lorial and Nestraya are alone within the circle of the Tree of Memories.

A soft glow appears ahead where the trunk of the massive tree rises from the forest floor. Lorial stares at it.

"We're to approach the light," Nestraya says softly.

At least she didn't call him king that time.

If only Father had explained more about this tradition to Lorial. They all assumed they would have more time. Father was barely past his two-hundredth birthday. Young still, for an elf. Strong. No one expected him to be cut down in his prime.

So many things Father had yet to tell Lorial.

"I don't know what to do," Lorial admits.

"I do." Nestraya guides him toward the light, and he lets her lead him. "Your father explained the joining ceremony to me several years ago. I'll walk you through as much of it as I can."

Lorial looks at her in surprise. Father told Nestraya and not him? Perhaps Father meant for her to guide Lorial on this journey all along.

The thought is a comforting one.

The closer they get to the ancient tree, the less the mist obscures their vision. The magic of the ground upon which they tread shows itself in the tiny flowers that glow like fireflies in the dark, illuminating their path. The flowers dance in the breeze, though the air lies still around Lorial. He ought to know—he has the power to command the wind, as his father did before him. Whatever breeze the flowers sway to, it exists only in their magical essences.

Lorial returns his attention to the tree as the silhouette of the trunk becomes clearer, no longer shrouded in mist. The glow emanates from a large knot in the center of the trunk, as if a branch was sheared off and magic left in its place.

It seems wrong to speak within such a sacred setting, but Lorial turns to Nestraya, anyway. "What am I to do?"

"Place your hand in the light. The tree should speak to you."

Lorial knits his brows at the oddness of the suggestion, but he does as she says, and words immediately fill his mind. Not spoken so he can hear them, but clearly conveyed nonetheless.

It is sooner than we anticipated.

Lorial glances at Nestraya. Is he supposed to respond?

Nestraya nods, and he turns his attention back to the tree.

"It is sooner than any of us anticipated, my sacred tree."

Indeed. Only fifteen years have passed since we first welcomed Restoval into our presence. A mere moment for us. Yet we sense his essence returning to us as his fathers did before him.

Lorial swallows at the tree's words. "Yes, my sacred tree. I bear the ashes of Restoval."

Never has a bearer of the king's essence come to us so young.

"I have great need of your wisdom." The light surrounding Lorial's hand has grown warm but not painfully so. It's a comfortable heat. Soothing.

Knowledge we can share, our young king. And truth. How you choose to use it is up to you.

"May I use it wisely, my sacred tree."

Not all do. We sense a purity of will in you, though, Lorial of Lostariel. And a humble, quiet strength. Is this your magic-bearer standing beside you? The power she exudes is blinding.

When Lorial glances at Nestraya again, nothing about her seems out of the ordinary. Is it possible the tree senses magic as light? If so, Nestraya would indeed be blinding.

"This is Nestraya. My...*estrassa*."

Nestraya turns wide green eyes toward Lorial but says nothing.

Surely she knows he views her as his chosen family. His *estrassa*. The only bond closer is that between binding partners.

Curious.

Lorial turns back to the light. What does that signify?

Restoval spoke of his estrassa *as well. He meant her for you.*

"He...what?"

This displeases you, our young king? That is difficult to believe. We can sense the threads woven between the words you do not speak. You long for more from her.

Lorial nearly drops the urn.

Curious.

This time, the tree doesn't elaborate.

"To whom exactly am I speaking, my sacred tree?" Lorial eventually asks as he pushes thoughts of Nestraya aside.

To the combined essences of your fathers before you, of course, our young king. Their memories and magic joined together as one voice. Today, the essence of Restoval will be added to our number.

Lorial stills. "Will I be able to speak to my father?"

It is but a representation, our young king. A manifestation of memories. Of a person's essence. There is no magic that would bring Restoval back.

No, of course not. Lorial deflates a little. Still, his father's wisdom, available to him here, in this place? No wonder Father frequently visited the tree when he sojourned in Darlei.

"What must I do, my sacred tree?" Lorial asks.

Your magic-bearer will guide you through the process, our young king. We wish you to understand that the joining which happens today will only happen this one time. You may converse with us whenever you choose, but never again will you be allowed to join your essence to ours until your own son carries your ashes beneath our branches.

His own son? Lorial glances at Nestraya. "I understand."

Then we are ready to welcome Restoval's essence back into our midst with you to accompany him on this final journey.

The light suddenly flickers out, and Lorial lowers his hand. "The Tree of Memories said—"

A lump forms in his throat, and Nestraya eyes him curiously. "What is it?"

"I can't speak of it." No matter how hard he tries, the words lodge in his throat.

"It's all right, Lorial," she says softly. "Your father was limited in what he could tell me as well. Are you ready to continue?"

Lorial exhales in relief and nods. "I'll need you to guide me."

"Of course. Remove the lid from the urn and set it aside."

He does as she instructs, and then, maintaining her handhold on his arm, she places her other hand on the willow, whose bark pattern resembles the fletching of the arrows she carries slung across her back.

Lorial can feel her power even before she speaks the Elvish words.

"As one journey ends, another begins. Carry these sons of kings together along the path of light one last time. May the former find rest while the latter takes his place among the Kings of Lostariel."

Threads of light encircle Nestraya's arms as she recites the words, flowing into Lorial and into the Tree of Memories, encapsulating them both. The light spreads to the earthen jar in Lorial's arms, and he gasps as the ashes contained within float from the urn like a specter in the image of his father's face, his long, silver hair fluttering in the breeze that now engulfs them.

Does Nestraya see it, too? Lorial tears his gaze from his father's visage, but Nestraya's eyes are closed as she concentrates on the magic pouring out of her.

When Lorial turns back to his father's ghostly form, his breath hitches. The ephemeral image swirls before him in a fully formed version of his father.

"Father?" Lorial's voice cracks, and Nestraya's eyes flash open as her own breath hitches. She must see him, too.

"Come, Lorial. It's time for me to rest and you to take my place." The specter extends his hand, and Lorial reaches for it. Just as his fingers pass through the non-corporeal representation of his father's memories—his essence—the world around them spins away. Father's grip becomes firm—as real as the hand Lorial clung to only days prior as his father lay dying in his arms.

The Tree of Memories transforms as if growing in reverse, the passage of time folding in on itself. Seasons whisk by too quickly to decipher, and a moment later, Lorial's grandfather appears beside them.

"So soon, Restoval?" he says as he lays a hand on both their shoulders.

Before Lorial can grasp what's happening around him, the swirling accelerates as generation after generation of Lostariel's kings appear beside them. Faces he recognizes from the gallery of portraits at Starhaven House in Celesta.

Then a final apparition appears before them, separate from the others, and Lorial's throat runs dry.

Zelovon. The first King of Lostariel. The first fire wielder. The one whose dual affinities for air and fire magic Lorial shares.

Then the swirling stops, leaving the Council Chamber at Starhaven in its wake to form the backdrop for this once-in-a-generation Council of Kings.

3
A COUNCIL OF KINGS

None of them are real. They're just memories.

But when Father grasps Lorial's shoulders and rests his forehead against Lorial's, it feels as real as any other embrace they've shared.

"My son," Father says. "This is not what I planned for you."

"I know," Lorial says.

"He is young."

Lorial looks up in surprise as Zelovon studies him. Never in all his imaginings did he picture himself standing eye-to-eye with the Dragon King.

"He is young, but he is strong," Lorial's grandfather says.

"Is he?" Zelovon continues to study him. "You say he has air and fire magic?"

"He does," Father says.

"Can he wield it?"

Lorial watches the scene unfolding around him, unsure what part he is to play in their discussion.

"He is in command of the elements he wields," Father says.

The assurance with which Father addresses the legendary king is startling. But then, Father feared very little in life. Is it surprising that he would fear even less in death?

"I am still learning," Lorial admits. "I have far to go to reach your level of mastery."

"In time," another of Lorial's ancestors says. "Everything in time."

"Tell me, young one," Zelovon continues, "Why have you brought Restoval to us so soon?"

Lorial glances at Father, and a sadness lingers in Father's eyes as he speaks. "I'm afraid my memories of my last moments were blotted from my essence."

Lorial shakes his head. "You spoke to me. At least, you tried. The...the wound made it difficult—"

Zelovon holds up his hand. "Where is Cyrelis?"

"Here, Grandfather." Another elf whose face Lorial recalls from the portrait gallery nods his head toward Zelovon.

"Your final memories were blotted out as well."

"Indeed, Grandfather."

"It was done as a mercy, Father. Your last moments were...distressing."

Unless Lorial is mistaken, the elf who speaks now is Cyrelis's own son, Filios.

"I ordered it myself," Filios adds.

All eyes turn to Lorial.

"Well?" Zelovon says.

"I had no hand in any blotting out of memories. I didn't even know about this place, or—"

Father puts his arm around Lorial's shoulders. "It's all right. You didn't know of this place because I didn't tell you. I thought I'd have more time."

"We all thought you'd have more time," Grandfather says.

"To the matter at hand, who would have done this?" Zelovon asks. "And to what purpose?"

"I don't know," Lorial says.

Father rests a hand on his shoulder. "Tell us what you do know of my final moments."

Lorial glances from his father to the other elves watching him expectantly and clears his throat. "It was a human raid. Your band of warriors was cut off, and most of your elves were taken down in their hasty retreat. One of their firearms wounded your heart. Nestraya"—Lorial pauses and takes a deep breath before continuing—"Nestraya said not even a heartbinding could save you. You died in my arms."

"Nestraya?" Zelovon says. "The *estrassa*?"

"The daughter of my heart," Father answers.

"Have they—"

"No." Father quickly cuts off the rest of Zelovon's question.

Lorial looks back and forth between the two elves. He and Nestraya? Have they what?

"Who else was present?" Grandfather asks, interrupting Lorial's thoughts.

Lorial turns to look at his father's father. "First Edgeron, along with a small band of warriors. All but Second Hothniel passed from the light."

Father staggers. "All of them?"

With regret, Lorial nods.

"Our hearts feel your loss, Restoval," Zelovon says, and the others murmur their agreement.

"But who blotted out Restoval's memories?" Grandfather asks.

Filios turns to Lorial. "Who prepared his body for the joining?"

Lorial shakes his head. "I don't know. I...Nestraya...I was overcome—"

Zelovon lifts a hand. "A king cannot afford to be overcome."

"He is little more than an elfling," Grandfather says. "He will find his strength."

"Lorial is good," Father insists. "He will be a great king, worthy of standing in this room among us."

"Will he?" This speaker leans against a wall, and Lorial shrinks when he recognizes the face of Polanis. The Shadow King. Aside from his pale skin, everything about him is dark, from his raven hair to his coal eyes.

"Would that we could blot you from our memories," Filios says.

"Lostariel was a dark place when I sat on the throne at Starhaven," Polanis says. "If not for me, she wouldn't have survived the Years of Torment."

"So you claim," Zelovon says.

"A darkness descends on Lostariel even now," the Shadow King continues. "Do you not feel it?"

Lorial gulps. "There is unrest—"

"There is more than that." Polanis straightens and saunters toward Lorial. "You must obliterate the humans. They're like an army of fire ants that has found its way into your bed. Insignificant until they realize they can bite you."

"Heed him not," Filios says. "Had my son heeded us, the Years of Torment would have been little more than days of discomfort."

"None of you were there." Polanis turns to face the others. "Even now, Restoval's memories seep within our group consciousness. The feelings of despair he hides from his young son mirror those my own father hid from me."

Lorial's brow wrinkles as he looks at Father. "Is it true?"

"No. I do not despair for Lostariel. Only for the pain my early passing causes the ones I love."

Polanis scoffs. "He lies."

Zelovon studies Father. "Your words, Restoval. They do not completely match the essence you share with us now."

Polanis opens his mouth again, but Zelovon silences him with a lifted hand.

"I despair because I left far too many things undone. Words left unsaid. You are all aware of the hope of Lostariel that stands on the cusp of greatness. The peace her sacrifice will bring."

Her? Of whom does Father speak?

"We are aware of your visions, Restoval," Grandfather says.

Visions? Father never spoke of visions. Not to Lorial.

"They have all come true so far," Father insists.

"Too bad you didn't envision your untimely demise," Polanis mutters.

"I meant to prepare her better," Father continues, ignoring the Shadow King.

Nestraya. He speaks of Nestraya. Prepare her for what?

"Will you tell the boy?" Zelovon asks.

"Tell me what?"

Father turns his eyes to Lorial, and as they gaze at each other, Lorial tries to make sense of the words uttered here tonight.

"I will tell you this, Lorial. Nestraya is everything. Trust her above all others, for through her, Lostariel will find peace once more."

"The Tree of Memories said you meant her for me."

Restoval turns to the others. "You told him this?"

"When last we spoke, you said you would tell him yourself," Zelovon says. "You did not."

"I thought I'd have more time."

"Tell me now, Father. Please. What of Nestraya?"

"She weakens," Zelovon suddenly says. "This Council of Kings is at an end."

Lorial shakes his head. "No. I'm not ready!" But the room around him is already starting to fade. "Father, no!"

Father reaches for Lorial. "You are ready, my son. You and Nestraya are better together than apart. The great hope of our people—it's not just her. It's—"

Father's words cut off as Lorial staggers in the light of the Tree of Memories. Nestraya sways at his side, and he reaches out to catch her before she falls.

"Forgive me," she whispers as her eyes slide closed. "I held it as long as I could."

Then she goes limp in his arms, and he tightens his hold on her as he lowers her to the forest floor.

"Nestraya!" Panic edges his voice. He leans his ear against her chest, but her heart beats steadily. Relieved, he gathers her close and weeps the tears he's been holding back since Mother told him to be strong. They burst from him like a flood.

It was too short. There was too much left unsaid. He gazes up at the light that once again shines from the trunk of the sacred tree. Gingerly, he lowers Nestraya to the soil and pushes himself to his feet.

Shoving his hand back into the light, he waits for the tree to speak to him.

Another time, our young king. We are weary. Let us rest.

"Tell me!" he cries.

Don't you already know the answer you seek? It is you, our young king. You and the estrassa*. Together, you are the great hope of Lostariel. Now let us rest. The joining has drained our magic. We must replenish it before you seek our wisdom again.*

With that, the light flickers out. Even the glowing flowers dancing on the forest floor have closed their blooms in sleep. Utter darkness surrounds Lorial, and he draws from his own inner spark to create a magical light by which to see.

Nestraya lies sleeping or unconscious where he left her, and as he returns to her side, a sinking realization worms its way through his stomach.

None of this. He can tell her none of this. The wisdom of his forebears is for him alone.

What is he to do?

4
CHOSEN FAMILY

Nestraya wakes in total darkness, and for a moment, she simply lies still and listens, trying to get her bearings. Tendrils of her life magic weave into the blackness surrounding her, searching for others nearby.

Her magic wraps itself around someone, and relief fills her at Lorial's powerful air magic. His familiar warmth and steady heartbeat.

Did they fall asleep together?

The air is heavy with the scent of the forest—the soil and decaying plant matter. Are they still within the protection of the Tree of Memories? How long have they been sleeping?

"Lorial?" she murmurs in a scratchy voice.

The sound of movement to her left where Lorial lies draws her ear as she returns her magic to its resting state. She still feels drained after the effort of joining the essences of Lorial and Restoval to the sacred tree.

Yellow light shines from Lorial's hand, and Nestraya blinks.

"Nestraya." He crawls toward her, worry illuminated in his gray eyes by the orb light in his palm. "Forgive me. I must have fallen asleep. Are you all right?"

"Just tired. I think your father was right. I need to work on my endurance."

They both grow quiet at the mention of Restoval as the reality of their loss weighs on them.

"I'll help you," Lorial says.

She nods gratefully.

Something about the way he looks at her unnerves her. What is he thinking?

"What happens now?" she asks. Hopefully, something he learned while connected to the tree will give him direction.

Lorial looks away. "I don't know. I think I have more questions now than I did before."

Disappointment fills her at his words, but she pushes it aside. He needs her to be strong now.

"I should return you to Windhaven. You'll wish to consult your First and Seconds before the humans launch a new—"

"I'm no warrior."

"You will be what your people need you to be, Lorial. Now, your father's First was lost in the attack, may he find rest. So you'll need to choose a new First. Second Hothniel is the highest ranking as both a commander and a high-born elf. His wounds were minor, so you should—"

"I choose you."

Nestraya stills. "You what?"

Surely she misheard him.

"I'll name you as my First. There's no one I trust more." His eyes hold a desperate sincerity that tugs at Nestraya's heart, but the expected custom is clear in this matter.

She gently shakes her head. "No, Lorial. You can't do that."

"I'm the king, am I not?"

"Of course, but—"

"But what? I'm free to choose my commanders and my advisors. My father was just killed, and someone..." Lorial's lips move, but no sound comes out.

"Someone what?"

Frustration etches his face. "I can't speak of it. Suffice it to say, I don't know who I can trust, other than you and Mother. I will name you as my First. It's the only option."

She frowns. What did Restoval tell him?

"Lorial, I'm not of noble birth. I'm not qualified—"

"It doesn't matter. You're *estrassa* to kings."

"But who will respect this decision? You'll be questioned for showing favoritism. People will...gossip about..."

His brow wrinkles, and she sighs. Surely he understands what people would assume. That she climbed to the top by climbing into his bed.

"Your reign would be tainted from the start," she whispers. "And everything I've worked for would be dismissed as...favors given to Lorial's bed warmer." She pushes the awkward words past her lips.

His eyes widen as her words sink in for him. "But there's no truth to such a lie. You and I aren't—"

"Truth matters little in such circumstances. You and your parents may see me as your equal, but I promise you no one else will."

"Nestraya, stop this nonsense. You're the most gifted magic wielder in all of Lostariel. You've earned your place—"

Nestraya shakes her head again. "People whisper already. They talk. I may be gifted, but gifted by whom? The fae? Or something more sinister? They tolerated my presence for your father's sake. Do not imagine they will continue to do so for yours."

For a moment, they simply stare at each other. He sees the truth in her words, doesn't he?

"I've made my decision," he says. "Please don't undermine my authority by refusing. There are things in play you don't know. I just...I need you to trust me."

That desperate sincerity is back, and she sighs. "I serve at the pleasure of my king."

"Thank you. Are you strong enough to walk now?"

"I believe so." She pushes herself to a sitting position, and their surroundings sway slightly in the dim light.

"Shall I carry you?" Lorial sends her a lopsided grin, and for a moment, all the grief of the past few days evaporates, and laughter bubbles from her throat.

"Now that would definitely contribute to the rumors which are sure to fly if you follow through on your foolhardy plan. Help me up, and I'll be fine."

He stands and extends a hand down to her, and she grasps it. As he pulls her to her feet, the forest spins around her, and he clasps her waist to keep her from falling. She looks at him in surprise.

"Are you all right?" he asks softly.

That unsettling feeling sweeps over her again at the intensity of his gaze, and she quickly looks away. "I will be shortly."

Still, he doesn't let go.

Up to this moment, their relationship has been entirely that of friendship. Family, even. His *estrassa*. And though she's never given voice to her feelings, she views him the same way. Her chosen family.

But this?

She pushes the unsettling thought aside. There's no future there.

And there never will be.

When they step through the willow branches and emerge from the circle of the Tree of Memories, it's nearly as dark without as it was within. Slivers of silver moonbeams cast dappled shadows on the forest floor, and lanterns illuminate Windhaven in the distance.

The elves who lined the path to pay their respects to their fallen king have dispersed, likely to their beds.

Clearly, a significant amount of time has passed since Nestraya entered the Tree at Lorial's side. Time is near meaningless within the Tree of Memories. Days could have gone by while the magic enveloped them.

Likely, though, it's been hours. The forest would feel older had more time passed than that.

Lorial's hand at her elbow steadies her as they return along the path to Windhaven House. They pass the charred remains of the guest wing, where no elves resided at the time of the fire, thank the fates. The rebuilding efforts have paused for the night.

When they reach the wing housing the royal family's private living quarters, Lorial's mother faces a window overlooking the Waters of

Pendarra that pass near the western wall of Windhaven at the edge of Darlei.

"We're back, Mother," Lorial says gently, and Miravel turns, hastily wiping wetness from her cheek.

"And your father's essence rests?" she asks.

Lorial nods.

"Thank you, my son." She rests her forehead against his, and Nestraya averts her eyes at the intimate display.

Miravel is far too young to be a widow. Perhaps soon she would have given Restoval another elfling, had he lived. Though they both claimed they were content with the two elflings the fates had bestowed upon them.

"My darling," Miravel whispers, reaching for Nestraya next. "The magic has weakened you."

"Nothing rest won't cure, Mera." The affectionate term for mother slips from Nestraya's lips before she can stop it.

"I wish you would call me such all the time, young one," Miravel says softly. "No more of this formality you've latched on to since you joined Restoval's warrior elves."

Lorial sends Nestraya a look of confirmed knowing, which she ignores. Regardless of how the royal family sees her, she is not one of them. Not really. And she never will be.

"Will you stay with us again tonight?" Miravel asks, and Nestraya wavers. She should return to her spartan quarters at the barracks, especially if Lorial clings to his ridiculous plan. The more space she can put between them, the better. But her cozy chamber here at Windhaven calls to her.

Miravel refused to clear it out when Nestraya left. She said Nestraya would always have a home at Starhaven and at Windhaven, regardless of whatever notions had taken root in Nestraya's young mind.

And as Nestraya sways in the corridor outside her old chamber, Lorial reaches out to steady her again, though he only holds her arms this time.

"You will stay here," he says with a surprising firmness.

Before Nestraya can argue, Lorial lifts her off her feet and carries her toward the door as Miravel swiftly opens it. He deposits her on her bed of moss, which appears to have been refreshed since she left it this morning.

Lorial seems loath to leave, but he straightens and nods. "I'll speak with you in the morning."

As soon as he's gone, Miravel closes the door and soon has Nestraya stripped of her warrior attire and ensconced in one of the luxurious sleeping gowns she left behind when she moved into the barracks. It reminds her of happier days when her pera and mera could protect her from the talk and the rumors of her conception and birth. When the world beyond the walls of Starhaven and Windhaven was exciting and waiting to be discovered, and she dreamed of the warrior elf she would become.

Now Pera is gone, along with the innocent girl he welcomed into his family so long ago.

To Nestraya's surprise, Miravel lowers herself to the bed and pulls Nestraya into her arms.

"Weep, my elfling," she says softly. "And then sleep."

And before Nestraya can help it, her tears flow freely as if she's once again the girl grieving the loss of a father taken from her before she was ready to say goodbye.

5
THE BARRACKS

Lorial passes a restless night. Images of his dying father wrestle with incoherent admonishments from his forebears, all with Nestraya as a constant presence just out of reach. When he tries to speak to her, she can't hear him.

And then it's morning. Birds chirp outside his chamber window as if all is as it should be.

Oh, to be a bird and fly away from all this.

He rises and clothes himself in the formal raiment reserved for official events. Perhaps if he dresses the part, his people will see more than a son attempting to fill the too-big boots of his father.

He's no elfling. He just needs to prove it to them.

A knock demands his attention as he tugs his vest into place. He turns to open the door only to find one of his father's clerks in the corridor.

"The Council of Elders has convened, my king," Jevoran says. He runs his eyes over Lorial's clothing and nods. "This may be as much of a battlefield as any you've stepped onto before."

"I assumed as much. Where's Nestraya?"

"Probably at the barracks, my king. Is that not where Third Nestraya resides?"

Lorial eyes the man, searching his face for any undercurrents of disdain. Was Nestraya right? Is she on the verge of being written off as a pet of King Restoval? Tolerated only so long as her master lived to require it?

Lorial's about to correct the man's assumption regarding Nestraya's sleeping arrangements the past few nights but thinks better of it. Perhaps announcing Nestraya has slept in the room next to his own chamber since Father died would be unwise.

"Tell the Elders I'll address them shortly," Lorial says instead.

Jevoran's eyes widen. "They await you even now."

"And I will attend them soon. You may go."

"Of course, my king." Jevoran bows and exits the private royal wing, and as soon as he's gone, Lorial knocks on Nestraya's door.

He heard her cries last night as he lay in his bed. The urge to go to her was strong, but Mother's soothing voice comforting their *estrassa* held him at bay.

When Nestraya doesn't answer, Lorial knocks again.

"I couldn't convince her to stay once she awoke this morning," Mother says softly from behind him.

He turns toward her. "She left?"

"You have your work cut out for you."

Lorial opens his mouth, but unsure how to respond, he closes it again.

"Be gentle with her, my son. She has wounds you know little about."

"Wounds?" He frowns. "Has someone hurt her?"

"If elves are skilled at anything, it's fearing that which is different. Your father did his best to protect her, as did her first father before him. Now, it's our job."

Lorial slowly nods. Has he truly been so oblivious to Nestraya's struggles?

"I need to find her. Where did she go?"

"To the barracks."

"Thank you, Mother." Lorial kisses her cheek before making his way out of Windhaven toward the warrior barracks on the outskirts of Darlei. A contingent of guards surrounds him as he walks, much to his consternation. He's used to being guarded, but not by four elves at once.

He's the king now, though. He'll have to accustom himself to such things.

"My king," a young elf barely past his gangly elfling years says. Surprise fills the youth's face when Lorial strides through the gate in the tree-grown wall surrounding the low-born warriors' quarters and practice arenas.

The noble-born warriors occupy their own homes in Darlei. Why Nestraya decided she belonged here rather than at Windhaven House when she joined the warrior ranks eight years ago has always been a mystery to Lorial.

Father and Mother weren't pleased with her decision, but they didn't stop her. If she went too many nights without appearing at a family dinner, though, Father wouldn't hesitate to march to the barracks himself and order her home for the evening.

"Where is Third Nestraya?" Lorial asks the boy.

"In the practice arena, my king. But—"

Lorial doesn't wait for him to finish before striding toward the open arena marked on four corners by tall fir trees and surrounded between them by lines of stones.

He easily spots Nestraya taking on two male warriors. Soil wielders, if the copious mud caking all three of them is any indication. Even fatigued, Nestraya seems to have the upper hand as she coaxes water into a spout swirling in a cyclone around the other warriors, containing their weaker attacks.

Soon, they yield, and she lets go of the magic.

"It's hardly fair to let her fight," one of the men mutters as he shakes water from his practice tunic. "Freak of nature."

Lorial stiffens.

"Take your sour grapes elsewhere, Fifth," the other soil wielder says. "And if I hear you say anything like that again, I'll put you on latrine duty."

The disgruntled elf glares at Nestraya as he marches past the stone border marking the boundaries of the arena.

"Don't listen to him," the other man says. "Not all of us hold with such backward thinking, and you know it."

Nestraya still hasn't noticed Lorial watching the entire exchange.

"Sometimes, I fear you're the only one among the warrior bands who doesn't look at me with disdain. Thank you for the match, Corivos. It was just what I needed."

"Any time. Perhaps one of these days, I'll win."

An odd tightening squeezes Lorial's chest as he watches their interaction. Why hasn't he offered to spar with Nestraya?

Probably because sparring isn't one of his preferred pastimes.

Soon, this Corivos leaves as well, and Lorial wanders into the arena.

"My king," Nestraya says in surprise.

"I thought we discussed this. Please—"

"How may I serve you, my king?"

It takes every ounce of patience Lorial possesses not to groan in frustration. Nestraya stands at attention before him like a wild hog that's been rooting in the mud. She's probably thirsty after water wielding. He spots her familiar water pouch sitting nearby and bends to retrieve it before handing it to her.

Perhaps, for now, he should just play the part she insists on thrusting upon him.

"At ease, Third Nestraya. Your presence is required at the Council of Elders, and I suggest you gather your belongings. You're being promoted beyond the ranks housed here at the barracks."

For a moment, they stare at each other, neither speaking as Lorial's guards pretend not to have ears.

"Very well, my king," Nestraya finally says, though she looks anything but at ease. "Do I have time to wash up?"

Thoughts of the waiting Elders cross Lorial's mind, but he pushes them aside. "Take whatever time you need."

She turns to go, but Lorial stops her with a hand to her mud-caked arm.

"That man, Corivos. Of what rank and family is he?"

Nestraya looks at Lorial curiously. "He's a Third from the family Hedellivys."

Hedellivys. A low-born merchant family but an upstanding one that never gave Father any trouble that Lorial can recall.

"Do you trust him?" Lorial asks quietly so his guards won't overhear.

"More than anyone but you and your mother," she whispers in return. "What are you thinking?"

"As First, you'll need a Second to be your personal advisor and field assistant. Perhaps if I promote him, too, that will help allay some of your fears? Unless you think someone would accuse him of warming my bed as well?"

A slight flush sweeps across the parts of Nestraya's face not covered by mud. "I think that unlikely. He'll need new housing, though. The only Seconds quartered here are the lower-ranked warriors' direct supervisors."

Lorial nods. He assumed as much. "Bring him with you. I'll quarter him at Windhaven."

"Do not imagine that promoting another low-born elf won't cause you more grief, Lorial. Though I appreciate the gesture."

Lorial pauses before whispering the words rattling around inside his head. "I would do anything for you, Nestraya. Anything to make you happy, even in our shared grief. Perhaps especially now. I long to see you smile again."

He wouldn't have dared speak such a thing in the past, but everything has changed. According to his forebears, Nestraya is meant for him. Now—somehow—he has to convince her of that.

Nestraya's eyes grow wide before her expression shutters. "Excuse me, my king. I'll clean up and collect my things and then report to Windhaven House along with Third Corivos."

She bows before sprinting toward the women's barracks, and Lorial sighs.

That went well.

6

COUNCIL OF ELDERS

Lorial paces near the door at Windhaven, waiting for Nestraya to arrive. Perhaps he should have waited for her at the barracks, but she wouldn't have thanked him for that.

Mostly, he's tried to avoid going anywhere near the makeshift Council Chamber. Rarely does the Council of Elders assemble in Darlei, but tensions with humans have been rising in recent years, as the events of the past week make obvious.

Father sent Lorial to attend to matters in the capital city of Celesta last spring, but it's been several years since the royal family took up their primary residence in Starhaven House on a more permanent basis.

For now, a meeting room has been converted into makeshift Council Chambers here at Windhaven House.

When Nestraya finally passes through the doorway, relief fills Lorial. Her companion, Corivos, steps past the ornate wooden door behind her as he takes in the understated elegance of Windhaven. Clearly, being in the southern home of the royal family is a new experience for him.

"We are here as ordered, my king," Nestraya says, and Corivos's eyes snap toward Lorial.

"My king." He bows. "It is an honor."

"The honor is mine. Has Nestraya informed you of your promotion?"

Corivos's head remains bowed. "She told me stories I find difficult to believe, my king, but here I am."

"Her 'stories' are true. She indicated you are to be trusted, and that's enough of a recommendation to me in these difficult times. You'll take on the role of Second to the First, serving at the pleasure of First Nestraya in whatever way she requires. Rooms will be provided to you here at Windhaven, and anything you need to fulfill your duties will be yours."

"I am honored, my king. I won't let you down."

"At ease, Second."

Corivos lifts his head as he clutches his meager belongings in his arms.

"I fear we've kept the Elders waiting far longer than prudent." Lorial sighs as he turns to Nestraya. "Put your things in the receiving room for now. We'll get you both settled later."

Lorial eyes Nestraya as she sets her belongings on the table in the formal receiving room near the western door to Windhaven. She's dressed like a common warrior. So is Corivos.

"Perhaps you should change first," Lorial says.

Nestraya glances at the open door where Lorial's guards watch. "And make the Elders wait even longer? My formal wear is here at Windhaven, or I would have donned something more appropriate already."

Corivos self-consciously smooths his uniform. "This is all I have."

"We'll soon remedy that," Lorial says. Indecision holds him in its grip as he gazes at Nestraya.

"We don't have time for this," she whispers. "Let's just go."

Reluctantly, he nods.

"Just follow my lead," Nestraya says to Corivos. "Don't speak unless spoken to."

"Yes, my First."

A look of long-suffering crosses Nestraya's face, and Lorial fights back a smile as he leads them from the room.

The walk to the Council Chamber is brief, and all too soon, the three of them stand outside the double wooden doors as Lorial's guards flank them. Lorial glances at Nestraya one last time before pushing open the doors and striding into the room his father presided over only a few days ago. The conversations around the long table pause as representatives from the high families glance their way.

"My king." Second Hothniel leans against his wooden crutch as he inclines his head toward Lorial. "We were unsure of your plans to join us and commenced without you some time ago. My Second will fill you in on everything you missed."

The room is silent as Lorial stares at Second Hothniel.

"Forgive me," Lorial says. "Did you say you began a meeting among the Council of Elders without your king?"

Some of the elves have the decency to look uncomfortable at Lorial's words.

Did they really start without him?

An elf Lorial recognizes as one of Hothniel's men hurries around the table to Lorial's side.

"Let me get you caught up on what you missed, my king." The man's words drift past Lorial's ears, but he barely registers them.

Surely he can't let this go, can he?

Several Elders eye him with something akin to pity, and the desire to become like that bird he heard singing this morning and fly away seems even more attractive now.

He's floundering, and it hasn't even been five minutes.

Nestraya closes the space between them and whispers in his ear, "If you do not take control now, you never will."

That was his fear.

"What would you recommend?" he asks her, ignoring the monolog being offered by Hothniel's man as the Elders around the table gradually return to their discussions.

"Take your place at the table. Say whatever you planned to say. Didn't you have a plan when you walked in here?" Nestraya asks.

He should have had a plan beyond dressing the part.

Nestraya presses her lips together at his silence before addressing the room. "Please, vacate the king's seat, Second Hothniel."

Hothniel looks at Nestraya in surprise, but he only hesitates a moment before abandoning the head of the table for the spot beside it.

Lorial exhales slowly. He can't expect Nestraya to do everything for him. "That is the seat reserved for my First, Second Hothniel."

Hothniel glances around in confusion. "Indeed, my king."

"First Edgeron has passed from the light, may he find rest," Lorial says as he stands at the head of the table. "I have chosen a new First to take his place. Nestraya." He gestures her to stand at his side.

Cries of outrage erupt from the men and women on his Council.

"Told you," Nestraya whispers.

"Quiet! Please." Second Hothniel lifts his hands, and the chatter dies down. "Lorial is young and inexperienced and perhaps unaware of the customs regarding such things. We will not hold his missteps against him. Now, as my Second has been trying to inform you, we have decided to authorize a set of raids on the human settlement of Feressa across the border. Perhaps if we take the battle to them..."

Lorial frowns and searches out Nestraya beside him as Second Hothniel continues speaking.

"It's King Lorial, Second Hothniel," Nestraya says firmly.

Second Hothniel chuckles and adjusts his crutch. "Of course, young one. A slip of the tongue. But I think we've established that it's First Hothniel."

There's a clear challenge in Hothniel's eyes.

"You are mistaken," Lorial says.

"My king," one of the other elves, a woman, says. "May we have a word with you? In private." She glances at Nestraya.

"No, you may not," Lorial says. "Now, I realize you are all struggling with the reality of our new existence. Perhaps we should reconvene—"

A series of groans rises around the room.

"King Lorial, I will be frank. You are ill-qualified for the role you're attempting to fill. As your advisors, we have agreed that a regency may be appropriate as you take on your new responsibilities."

Lorial's eyes widen in shock at Elder Terrelin's suggestion. As the eldest member of the Council, his words have the weight of experience and wisdom behind them.

"A regency?" Lorial frowns.

"Just for a few years. Perhaps a decade or two, while you focus on the personal pursuits more suited for a royal son of your age. A binding partner and an heir, to start. These things should have predated your rise to the throne, but as no one anticipated your father's untimely death, the unfortunate truth is that you are not yet ready to step into his place."

The elves at Lorial's table await his response, but words escape him.

"This is unacceptable," Nestraya says.

"You have no authority in this room, fae slops," someone calls out, and Lorial tenses.

"Who said that?" Lorial demands, but no one speaks up.

"It was him." Corivos points to the son of one of the noble houses from the north.

"Guards, remove him," Lorial says.

"From the room, my king?" the head guard asks.

"From Windhaven House."

The guard reluctantly steps toward the elf in question.

"This is outrageous," Second Hothniel says.

"I will not tolerate such words in my Council Chambers or anywhere else, and neither did my father. Or have you all forgotten so quickly where your loyalties lie? Tell me you could look my father in the eye were he here to witness your conduct today."

A visible discomfort descends upon a number of the Elders, and Lorial gestures the guard forward again. This time, no one intervenes, and the offensive man shakes off the guard before storming from the room under his own power.

"If I may, my king," Corivos whispers in his ear. "The last regency in Lostariel was between kings Cyrelis and Filios when Cyrelis became too ill at his end of days to perform his duties. Lostarien law on the matter asserts that a regency must be agreed upon unanimously by the Council of Elders along with whoever held the title of First when such an arrangement was brought to the reigning king's attention."

Lorial looks at Corivos in surprise.

"I'm something of a historian, my king."

"Indeed, thank you, Corivos."

Lorial turns to the Elders. "Let us vote on the matter of a regency. First Nestraya, what say you?"

More words of argument arise from the table, but Lorial turns to Corivos. "Enlighten us, Second Corivos."

"Who's he?" Second Hothniel asks in disgust.

"He's my personal Second," Nestraya says.

"This is ridiculous," someone mutters.

"Go on, Second Corivos," Lorial says.

After swallowing, Corivos repeats the words he shared with Lorial.

"Is this true?" one of the elves asks Terrelin, and Terrelin sighs.

"It is. You have made your point, King Lorial. I caution you, though, my young king. This mantle you take upon yourself is a heavy one. Certain exceptions aside"—he glares at Second Hothniel—"we only want what's best for you and the future of Lostariel. Your father, may he find rest, did not adequately prepare you to become king at such a young age. Please do not so quickly spurn the wisdom of your Elders."

Lorial shrinks a little as he nods. "Of course not, Elder Terrelin."

"Now, with your permission, my king, I recommend we adjourn for today and reconvene in the morning when cooler heads might prevail. Please provide us with the respect of being on time."

"Yes, Elder Terrelin. My apologies for making you wait so long today." He glances at Nestraya. "I know I have much to learn. I appreciate your patience as I do so."

Murmurs of acceptance rise around the table, and one by one, the room empties until it's just Lorial and Nestraya and Corivos left along with Lorial's guards.

"You may leave us," Nestraya says softly to the guards. "Take up your station in the corridor."

"Of course, my First."

The guards shuffle out, and the door closes as Lorial drops to one of the chairs and braces his forehead against his hands. "That was a disaster. Perhaps they were right. I'm not ready for this."

"You are, Lorial. But tomorrow, we won't wander in without a plan."

Lorial glances up at Nestraya, and she crosses her arms as she looks down at him.

"Thank you," he whispers.

With a sigh, Nestraya lowers herself to the chair beside him. "I promise, you are not alone."

7
FIRST NESTRAYA

Lorial rubs his eyes again, and Nestraya looks at him with compassion.

"You should rest. It's been a long day," she says quietly as Corivos dozes on the small sofa in Lorial's study.

"How did I not know all of this?" Lorial asks. "Was I willfully ignorant?"

Their eyes meet across the maps marked with records of raids by the humans and information from their own spy network about attacks on human soil by elves.

"You aren't a warrior, Lorial. Restoval knew that. He never held it against you."

"But this...I should have at least been aware of his suspicions."

"Perhaps."

It was only recently that Restoval even revealed his concerns to Nestraya that renegade elves have been inciting the humans to attack. Few other explanations for the human complaints against the elves make sense.

And now Restoval is dead.

Dare she confess her own unease about Restoval's passing to Lorial?

"Lorial," she says softly as she reaches for his hand, and he looks at her in surprise. Perhaps she shouldn't have touched him.

She relaxes her hold, but he threads his fingers between hers before she can stop him.

What's going on here? This can't happen.

She tugs at her hand, but he holds tight

"Lorial—"

"What were you going to say?"

She stares into his gray eyes in the glow from the orb light hovering beside his desk.

"Please don't," she whispers.

He looks almost stricken as he drops her hand, and she sighs again. Perhaps tonight isn't the best time to bring up Restoval's death.

"Forgive me," he says. "Finish, please."

After a moment's hesitation, she plunges forward. "Something about your father's death leaves me uneasy. As if all is not as it seems."

Lorial opens his mouth, but no words come, and he curses. It's so out of character for him that Nestraya jumps.

"Forgive me," he says again. "It's the Tree of Memories. I can't speak the words I wish to say."

"Curse all you want. I've heard worse walking from the barracks to the mess hall on a rainy day." She offers him a sad smile, and amusement lights his eyes, though it quickly fades.

"I learned something in the Tree of Memories that leaves me uneasy about his death as well. Do you know who prepared his body for the joining?"

Nestraya frowns. "I don't. Would you like me to find out?"

"If you don't mind. I need to know everyone who had contact with his body before his ashes were placed in my arms yesterday."

"You needn't ask if I mind. As your First, I am yours to command, my king."

Nestraya meets his gaze again, and something unspoken hangs in the air around them before Lorial speaks.

"Today, when that man insulted you—"

"It was nothing I haven't heard before," Nestraya assures him.

"How long?"

She shakes her head. "I don't understand."

"How long have you been listening to their lies?"

She leans back in her chair. "They aren't lies. I am what I am."

A fierceness overtakes Lorial's face, catching Nestraya off guard. "You are *estrassa*. My *estrassa*. Daughter of Restoval and Miravel."

A sad sigh escapes her lips. "I am what I am."

"You shouldn't heed their words. This...this lowering of yourself is cruel to everyone who has ever loved you. Don't throw that love away because some uncouth ass who's jealous of you and afraid of things he doesn't understand tries to convince you you don't belong."

How many times did Restoval say the same thing to her when the taunting began the year she started her warrior training?

"You don't understand, Lorial. I—"

"You are *estrassa*."

If only it were that simple.

"Goodnight." She stands. "I'll see you in the morning."

He opens his mouth to speak but eventually nods instead. "Goodnight."

She rouses Corivos and shows him to the room Miravel had prepared for him before making her way to her own bed. She should ask for different rooms far from Lorial's, but tonight she's too tired to do more than collapse onto her moss mattress and let sleep claim her.

In the morning, Nestraya dons the black leathers Restoval and Miravel commissioned for her when she finished her warrior training. The supple trousers, tailored to her body, fit like a second skin, and the overdress hangs near her knees in the back and stops at mid-thigh in front. Knee-high black boots make her legs seem even longer than they already are, and the high tail she gathered her hair into atop her head only adds to her height.

She fingers the ayervadi leather with its subtle stretch and inexplicably breathable qualities.

Fit for a princess.

She never wore it before Restoval died. It was out of place among the warriors at the barracks.

And she was out of place at Windhaven.

Or so she managed to convince herself.

Lorial's words from last night travel over her again, and she blinks back a tear as his voice in her head becomes Restoval's instead.

Pera. Her pera.

A knock at her door draws her back to the present, and she carefully wipes any wetness from her face without smudging the shimmery black korathite she used to line her eyes. Then she crosses her chamber to answer the knock.

Lorial stands in the corridor, and when he sees her, he does a double-take. His eyes sweep over her, lingering in a way he's never looked at her before.

It both warms and unsettles her.

"Nestraya—"

"More appropriately dressed for a Council of Elders?" she asks before he can finish his thought, and he swallows.

"Yes. You look every bit the daughter of Restoval. A fierce warrior elf princess."

Nestraya inclines her head as she closes the door behind her. There's little point in arguing about the princess part.

"And you're stunning in all black to match your glorious hair," he adds.

She stills with her hand on the door, but before she can say something—anything—to discourage this strange new infatuation he seems to be developing, Miravel joins them in the corridor.

"Oh, my darling. You look just as I imagined when we gifted you this. It suits you."

Nestraya keeps her eyes locked on Miravel and away from Lorial. "Thank you. I'm sorry I never wore it before..." Her voice drifts off as the words lodge in her throat, and Miravel reaches for her hand.

"It's all right, young one. He understood."

Corivos waits for them just outside the royal wing, and he also wears much more appropriate clothes for a warrior of his new station, though where Miravel sourced the fine leathers on such short notice is a mystery.

Unless they once belonged to Restoval.

"Thank you for your hospitality, my queen." Corivos bows his upper body toward Miravel. "And for the leathers. I feel as though I've entered a strange dream beyond my wildest imaginings, though I would trade it all to have our king Restoval among us again."

"You honor him with your kind words," Miravel says.

Corivos lifts his brows as he takes in Nestraya's altered appearance, but he says nothing.

After a hastily eaten breakfast of venison sausage and wild berries, they part ways with Miravel and make their way to the Council Chamber.

Hopefully, today's meeting goes better than yesterday's.

"No," Lorial says again, and an edge of frustration colors his voice.

"You are not a warrior, my king," Second Hothniel says. "We must strike hard and fast as I have already tried to explain to you."

Lorial sends a pleading glance Nestraya's way, and she takes mercy on him. "We will not attack the innocent people of Feressa for the sins of a band of human raiders. We need more intel before we make such a bold strike. Who sanctioned the attack on Windhaven? Where did the humans get their information?"

"They killed the King of Lostariel," another Elder says. "Does it matter who sanctioned it? We can't just stand by and wait for them to return."

"I'd like to hear your thoughts, Elder Terrelin," Lorial says.

"Violence begets violence, but sometimes it is impossible to avoid."

Voices around the room affirm his words, and Lorial rubs his eyes and stifles a yawn. Has he been sleeping at all?

"I will take your words under advisement," he says.

"And our other advice?" Elder Terrelin asks as he folds his hands on the table. "Never has an elf ascended to the throne of Lostariel without an heir of his own. Have you given thought to a swift rectification of this concerning situation, my king?"

Nestraya stares straight ahead, refusing to meet Lorial's eyes. As his First, this matter doesn't concern her.

Though judging by his words to her this morning, Lorial might disagree.

He's a foolish elf if he does.

"Perhaps one of our own daughters or granddaughters would suit," Terrelin continues.

"I'm not convinced this needs to be settled so soon after my father's death," Lorial mumbles, and Nestraya ventures a glance in his direction. Even the tips of his ears are pink, and she can barely refrain from smiling at his obvious embarrassment.

He shouldn't be surprised, though. His binding, and the resulting union that brings forth an heir for Lostariel, are very much within the purview of the Elders' concerns.

"Perhaps you would benefit from a season in Celesta," Second Hothniel suggests. "Leave your...First to handle your warriors here while you focus on finding a binding partner from among our noble daughters."

A few nods and murmurs of agreement follow the man's words.

"I'm not leaving Darlei at present, though I will consider your advice. Shall we adjourn?"

As the elves file out, one of them spits on Nestraya's boot, which she ignores. Thankfully, Lorial doesn't seem to notice.

"Well, today's meeting went much better, I think," Corivos says once they're alone again.

"Yes." Lorial has a faraway look in his eyes. "Is it true? Has an elf king never come to power without a son of his own?"

Corivos clears his throat. "I believe Elder Terrelin's words match the historical record."

Lorial sighs and turns to Nestraya, and a sense of foreboding fills her.

"Then I suppose I have my work cut out for me." He stares into her eyes long enough to convey a message Nestraya has no desire to comprehend.

"Shall I assemble a list of noble daughters for you to consider?" Corivos offers, oblivious to the tension between Lorial and Nestraya.

"Yes, Corivos. That would be helpful," Nestraya says. "Wouldn't it, my king?"

Without waiting for Lorial's response, she makes her way from the room.

8

EMERALD EYES

The next afternoon, Lorial sits in his study, trying to focus on his father's notes and papers. His clerk has come and gone with various things for Lorial to sign along with accounts on the state of affairs elsewhere in Lostariel.

All he can think about is Nestraya.

By the time he rose this morning, she had already eaten and left Windhaven. For what purpose, no one could tell him. She took Corivos with her, though, which was a relief.

Not that she needs protecting.

Of course, Father didn't either. Until suddenly he did, and a band of retreating humans with muskets took down Father's most elite warriors with little effort or forethought.

Nestraya's right. Something doesn't add up. Which just increases Lorial's worry about where she is and what she's doing.

His air magic lies restless within him. He needs to get out of Windhaven. Feel the wind on his face. He's been cooped up inside too much the past few days. Perhaps Nestraya will spar with him. He did promise to help her work on her endurance. Visions of her in that linen tunic in the arena at the barracks flit across his mind—the linen wet and caked to her body. Every curve. Every line.

Thoughts he's never let himself dwell on before.

An image of an elfling with Nestraya's dark hair and emerald-green eyes forms in Lorial's mind.

He rubs his eyes to clear his head. How is he supposed to convince Nestraya to bind with him if he can't tell her what he learned in the Tree of Memories? She didn't want to become his First. Convincing her to become his queen will take an act of the fates.

He won't be able to put the Elders off forever about the matter of an heir, though. Still, he certainly won't be courting the favors of their daughters or granddaughters, either.

A knock interrupts his thoughts.

"Come in," he calls.

Hopefully, it's Nestraya.

Relief settles over him when she strides into the room with Corivos on her heels. She's wearing the black leathers again, and the sight is enough to start Lorial's heart racing the way it did yesterday when she stepped out of her chamber.

"I've been to the Healing Center," Nestraya begins with no preamble as Corivos closes the door behind him.

Lorial leans forward. "And?"

"And Restoval's body was brought to the Healing Center along with his fallen warriors, may they find rest. A healer examined his body thoroughly and recorded his death by human musket fire—a wound directly to his heart, as I ascertained on the field."

Lorial's chest tightens at her words, and her lip wavers, but she continues.

"Then a fire wielder prepared his remains for the joining ceremony, and I personally collected them before the ceremony began."

"And who had access to his body before it was..." Lorial swallows.

"Only the transport elves, the healer who examined him, and the fire wielder. Corivos took down a list of names."

Corivos hands Lorial a note with the names of six elves, none of whom Lorial recognizes.

"Do you know any of these people personally?" Lorial asks.

"From my healing training, I know two of the transport crew and Healer Cadowyn, who examined Restoval's body."

Lorial nods. "And?"

"And they're certified healers." She shrugs. "They take an oath to harm no one. I wouldn't suspect any of them of ill will, but I assume you have reason to think someone did something nefarious with Restoval's remains since you sent me on this mission."

Lorial rubs his eyes. "I wish I could tell you more."

"I know. Am I correct in surmising that someone dallied with Restoval's final memories?"

Lorial looks up at her. She's so brilliant. She always has been.

He opens his mouth, but once again, the words won't come, and he sighs. "Judge my response as you will."

"So we're dealing with a life wielder," Corivos says. "No one else could alter memories like that, which eliminates the fire wielder. He only possesses an affinity for fire, which I confirmed with multiple people." Corivos points to one of the names, and Lorial draws a line through it.

"Thank you for being thorough," Lorial says.

"I mean to earn the rank you and the fates have bestowed upon me, my king. I can't even begin to tell you what your generosity means to me and my family. Few low-born elves achieve the rank of Third, let alone Second. I am—"

"Corivos, hush," Nestraya says. "You're rambling."

"Right. Forgive me, my king."

Lorial waves his apology away and gazes at Nestraya. "I hold little with these ideas of low and high birth."

"Then you are an anomaly, my king." Nestraya lifts her chin as she meets his gaze.

"Perhaps." Lorial leans back in his chair and studies the list again.

Five elves, all healers. What purpose would any of them have for blotting out Father's last memories?

He tosses the list aside and rubs his brow. His continuing inability to sleep seems to be manifesting as a headache.

"Are you well?" Nestraya asks as she watches him.

"You're assessing me, aren't you?"

Wisps of her magic crawl over his skin. If only it were her hands.

He quickly banishes the thought.

"You're flushed," she says. "And tense. Perhaps we should return to the Healing Center—"

"I'm fine. It's just a headache."

"Well, I can help you with that. It's a simple healing technique."

Lorial studies her. Father ensured she had as much training in the healing arts as she could get as a life wielder without entering the Healer's Circle and taking the healer's oath. It wouldn't do for a warrior to swear to do no harm.

Still. The thought of her using her healing magic on him...

"I have some work to do on that list of binding candidates I promised," Corivos says. "If you'll excuse me, my king. My First."

All too soon, Lorial is alone with Nestraya, and she steps around his desk. "Lean back."

After a brief hesitation, Lorial does as she says.

"Where does it hurt?" she asks.

"Along my left brow."

"Here?" She lays her thumb over his eyebrow, and her touch burns like fire, though her magic is gentle. "You're flushed again. Are you sure you don't want me to summon a healer?"

Threads of her magic seep into his skin, soothing and relaxing his tense muscles, and he closes his eyes and groans.

"I don't need a healer. I have you," he murmurs. "I don't need anyone else when I have you."

She immediately removes her hand from his forehead. "That should be enough for the headache. I'll just—"

"Stay?" He opens his eyes and looks up into her green ones. That vision of an elfling with emerald irises dances across his mind again.

She quickly looks away. "Lorial..."

"What?"

"This...whatever this is that you seem to be encouraging between us. It needs to stop."

Now she's flushed. It only adds to her allure.

"Does it?" Lorial asks.

"Does it what?"

"Need to stop?"

Her gaze swings back toward his. "Yes. It does. As soon as you can arrange it, you will bind with one of the high-born elves on that list

Corivos is assembling for you. And whatever exists between us will be nothing more than the friendship it's always been."

"What if I don't want to bind with any of the women from that list? What if"—he rises and leans over her where she sits against his desk—"I want an elfling with ebony hair and emerald eyes?"

He's never been this bold with her. His heart pounds as he awaits her response.

Her mouth opens and closes, and she swallows. "Lorial, you speak nonsense," she eventually manages. "Whatever ideas you're entertaining, nip them in the bud right now. I will never be that for you."

He deflates at her response. Not that he expected anything different. "You could be."

"I could not. Please, let it go."

"Why not? What's stopping you?"

Her chest rises and falls as she presses her lips into a thin line. "I think you know."

"And if none of that matters to me? I don't care, Nestraya. I don't care where you came from or what you think you are. You are *estrassa*. My *estrassa*."

"Then let me be your *estrassa*. Don't ask me to be more than that. You won't like the answer you receive."

Before he can respond, she pushes him away and flies from the room, and he groans.

He should have kept his mouth shut.

9

MEETING OF THE SECONDS

Later that day, Nestraya paces her chamber. The last thing she wants to do after what passed between her and Lorial earlier is face him at dinner.

Or ever.

What was he thinking? Now everything between them will be awkward.

The way he looked at her. The way he hovered over her as she sat on the edge of his desk—close enough for her to smell the soap he uses.

The words he spoke.

Nonsense about elflings, of all things.

There's no point in even entertaining the thought. It's impossible. He deserves better than a queen his Council spits on as they pass.

Not to mention the fact that she doesn't return whatever feelings he seems to harbor for her.

Does she?

Of course not.

Besides, there's no future for them together, so there's no reason to give it another thought.

Of all the idiotic things for Lorial to do. Talk of elflings. She shakes her head. The sooner he binds with one of those women from Corivos's list, the better.

With a groan, she drops to the edge of her moss bed. She can survive without dinner tonight, can't she?

And breakfast tomorrow?

Perhaps she'll never eat again.

This is ridiculous. She's First Nestraya. *Estrassa* to kings.

She'll just go and pretend nothing is wrong.

Before she can think better of it, she strides toward her door and flings it open.

And there he is with wide eyes, his hand raised to knock.

"Lorial."

"Nestraya." He lowers his hand. "I thought I might accompany you to dinner."

There's a hopeful look in his eyes that both tugs at her heart and makes her want to douse him with her water magic as she did when they were elflings.

"Should I erect a barrier to protect myself?" The corner of his mouth ticks up. "You've got a threatening look in your eye."

"Perhaps you should. It seems my words earlier were less clear than I thought."

"Or maybe I just decided to ignore them. Shall I anticipate water or plant magic?"

The hint of a smile sneaks unbidden across her face. "Perhaps both." Then the air shifts around her, teasing her high tail of hair and whipping at the edge of her split skirt, and she crosses her arms. "You really want to spar in the corridor?"

He shrugs. "My air magic is restless."

"Because you don't use it enough."

"I'm using it now."

"I noticed. I thought we were supposed to be walking to dinner."

"Were we?" The wind dies down, and he grins at her.

She just shakes her head and strides past him as he hurries to catch up.

She could strangle Lorial. He must be insane, making her his First.

"Your Seconds are assembling as we speak, my First," Corivos says as Nestraya paces former First Edgeron's office at Windhaven. She had Corivos pack up the man's personal effects and deliver them to his family yesterday, but the room still doesn't feel like it belongs to her.

It's too...heavy. And tinged with First Edgeron's destruction and fire magic. It rubs at her own opposing magic, nearly suffocating her.

He was strong to have left so much magic behind as if it seeped from his pores while he sat behind his desk. To think he went down so easily to a band of Nunian raiders.

"First Nestraya?"

"Yes, I know. They're waiting." She sighs. "I'm sorry. I'm just...not sure I can do this."

"For our king Restoval?" Corivos lifts his brows, and Nestraya meets his gaze.

"Your mother must be excellent at guilting you into things for you to have such skills."

Corivos grins. "My grandmother, actually. Are you ready?"

"No."

"Neither am I. Shall we face the angry hordes together?"

"Corivos, what would I do without you?"

He smiles and holds the door for her as they make their way to the makeshift Council Chamber, which she had Corivos commandeer for this Meeting of the Seconds.

She sat in on First Edgeron's meetings at times during her training, at Restoval's insistence. Not that her presence was more than tolerated and ignored, though First Edgeron was always kind to her.

Play a part. Restoval once told her that's how all great elves begin. If you don't know what you're doing, fake it until you do.

As she approaches the Council Chamber doors, she lifts her chin and straightens her back, keeping her arms slightly away from her body and her stance wide.

"Seconds," she says as she passes through the doorway. "Report."

For a moment, only wide eyes greet her. If they expected a wilting flower, they won't get one.

"You, tell me our latest scouting intel." She points to the head of their intelligence brigade. He's a young elf, though still much older than Nestraya. He's new to his position as well, which is why she chose him to speak first.

Less chance of him asserting some misplaced authority over her.

"Of course, my First. The human raiders who burned Windhaven haven't been seen since they crossed the border back into Nunia. Word is, they may be amassing troops in Feressa. Their new locomotives have enabled quick transport of troops to the border—"

Nestraya frowns. "Locomotives?"

"Uh, yes, my First. Carriages that run along tracks."

"How do they power such things?"

A few snickers rise around the room, but she dons her best imitation of Miravel's no-nonsense glare, and the laughter stops.

Clearly, she's out of the loop here.

"Steam," Second Hothniel says. "Which you would know if you belonged in this room."

Nestraya tenses but ignores him. She'll have to ask Corivos to research this new technology. She's heard of the humans using steam to power other machines, but a carriage capable of traveling at high speeds that close to the border is a frightening prospect.

"Continue," she tells the head of intelligence.

"Our most recent reports indicate the humans are not yet aware that the elves they killed belonged to the king's elite warriors and included the king himself."

Nestraya frowns. Restoval's silver hair was easily identifiable, even to the humans. "How could they not know?"

"It was a wild retreat," Second Hothniel says dismissively. "Disorganized at best. The humans were acting like barbarians, attacking anything that crossed their paths like rabid dogs. They didn't even wait to see the outcome of their actions."

Nestraya glances at Corivos, but he shrugs. Second Hothniel was the only one there who lived to tell what happened. They have little reason to doubt him.

It just seems like such an unlikely account. To take down the king's elite warriors without even realizing what they'd done? Without recognizing Restoval, the King of Lostariel? When they knew to target Windhaven?

"There is evidence that a change in power might soon occur in Nunia," the intelligence head says, drawing Nestraya back into the conversation. "The king's son has taken on many of his father's duties during the past month. Rumors of the king's failing health are widespread."

Great. Just what they need. A hot-headed young prince eager to prove himself. At least Lorial hasn't the stomach for battle, unlike these humans. He's not going to escalate a war to make a point, especially not with Nestraya standing as his First. They'd already be attacking Feressa if Second Hothniel had his way.

"I want you to keep your eyes on Feressa," Nestraya says. "If you see any sign of the prince amassing an invasion force, I want to know about it the minute after you do."

"Understood, First Nestraya."

The meeting continues with begrudging cooperation from most of the elves now under her command. None deign to spit on her as they pass out of the room, so she'll consider that a victory.

Once they're gone, she drops to a chair and sighs.

"You did well, my First," Corivos says.

"I played a part. Nothing more."

"I couldn't tell." He lowers himself to the chair beside her.

"Thank you for doing this with me."

"I serve at your pleasure, my First."

"To that end, will you research steam locomotives for me? I'd prefer to avoid playing the idiot in the future as much as possible."

"Of course, my First. I'll start now."

She chuckles at his eagerness as he departs, and just as she's about to go find Lorial, the door closes on its own.

A niggle of fear twinges in her belly as she grasps at her magic and searches the edges of the room.

Then the hair atop her head catches the breeze, and she groans. "If you tell me you were here the whole time, I'm going to douse you."

Lorial suddenly appears far too close to her for comfort, but she refuses to give him the satisfaction of reacting to his nearness.

"You were magnificent," he murmurs.

"You were not invited. Did you not trust me to handle it? You're the one who insisted on thrusting me into this position."

"It wasn't you I was worried about. It was them. I wanted to make sure nobody spat on you today." Anger clouds his eyes, and Nestraya sighs.

"I've experienced worse, I can assure you. I can't believe you pulled that off. Have you been practicing?"

"A little. Father—" Lorial sighs. "Father was working with me before he died." He straightens and approaches the window, looking out into the forest. "There aren't many air wielders left to teach me now."

Nestraya stands and joins him. "I'll help you however I am able," she says softly.

He nods, and for a while, they just gaze out over the forest together.

Eventually, Nestraya speaks. "Do you trust Second Hothniel's account of the human raiders?"

"No."

"Neither do I."

Lorial turns toward her, but before he can speak, the head of intelligence bursts through the door.

"My king. First Nestraya. Nunia marches on Lostariel. They say elves have attacked Feressa."

10
MARCH THROUGH THE WOODS

Lorial holds up his own warrior leathers. He's only worn them once before.

The night Father died.

Father's blood still stains the expensive clothing.

Nestraya glares at him. "You're not coming."

"I am." He pulls his formal shirt off over his head. He'd have to be blind to miss the way Nestraya's eyes sweep over his bare chest, and heat creeps up his neck. "With as much as you've been pushing me away, you seem more than content to stand there and watch me undress."

"I'm not watch—" She groans. "Lorial, you are not a warrior. Putting on the clothes doesn't change that, and you know it."

He fastens the underlayer before reaching for the leather jacket and sliding it along his arms. "I'm the king now. I'm not an elfling. I'm not helpless."

"I didn't say you were."

He sits on the edge of his bed and tugs off his boots. "You thought it."

"You just...you need more training before you run headlong into the wrong end of a musket."

Boots off, he stands again and raises his brows as he reaches for the fastening at the waist of his formal trousers, and she finally turns away.

When she followed him from the Council Chamber, he didn't think she'd stride into his personal rooms behind him.

And then she stayed.

And now he's getting dressed in front of her.

So much for avoiding giving the wrong impression to people. Not that anyone knows they're here. Alone. While he strips out of his formal clothes.

Moving quickly, he exchanges his wool for leather.

"Are you decent yet?" she asks as he pulls his boots on.

"Yes."

She turns back to him. "Now, as I was saying—"

He reaches for his bow and quiver, followed by his cloak.

"Lorial! Are you even listening?"

"Yes. You're beautiful when you're mad. Let's go."

Her jaw hangs, but he doesn't wait for her response as he pushes her toward the door, only to find Mother standing in the corridor. Her brows rise, and Nestraya steps away from Lorial.

"This is not what it looks like, Mera. Miravel."

Lorial resists the urge to smile. She's flustered.

"Is it not?" Mother asks. "Pity."

Nestraya chokes, and Lorial's mouth quirks up despite his best effort to keep a straight face.

Then reality comes into focus again.

"Mother, the humans—"

"I know. Corivos informed me. I'll be safe here for now. Let me hold you both before you go." She wraps an arm around each of them. "I love you so much, my elflings."

"And I, you," Lorial whispers.

"Mera." It's all Nestraya says. It probably means more than anything else she could have uttered.

After a few more moments, Mother lets them go. "I expect you both to return to me in one piece. Do you understand? I will not lose either of you tonight."

"We'll do our best," Lorial says, though of course he can't promise her anything.

And she knows it.

He kisses her cheek and then starts down the corridor.

"Lorial, wait," Nestraya says.

He doesn't slow. "This conversation is over."

"You oaf of a man. I need to gather my things."

He stills. When he turns, Mother looks amused, which is refreshing after the week they've passed together.

It leaves him feeling guilty, though, as well.

Soon enough, Nestraya flies from her chamber with her own cloak and bow. "Now we can go."

By the time they reach the barracks along with Corivos, the various bands of warriors have already assembled. Second Hothniel addresses the joint forces of high- and low-born elves, and Lorial frowns.

"He should not—"

"I know," Nestraya says.

"You—"

"I know. Can you see now why I fought you on this, my king? It was never going to be easy."

"We don't make decisions because they're easy. We do what we know is right."

"You sound like Restoval," she says softly.

"That is high praise, *estrassa*."

She sighs. "Excuse me."

As he watches, she strides toward Second Hothniel and lifts her voice so it carries across the forest. "Thank you, Second Hothniel. I will take it from here."

The man looks loath to relinquish command of the warriors, but he inclines his head and takes a step back.

"Elven warriors," Nestraya calls out, and more than one grunt of disgust echoes toward Lorial's ears. Nestraya ignores it all, though. "Our only goal today is to defend Lostariel and the Wildthorne Woods from attackers. We have lost far too much already—"

The booing grows louder, and Nestraya's anger builds.

She's magnificent when she's angry.

"You will maintain your silence until I give you leave to speak. Is that clear? This is not up for debate. If you cannot follow my orders, take your leave and return to your mother's breasts like an elfling. I have no use for such cowards in my bands of warriors."

Lorial stares at her in shock, as do most of the warriors standing before her. She...sounds just like Father.

And she thinks she can't do this?

"Now, I don't know what you've been told, but our king Lorial hopes we can settle this peacefully. You will not engage the enemy so long as they stay on Nunian soil. Is that understood?"

A resounding affirmation rumbles around them, and Nestraya nods. "Good. We will separate into two squadrons as planned. Second Hothniel will lead the high-born bands, and Second Weforyn will command the low-born warriors. We head out tonight."

A round of cheers erupts from a number of warriors, and Nestraya makes her way back to Lorial as the bands prepare to move out.

"You sounded like Father," Lorial says once she's by his side again.

"I was pretending to be him. I'm just relieved it worked."

"I think we all are, my First," Corivos says. "Do we really trust Second Hothniel to lead the high borns?"

Nestraya sighs. "No. But the backlash if I relieved him would have rivaled anything we've seen so far. Keep a close eye on him."

Corivos nods. "Yes, my First."

"What intel do we have on the reports of an elven raid on Feressa?" Lorial asks.

"That's all the information we have, my king," Corivos says as they mount the leather-clad horses grooms lead out to them. "No word on who these elves were or if they truly set foot in Feressa. The human prince has declared it an act of war."

Nestraya frowns. "And attacking Windhaven and killing our king wasn't?"

"We have received no communication from Nunia regarding either of those events," Corivos says. "I checked with the head of intelligence myself before he left Windhaven."

"How were you not promoted to Second long ago?" Lorial asks.

"You forget to whom you speak, my king. I am a low-born elf."

Lorial studies the man. There's no rancor in his words or expression. Mere acceptance.

"Lorial," he says to Corivos.

"I beg your pardon, my king?"

"Call me Lorial in private. Together, we three are simply elves."

Shock wends across Corivos's face, but he doesn't argue.

"Head out," Second Hothniel calls, and Lorial nudges his horse forward along with the warrior bands.

His warriors.

A sick feeling lodges in the pit of his stomach, but he pushes it away.

A king doesn't have the luxury of being overcome.

They travel well into the night, making camp halfway to the border to rest the horses. The latest reports from their spies in Nunia indicate Prince Gerault is still amassing his troops outside Feressa. They have time to rest for a few hours.

Not that Lorial can sleep.

"You should lie down, my king," Nestraya says softly as she approaches him where he stares off into the murky woods beyond their bands of warriors.

He doesn't respond.

"Would you like me to help you sleep?"

Images of her curling up beside him flit through his mind, and he looks at her in surprise.

"Every warrior-class healer knows how to induce brief sleep," she says.

Of course that's what she meant.

He shakes his head. "I need to stay alert."

"Very well." She stands at his shoulder, and he returns his gaze to the forest.

"Do you think I'm doing the right thing? Humans killed my father mere days ago. Should I not fall on them with the full force of my elven warriors?"

"I don't know, Lorial. I can't shake the feeling that something doesn't add up about your father's death. It would be foolhardy to send our warriors to face human firepower before we find out the truth. If the Prince of Nunia truly has no knowledge of what happened, it's possible the human raiders were mercenaries of some sort. Restoval wouldn't march into battle with magic flying and muskets blazing without all the facts."

"I should have visited the Tree of Memories before we left Darlei."

The thought didn't even occur to him until they were underway.

When she doesn't respond, he turns to look at her. The glow from the many lanterns suspended around their makeshift camp shines on her shortened braid and across her peach cheeks as a sudden, overwhelming longing pinches at his heart.

"Nestraya."

"Don't. Please don't. Don't ruin everything we are to each other by grasping at something we could never be. You are the king. I am the fae-touched daughter of a common elf. There is no future for us."

"You are the daughter of Restoval's heart."

Lorial wasn't sure if the magic would let him repeat his father's words from the Tree of Memories. It's no secret, though. She must already know that's how Father saw her.

She turns her face away. "But when people look at me, they don't see a princess. They see a freak reaching above her station."

"I see a beautiful woman," Lorial whispers. "Brilliant and strong. Loyal and true. Everything a queen should be."

Nestraya sighs and meets his gaze. "You delude yourself, my king."

Before he can respond, she turns and strides into the darkness as he watches her disappear from view.

11

ALONE

"Wandering alone, my First?"

Nestraya freezes at the derision in the man's voice. She was so distracted by Lorial's words playing in her head that she didn't sense the approach of the elf whose dagger at her side threatens to slide between her ribs.

"What do you want?" she asks.

"I want many things." He slides his arm along her waist as fear squeezes its tendrils around her heart, but she dares not move. Not yet. Not until she has a better grasp of his magic and what she's facing.

He must not be very powerful if she can't sense his magic this close to him. His rank breath rises beside her cheek, where he leans close as he pulls her back to his chest.

She can feel Lorial's air magic from across rooms—this man has very little magic at all. He's weak. That's probably why he resorted to using a weapon to subdue her.

"You must be good to him for him to grant you so many favors," the man says.

"You speak nonsense."

"Do I? Would he continue to elevate you if you were to bestow your favors on another? Fae slops?"

Panic threatens her calm as she forces herself not to fight back. "Again, what do you want from me?"

"I think you know what I want."

Just as his hand slides upward along her leathers, she gets a smoky hint of fire magic.

Perfect.

If she can distract him long enough to disarm him, his magic will be no match for her water powers.

"Not here," she whispers as she lays her hand over his to slow its upward progression. "Not where my king might discover us."

"Does he know you perform for the highest bidder?" the man presses his lips to her neck, and she pushes back the revulsion that threatens to upend her stomach contents.

"Put the dagger away, and it will be our little secret."

The point of his blade presses deeper into her ribs, puncturing her ayervadi leather.

"I don't think so, fae slops. You disgust me. Did you really think I'd fall for your wiles as our weak kingling has? As if I would lower myself to tryst with you." He spits across her face before wrenching her arm behind her back. "You're coming with me."

So much for distracting him.

Reaching out with her plant magic, she sends shoots of roots and vines toward his arms and legs. As he trips, his dagger slices her skin, but it's merely a flesh wound, and she doesn't hesitate as she spins away from him.

Pulling forth water from a nearby creek, she blasts the man where he hovers, dangling from the vines that wrap themselves around his body. Any spark he attempts to bring forth is easily overpowered.

Just as she's about to pull back on her water magic, a hand rests over her hair, and the dim light of the forest fades.

A life wielder. And a powerful one. With...stone magic? She should have been searching for other elves nearby.

It's the last thought that fills her mind before darkness engulfs her.

Lorial watches the forest where Nestraya disappeared, but as morning light trickles over the Wildthorne Woods, she still hasn't returned.

Finally, turning toward the warriors where they break camp, Lorial seeks out Corivos.

"Where is Nestraya?" Lorial whispers so no one else will hear.

"Scouting ahead. She sent word that we're to meet her near the border."

She left? Without telling him?

"Are you all right, my king? Lorial?"

"Yes. Just concerned about what awaits us."

And Nestraya.

They have scouts. Why would she feel the need to wander off alone? Did his words truly upset her enough for her to leave without telling him?

At least she sent word to Corivos.

"We're four hours from the border," Second Hothniel calls out to the warriors. "We will taste victory before this day ends."

A cheer erupts from many of the warriors, though several low-born elves frown and whisper amongst themselves.

"Corivos—"

"I heard. What would you have me do? I fear few among the high-born elves would listen to me."

"Would they listen to me?"

"You're their king."

"I'm not convinced Second Hothniel realizes that."

Before Lorial can address his warriors himself, one of their scouts gallops into the camp. "Humans have crossed the border!"

"Already?" Lorial says. "I was assured we had time."

"I warned you it was unwise to stop last night," Second Hothniel says. "Warriors, mount up! We fight to avenge our king!"

"Wait!" Lorial cries.

Where is Nestraya? She should have returned when the scout did.

But his warriors are already assembling behind Second Hothniel.

"You don't belong here, my kingling," Hothniel spits out. "Perhaps you should run to your mother's breast like your weak pet. Wait. That's right. She's just a dog off the streets. A mongrel. How much did her disgusting whore mother pay a fae lord to impregnate her? And now, at the first sign of trouble, your strumpet is nowhere to be found, is she? My men saw her making her way back to Darlei. Not even she will fight by your side. You are all alone."

Shock turns every muscle in Lorial's body to pudding as Hothniel's words prick him like knives.

Then anger. So much anger.

"Hothniel, you are hereby stripped of your rank and command. You will leave my presence and never return."

Hothniel laughs, and soon other elves join him before he turns away from Lorial. "Move out, warriors! We fight!"

"Do something!" Corivos hisses, but Lorial just watches in helpless shock as his bands of warriors push past him.

He failed.

But Nestraya wouldn't abandon him. Would she?

Pain slices across Nestraya's ribs as she wakes in total darkness on cold stone. She reaches for the wound from the elf's dagger, and sticky warmth spreads across her fingers. Perhaps the damage was worse than she thought.

Reaching out with her life magic, she does her best to knit the wound, though the lack of light makes it difficult. It will probably leave a scar. Thoughts of Lorial's reaction fill her mind, but she pushes them away. She's not his, and even if she was, he wouldn't care about a scar.

What a ridiculous thing to be concerned with right now.

Far more pressing is the question of where she is and who brought her here.

And why?

With her wound healed well enough, Nestraya feels around in the dark. She's definitely on a stone floor of some sort, and no one else, elf or human, seems to be nearby. She'd be able to sense them with her life magic.

The floor is rough and uneven, not smooth as she'd expect from a dungeon of some sort. A cave, perhaps? The air is too stale and dark for her to be outside.

Gingerly, she crawls along the ground, trying to get a sense of her surroundings, when a stone wall rises in front of her.

She pushes herself to her feet and follows the wall with her hand as she steps forward. Occasionally, she trips, but each time, she catches herself.

The wall stretches much farther than she would expect given the staleness of the air, but, unsure what else to do, she continues moving forward.

Is she underground? There are no stone structures or caves this large near Darlei. At least, none that she's aware of.

She trips again, and as she reaches down to search for whatever caught her foot this time, her hand brushes against a tree root protruding through a crack in the wall.

Perhaps she can use that to help her escape. She'll have to return to it after she reaches the end of this tunnel or whatever it is.

She pushes forward, taking small steps, shuffling carefully along, until she trips again. Reaching down, she feels another root extending in front of her, and she frowns. It's shaped remarkably like the first root.

That's impossible, though. Isn't it?

A little farther, and then she'll turn around.

As she shuffles forward, soon enough, her boot knocks against yet another root, and her stomach knots as the reality of her situation sinks in.

It's not a tunnel. It's a sealed cave.

And she's been going around in circles.

12
STONE MAGIC

Stone magic.

A sick feeling pools in the pit of Nestraya's stomach. It's almost as rare as air magic.

She should have sensed him coming. Was she really so focused on the elf with the dagger that she didn't notice Second Hothniel sneaking up on her? Plying her into a brief sleep with his life magic? Why wasn't she paying more attention?

He must have grown this cave around her. It's solid with no way out. But why?

The roiling in her stomach grows as something else occurs to her.

Another elf was present when Restoval's body was collected by the healers. Second Hothniel was injured. The same elves who gathered the dead, may they find rest, treated Second Hothniel before transporting him to the Healing Center.

Hothniel carries the same warrior-class healing certification as Nestraya. Blotting out Restoval's last memories would have been an easy skill for him to master.

To hide the truth of Pera's death.

It wasn't humans who killed him, though a human weapon may have been responsible.

It was his own Second.

He was betrayed.

The emotion of the past few days chokes her as sobs grip her body. She thought she cried all her tears when Mera held her the night of the joining ceremony, but clearly she didn't.

Images of Lorial flash before her eyes, and fear clutches at her.

Lorial. He's in danger. Even more danger than they realized.

Using the breathing techniques she learned from Pera to re-center herself, she calms her tears. There will be time to mourn later.

Lorial must think she abandoned him. She needs to find a way out of here. If only she had fire magic to light the cave.

Why trap her here to start with, though? Why not kill her and be done with it?

Leverage, perhaps? Lorial would do anything to protect her, foolish man that he is. Especially since he fancies himself in love with her.

And Mera. What would Mera do if she knew Nestraya was in danger?

Second Hothniel is a widower. His own binding partner died just last winter of some mysterious illness.

Whistling wind. Did he kill her, too?

Mera is young. Not yet two hundred. Beautiful.

Binding with her would legitimize whatever regime change Hothniel has planned.

And Mera would do it to save Nestraya.

Bile rises in her throat like a human projectile, and Nestraya doubles over as the meager contents of her stomach make a reappearance.

She's stronger than this. Isn't that what Pera told her the night he died? As he walked her back to the barracks right before she sensed the humans nearby.

"You are so strong," he murmured as he wrapped his arm around her shoulders. "You will do great things, I have no doubt. Someday, the name Nestraya Westaria will be sung as one of our heroes of legend."

"First of all, I think perhaps you've had too much to drink," she said to him. "And second, that's not even my name. Westaria is your name."

"It will be your name."

He started to say more, but she'll never know what. She interrupted him with her cry of humans nearby.

And then he was gone with his elite warriors. And the next time she saw him, he lay dying in Lorial's arms, his mouth so full of his own sticky blood that his words came out garbled before they ceased.

What would he have said? Would she have listened?

She needs to be strong now. For Pera. For Mera and Lorial.

Wiping the back of her hand across her mouth, she assesses her situation. Water will cut through stone, but it takes time, and she would become dehydrated long before she freed herself without a source of water nearby.

Her life magic is useless right now.

That leaves her plant magic. And that root Hothniel overlooked when trapping her in here. A weed can push apart rocks when given the chance. A root can upend a foundation.

Surely it could break a wall of stone.

She runs her hand along the cave wall again until she finds the root. Grasping it, she reaches out with her magic, coaxing it to grow. Not fast—she doesn't want to damage it. But slowly. Steadily.

It's hard to tell if her efforts are even helping, but before long, a tiny sliver of light forms in a crack in the stone.

It's working.

She keeps pushing, encouraging the root to push apart the stone, and the hardy tree keeps growing.

Then a loud crack rends the air as the sliver of light spreads faster than her eyes can follow it up the wall to the roof above.

Whistling wind. She's going to be buried in rubble.

She pulls back on her magic, but it's too late. The crack grows as she hurries to the other side of the cave. Webs of lines branch off in all directions, and just as the stone ceiling starts to cave in on itself, she steps in the puddle of sick, and her feet fly out from under her. Her head hits the stone floor, and everything goes dark again.

"Lorial, there!"

Lorial follows Corivos's gaze to a strange mound of stone in the middle of the forest.

"That doesn't belong there," Corivos continues. "And the tree beside it is growing."

Together, they rush forward as Lorial tries to make sense of what he's witnessing.

Plant magic. Is Nestraya inside the stone mound?

A crack forms in the stone wall, and Lorial looks on in horror. What is she trying to do? Kill herself?

"Nestraya!"

Corivos lifts his hands toward the rock. "My stone magic is weak. I can't hold it for long."

"I thought you were a soil wielder."

"I am. I'm not allowed to claim a second affinity. That doesn't mean I don't have one. My father made me swear not to let anyone find out. Help me. Please!"

There's no time to ponder his words. Lorial reaches out with his air magic to lift the crumbling stone and fling it away before it caves in on itself, and Corivos staggers beside him.

They both rush forward, picking their way over tiny bits of debris that now litter the stone cage. And in the midst of it, beneath a layer of dust and pebbles, lies Nestraya. Not moving. Not doing anything.

"Nestraya!" Lorial drops beside her. As he gathers her to his chest, a warm wetness seeps onto his hand, and dread fills him. When he pulls his hand away, he expects to see crimson.

But it's not blood.

"What...?" He sniffs it, and his stomach nearly revolts.

"I think it's vomit," Corivos says. "But she has quite the goose egg."

Lorial presses his fingers under her nose, and her warm breath fills him with relief. "She's breathing."

Suddenly, she coughs and pulls her face away from his hand. The one with the sick on it.

Her eyes blink open, and Lorial doesn't even try to hide the tears streaming down his face. "You will not die. Do you hear me, Nestraya?"

"You're alive," she breathes. Then she coughs again and reaches for the back of her head. "I fell." Threads of her magic encapsulate her hair, and after a minute, she sags in his arms and drops her hand. "That's better."

"You almost killed yourself. If Corivos hadn't been here to hold the stones while I gathered my senses, you'd be under a pile of rubble right now."

"I knew you were hiding stone magic," she murmurs. "All those pebbles you slip in the soil and fling at me while we're sparring."

"I'm sorry," Corivos whispers, looking more than a little overcome himself. "I—"

"I understand," she says. "You can stop clutching me, Lorial. I'm fine now."

"I will never let you go again. Never."

"Don't be an idiot. Help me up."

He pulls her to her feet but doesn't let go of her hands. They're both covered in sick, but he can't bring himself to care.

When Second Hothniel rode off with the elven warriors, Corivos was all that held Lorial together. He insisted Nestraya wouldn't have abandoned Lorial and managed to grow terror in Lorial's heart like he's never experienced. Even when Father died.

And now that Nestraya's safe, Lorial couldn't care less about pretense or appearances anymore. Without hesitating, he wraps his arms around her, and she stiffens.

"Lorial—"

"Who did this to you?" Lorial buries his face in her hair. It smells like vomit, but so does he.

"Lorial!"

Corivos clears his throat as he brushes off his hands. "I imagine it was Hothniel. He's the only other stone wielder I've met in the warrior bands."

Nestraya slides her palms along Lorial's arms, untangling him from her and taking his hands within hers. He threads his fingers between her smaller ones before she can let go, and long-suffering fills her eyes, but she doesn't push him away.

He probably should let go, but he feels as though she might fade away if he doesn't hold on to her.

"I didn't see him, but I'm sure it was Second Hothniel," she says. "I think...I think he killed Pera, too. And blotted out Pera's memories to hide it."

13

THE KING'S ELITE WARRIORS

Nestraya watches the series of emotions that sweep across Lorial's face at her words.

"He betrayed Father? Murdered him? Father trusted him. And now he's commandeered my bands of warriors and marches on Nunia as we speak."

"He what?" Nestraya looks from Lorial to Corivos.

"It's true," Corivos says. "Lorial tried to relieve him, but he just laughed. All the high borns followed him and about half of the low borns."

No wonder Lorial looks broken.

"It seems I've failed," Lorial whispers.

"No. No! This is not over. You are not giving up."

"They won't follow me, Nestraya. I'm little more than an elfling in their eyes. I wield the affinities of the Dragon King, but I can barely manage half the magic Zelovon mastered. I'm not a warrior, as you've pointed out again and again. They won't follow me. The line of Westaria ends with me."

"Don't be ridiculous. What would Pera say to you now?"

For a moment, Lorial stares into her eyes as if searching for something. "I think he would say I need you. They might not follow me...but some of them might follow us."

She scoffs. "Now you're spouting nonsense. Come on. You can spout nonsense on the way to fix this mess." She tugs her hands away from him and glances at the sky to get her bearings before striding west toward camp. "A few hours. I was only gone for a few hours."

She looks back to make sure they're following, and they both smile at her.

"Well, come on."

By the time they arrive back at camp, only a few handfuls of low-born warriors remain. Nestraya recognizes all of them as those who've never insulted or spat at her.

"First Nestraya. King Lorial," one of the elves says.

"You said half," Nestraya whispers to Corivos.

"I may have exaggerated."

"Where are my Thirds?" Lorial asks.

What is he doing?

Three of the fifteen step forward.

"You three are now Seconds. The rest of you are Thirds. Four to a Second. For your loyalty...I—"

"My king," one of the new Seconds says. The others echo her call.

"We may not live to see tomorrow," Lorial says. "But if we do, you will be my elite warrior band. When everyone left, you stayed. I will not forget."

Nestraya glances from him to the elves and back again.

"How many of you are hiding a second affinity?" he continues.

At first, no one speaks, but then Corivos steps forward. "I am a soil and stone wielder."

A series of whispers rise around them, and then one of the women lifts her hand. A new Third. "I have little mastery, but I wield destruction magic in addition to plant magic."

"You wield destruction magic, Third Derazyn?" Nestraya says. It must be weaker magic, or she would have sensed it.

"I do. I haven't been trained to use what little I have, but I can…I can do this." She holds her hands toward a fallen log in the distance, and Nestraya jumps when the top layer explodes in a cloud of decaying wood.

"And you chose plant magic?" Nestraya asks.

The woman shrugs.

Nestraya turns to the female Second, the only other member of their band with destruction magic. "Third Derazyn is under your command. Teach her as much as you can while we travel."

"Yes, my First."

"Anyone else?" Lorial asks.

When no one is forthcoming, he turns to Nestraya, waiting for her to announce a plan, probably.

"Second Corivos will reassign the rest of you. My new Seconds, join me and our king while we discuss our battle plan."

"What is our plan?" Lorial whispers near her ear.

"I have no idea."

The three Seconds approach, and Nestraya clears her throat. "Our priority is to protect our king."

They nod and continue to look expectantly at her.

"We need to take down Hothniel," she eventually says. "Cut off the head, and hopefully, the body will fall. I'm open to suggestions."

They stand there discussing their options, and all three of her new Seconds impress her with their strategic thinking. Especially Second Quilian, the oldest of the three.

The horses are gone, so they'll have to go on foot. By the time they pull out, they have a vague plan. It's not much, but at least it's something.

The sound of musket fire reaches them before Nestraya senses the presence of humans. One Third, another elf with life magic, was sent ahead to scout out the scene, and he quickly returns bearing the news they all feared.

The battle rages at the outer edge of the Wildthorne Woods, and people are dying.

On both sides.

"Hothniel leads the elf warriors," the scout, Third Rafelis, says. "As far as I could tell, he's stationed the low-born warriors at the front lines while the high-born elves attack from afar."

"Farther from the human firearms," Nestraya says.

"Indeed. It might work in our favor, though. Hothniel will be easier to target away from the front lines."

"And the human prince?" Corivos asks. "They say he has brown hair that shines red in the sun."

How does he know these things?

"The smoke from the muskets made it difficult to see the human lines, and they all wore caps of some sort. One man seemed to be giving orders, but I can't tell you if he was the prince or not."

Nestraya nods. "Thank you, Third. You may return to your band of warriors."

The man bows his head and spins to rejoin the other loyal elves.

"So we flank him," Lorial says. "We each ride with one of our three bands, coming from the north, the east, and the west."

Nestraya shakes her head. "We do this without you. You have no heir. If you die on that battlefield, this will all be for naught."

Lorial purses his lips as he stares into her eyes. "Emeralds," he whispers. "And ebony."

Corivos glances between them, confusion in his eyes, but he says nothing.

"Put that image aside, my king," she says softly.

He shakes his head. "Never. It's all I have to hold on to right now."

She sighs. "Then cling to this fantasy of yours and stay alive, my king. We do this without you."

This time, he doesn't argue, which is a little troubling. She didn't think it would be that easy. Hopefully, he's not planning something heroic and idiotic. That's the last thing she needs to worry about right now.

Nestraya takes the least experienced Second under her wing and sends Corivos with the other young Second.

The third band is led by Second Quilian, who, Corivos informed her, is one of the most experienced low-born elves in the entire warrior ranks. His loyalty to his king is a boon for them all. The more Nestraya speaks to him, the clearer it becomes that the only reason he didn't surpass the rank of Third until now is because of his status as a low-born elf.

"We all have our orders," Nestraya says. "If things go south, get out of there. You all are too valuable to lose here today. Do you understand?"

"Yes, my First," the loyal elves say.

As the three bands separate, Lorial sneaks up behind Nestraya, though she's been keeping her life magic active and easily senses him. The only time she can't sense him and his powerful air magic is when he's cloaking himself with it.

"That goes for you, too," he whispers in her ear. "You are far too valuable to lose, Nestraya. *Estrassa.*"

She turns to face him. "I will do everything I can to return to your side, my king."

His gray eyes stare down at her with an intensity that steals her breath away.

"Why do you keep calling me that?" he asks.

"To remind you of the gulf that exists between us, my king."

He takes a step closer. "It's not working."

To her shock, he slides his hands along her jaw, framing her face as he leans close. Surely he isn't going to kiss her here, in front of his band of elite warriors.

Or anywhere, for that matter.

But instead of his lips, he presses his forehead to hers. It's still an intimate sign of affection, but one appropriate for a sister and not just a lover, as a kiss would have been. Her tense muscles relax, and she closes her eyes.

"Return to me," he says softly.

Then he lets her go, and something deep in her belly flutters.

She pushes the sensation from her mind. Every single one of her warrior elves seems very intent on everything except her as she joins her band. With one last glance at Lorial, she and her five companions head west through the woods toward the musket fire.

14

CEASEFIRE

As they tread lightly through the woods, the familiar brush of Lorial's air magic lingers in Nestraya's mind. His fire magic is more than adequate, but his air magic overpowers everything else when he's near. It's familiar, like home. So reminiscent of Pera's air magic.

Not every life wielder can feel magic the way Nestraya can. And not every elf has strong enough magic for her to sense, especially if one of their affinities is stronger than the other one, like Corivos with his weaker stone magic.

Healer Cadowyn once told Nestraya her own magic was overwhelming. All three affinities drowning out everything else.

She stops short.

What if Hothniel can sense her coming? He's a life wielder. A strong one.

Will her presence jeopardize their entire mission?

"What is it, my First?" Second Yedelis asks.

"Hothniel will sense my magic."

"Even with all the other elves nearby?"

"I don't know. It's possible."

The Second purses his lips before calling for one of his Thirds, another life wielder, the scout they sent out earlier. "What sense do you have of First Nestraya's magic?"

The man glances from his Second to Nestraya and back again. "It's stronger than almost anything else I've ever sensed, my Second."

"Noticeable even among other elves?" Nestraya asks.

"It depends. When our king Lorial is near, his air magic blunts my sense of you to a small degree. And it's easier to dismiss when you walk among other high borns, especially those with powerful magic. But right now, your magic masks that of everyone else in our warrior band."

Lorial's air magic is stronger than her three affinities? That's fascinating. She has little time to dwell on it, though.

"Perhaps we could use this to our advantage," Nestraya says. "If I distract Hothniel, he might not sense the rest of our warrior band approaching."

"Are you sure that's wise, my First? With all due respect, we can't afford to lose you," Second Yedelis says.

"I can take care of myself."

Probably. Though Lorial might disagree, especially after what happened earlier with the cave.

In any case, it's their best chance.

"I'll go first," Nestraya says. "The rest of you stick to the plan. No matter what happens to me, protect your king at all costs."

"Understood."

Nestraya moves to the front of their band, and after she's put some distance between herself and them, she reaches out with her threads of life magic, searching for a stone wielder on the battlefield ahead.

The closer they get, the louder everything becomes. Musket fire and words yelled in Elvish and, more distantly, Nunian. She recognizes some of the human language from the tutoring Restoval insisted on. She should have paid more attention. Lorial was always better with language lessons than she was.

The faint essence of stone magic greets her. Too strong to be Corivos.

She slows her steps and quietly presses forward. Elven shouts of "Attack!" and "Strengthen the left flank!" rise to greet her. If she's not mistaken, that's Hothniel himself giving the orders. If he senses her, he's given no indication.

Stepping past a few more trees, she stops, and her stomach clenches at the battlefield rising before her. While the high borns hide behind trees, Hothniel sends line after line of low borns into the fray to draw the musket fire. If the piles of bodies growing at the front of the human lines are any sign, his plan is working as high-born elves attack the distracted Nunians from afar, but too many elf warriors lie near the dead humans to make it worthwhile.

The loss of life is staggering. This isn't what Restoval would have wanted. It's a good thing Lorial isn't here to see this. He'd probably lose all sense and do something stupid to try to keep everyone from killing each other.

No, the best plan is to take down Hothniel. The elves and humans alike look frightened—overwhelmed and in shock. With Hothniel out of the picture, a temporary ceasefire should be possible.

Perhaps they could reason with the humans. Find a peaceful solution. Figure out who's responsible for the rogue raiding parties crossing the border in both directions and put a stop to it.

Though she's pretty sure she already knows who's responsible.

They have to take down Hothniel.

She reaches for her bow before remembering she left it behind as she wandered off into the woods last night. It was gone when she returned, probably stolen by Hothniel's men trying to make it look as if she'd truly abandoned Lorial.

Hothniel would almost certainly sense her magic if she tried to use it from here, though.

She'll have to let one of her warriors take him down while she distracts him, just as they discussed.

As Second Yedelis approaches, Nestraya steps out from behind the tree and runs toward the fighters. She can faintly sense Corivos nearby. Hopefully, he holds steady.

Then that familiar rush of air magic engulfs her, and she gasps.

Where is he?

Oblivious to the chaos around her, she scans the scene, searching for his silver hair. She spots him running toward the fray.

"Ceasefire!" he cries. "We can end this peacefully! Too many people have died here today!"

Stupid, stupid, heroic man. He must have cloaked himself and followed her.

Hothniel has noticed as well if that smirk on his face is any indication. Then the vile man's brows lower, and he turns and looks straight at Nestraya.

Mustering her plant magic, she reaches toward Lorial, whose presence has so surprised the front lines that the low-born elves have backed off.

At least they aren't trying to kill him.

The human leader yells something in Nunian, but Nestraya can't make it out as she digs down for her plant magic to pull Lorial out of the fighting. It's weak, though, after her exertion in the cave.

Water magic, it is. She searches their surroundings until she locates a creek nearby and coaxes the water to her. It's little more than a trickle. The other water wielders must have already drained it.

At best, she'd be able to douse Lorial with it, which won't help anyone. Stupid, stupid man.

Stones start flying her way, and she dodges them as she takes off toward the fray. Then other magic and elven weapons home in on her. The rocks fall shy of touching her, and mounds of soil rise to protect her as she runs.

Corivos.

She doesn't take the time to seek him out as the temporary ceasefire Lorial called for holds at the front lines.

Maybe it will work.

She'd feel a lot better if Lorial was more practiced at holding those shields he's been working to master since they were elflings.

"Lorial!" she cries as she follows him onto the battlefield.

He turns to look at her, his concentration wavering, and just as she reaches his side, the unmistakable blast of a nearby musket tears at her ears.

The ball pierces a weak point in Lorial's shield, and his left shoulder rips backward as he falls against her.

"Lorial!" she screams.

The human leader yells something unintelligible, and the cries of elven warriors erupt around them as Nestraya lowers Lorial to the ground.

The sounds are distant, as if muffled, and the battle cries and resumed musket fire fade into the background.

Blood seeps from Lorial's shoulder, and his eyes grow large as he looks at her.

"Don't die. Please don't die." She reaches for her life magic, pushing past the noise of everyone around them as she presses her hand against his wound to stop the bleeding. Oblivious to everyone and everything else, she closes her eyes and uses her magic to see into his wound. The seared flesh. The jagged tear.

Please, not his heart.

She follows the trajectory of the musket ball, searching for it within his body, but it's not there.

It passed through his shoulder.

It must have missed his heart.

She almost tips over in relief, but she manages to keep her head.

The bleeding. She needs to slow the bleeding.

She's not trained for this. She could knit the flesh back together, but would he continue to bleed internally?

Then someone grabs her, and her eyes flash open. It's Corivos. Their warrior band surrounds them on every side, magic and arrows flying outward in all directions.

"Does he live?" Corivos asks.

Nestraya nods and glances at Lorial's face again. It's pale. Too pale. And he's lost consciousness.

"We have to get him somewhere safe." Relief fills Corivos's voice, but Nestraya shakes her head.

"We can't move him."

"If we don't, someone will break through our warrior shield. We're being attacked from both sides. We've already lost one of our warriors."

"What?"

"Hothniel has retaken control. If we don't retreat, we'll all die. Can he be moved?"

Despite Nestraya's best efforts to stem the bleeding, the pools of blood on Lorial and the ground beneath him continue to grow larger. He's weakening. She can feel it.

But if they stay, he'll die.

"Third Rafelis," she calls, and the scout drops back within the circle as their ranks close to fill the gap.

"How can I help?"

"He's losing too much blood. I need you to press on his wounds with your magic while we lift him. I'm going to try replenishing his blood with my life magic as we go. It may not work, but I don't know what else to do. I'll do my best to keep his heart beating until we can get a real healer to help him."

Third Rafelis nods, and Corivos and two other elves lift Lorial as Rafelis works his magic to stop the bleeding. Nestraya takes Lorial's hand in hers and focuses on his weak pulse, pressing his body to replenish its life force and make more blood.

Her efforts seem to strain his heart more than help him.

As a group, they hurry off the battlefield toward the woods, their warrior elves fighting back any lingering attacks, but the battle raging all around them with the humans soon draws everyone's attention away from the fleeing elves.

Hopefully, Hothniel doesn't send one of his elites to finish the job the human musket failed to accomplish.

If they don't get a healer here soon, though, it won't matter.

15

FOR OUR KING

They carry Lorial to a copse of trees at the top of a small rise, where they'll have an easier time guarding him. His heart grows weaker by the second, and panic looms at the edges of Nestraya's mind as she feels him slipping away.

"My First, I've stopped the bleeding," Third Rafelis says, though he keeps his magic in place as Nestraya clears her throat and nods.

"He's weak," she whispers. "I fear my magic is all that keeps his heart beating, and I don't know how long I can hold it like this. We need a full-fledged healer."

"You three, hurry back to Darlei. Find someone," Corivos says.

Thank the fates for Corivos.

The three warriors take off into the woods.

"I don't know if they'll find someone in time," Nestraya whispers to Corivos and Rafelis.

"Heartbind with him," Corivos says.

Nestraya swings her eyes toward Corivos. "What?"

"A heartbinding—will it save him?"

Nestraya looks back at Lorial's pale face.

"It might," Rafelis says. "At least it would buy us time. But it's dangerous. If it doesn't work, and he dies, First Nestraya—"

Nestraya shakes her head. "I can't bind with him. I'm…low born. Fae-touched. I…I can't—"

"Would you watch him die instead?" Corivos asks.

"Would he consent?" Rafelis asks. "A heartbinding between two not already bound...it's a tricky thing, especially since he's unconscious. His heart would have to accept First Nestraya as his binding partner."

"Have you seen the way he looks at her?" Corivos asks. "I doubt his refusal will be the problem."

They both look at Nestraya.

"Will you do this, my First?" Corivos asks softly. "For our king. For Lostariel. For Restoval and Miravel."

A tear escapes Nestraya's eye, and she hastily wipes it away with her grime-covered, bloody hand. "Yes."

If she doesn't...his heart already grows weaker. They haven't much time.

"Corivos, take command. You are acting-First until we wake, assuming we wake. If not...you must protect our queen Miravel with your life. Swear it."

"I swear it, Nestraya. With my life."

"Do you know the words?" Rafelis asks, and Nestraya nods. Every warrior-class healer is drilled in the words of the heartbinding.

Is she really doing this? Binding with Lorial? Saving his life, yes. Hopefully. But becoming his queen? Bearing his elflings?

Once she does this, there will be no turning back. For either of them.

"He grows weaker, my First," Rafelis says. "We must hurry." He lifts Lorial's other hand toward her, and she grasps it as well.

Palms together.

Will his heart consent?

Is there any doubt?

She takes a deep breath and utters the ancient words. "My heart is for you. There is no other."

A tingling begins at their connected palms.

"My soul is a well unto yours. May you find refreshment in me."

Light bursts from their joined hands, wrapping itself around their arms.

"My light will fill your darkness, and when my light wanes, yours will guide me."

Nestraya gasps as the light grows, tugging at her life magic, but she doesn't stop.

"My heart to yours. Your soul to mine. Our bodies as one until the beating of our hearts fades."

The light seeps into their chests, burning. Lorial moans, but he remains unconscious. Hopefully, this doesn't strain his heart too much.

She pushes past her own discomfort at the burning light, as well as the full implications of everything she's promising him, to utter the final words.

"From this moment on, our two hearts beat as one. I bind myself to you until my end of days."

Then everything goes dark. The sound of musket fire fades away along with the coppery sweet smell of blood. The deep musty scent of the Wildthorne Woods. The burning pain in her chest and the feeling of Lorial's limp hands in hers.

A cool breeze flows around her, tugging at wisps of her hair as it flows freely, untethered from its braid. The ground is hard beneath her. Lines run along her back, like the slats between boards.

She forces her eyes open, and her stomach lurches as she struggles to get her bearings.

Stars. Inky blackness in every direction, as if she might fall into the embrace of the night sky.

It's chilly, but a soft blanket covers her, and she pulls it closer.

This must be the heartlanding.

Their heartlanding.

But where is Lorial?

Sudden movement beside her draws her eyes, and she turns.

Lorial sits next to her, his own blanket puddled at his waist, exposing his bare chest to the night air as he gazes around and then looks toward her. "Nestraya? Where—"

"The heartlanding," she whispers. Her voice is quiet as if by speaking softly, she can will it to be untrue.

"The...I don't...I don't understand."

"You were dying." She pushes herself up, and the blanket falls away, revealing an unfamiliar garment of ayervadi leather with a low neckline that leaves her arms and shoulders bare.

Lorial's eyes widen as they sweep over her, and she pulls the blanket higher. He has the decency to look away.

"So you...performed the heartbinding to save me?"

"Yes." Her voice sounds timid. Weak.

What she really is...is angry. Angry at life. At Hothniel for taking her pera.

At Lorial for getting himself shot.

She glares at him. "I know you wanted to bind with me, but running into a battlefield in order to put yourself on death's door is hardly a fair way to get what you want."

His gaze swings back to her, and for a fleeting moment, she stares into his eyes before turning away.

If she wasn't afraid to see what she's wearing on her lower half, she'd throw the blanket at him.

"I'm sorry," he says softly. "Please tell me we aren't both going to die now."

"I don't know."

"Nestraya, why—"

"To save you, you oaf of a man. All right? I already lost my pera. I couldn't lose you, too."

"But—"

"Be happy. You got what you wanted, didn't you?"

"But not like this. Never like this."

"It is what it is. If we survive this—if we fight for your throne—if there's anything left to fight for once Hothniel's finished sending elves to be slaughtered, then I will be Queen Nestraya. The fae-touched. Low-born—"

"Mine."

She looks up at him again, trying not to let her eyes linger on his bare chest. Not that it makes much difference now. They're bound.

And he needs an heir.

Whistling wind.

It's Lorial. Can she be that to him? See him that way? The way he seems to see her?

Can she even bear elflings? Her mother struggled. What if she does, too?

"So this is our heartlanding?" he asks, and Nestraya follows his gaze. They're on some sort of platform above the trees. Built for stargazing, perhaps?

A spiral staircase leads somewhere below the platform.

Not a lot is understood about the heartlanding. It's a private place for a couple who have been heartbound—whose hearts beat as one. It's a construct of their minds—a place to rest. To...bond. To grow closer.

And they'll find themselves here whenever the magic thinks they need it. At night as they sleep. Now, while Lorial recovers—or they both die.

Either way.

But no one who's ever visited a heartlanding has been able to speak of it in more than the vaguest terms.

It's a place for them alone, where all secrets are laid bare.

And all secrets are kept.

"Are you warm enough?" Lorial asks softly, and Nestraya tugs the blanket tighter.

"You're the one sitting there half-naked."

Hopefully, it's only half.

His cheeks redden, and she looks away.

Yes. They're off to a great start. Surely there will be elflings soon.

She needs to stop thinking about elflings.

"Perhaps there are warmer clothes below," he says.

She glances down at herself and nods. "I hope so."

And perhaps something to tie back her wayward hair. It's long here—as it was before she cut it when Pera died. And the wind seems to delight in playing with it.

Unless that's Lorial. She turns toward him, but his magic is quiet.

So just the wind.

"Right. Let's see what's below," she says.

He nods and stands, and, to Nestraya's relief, he's wearing his ayervadi leather trousers. He offers her a hand, and she reluctantly takes it as she clutches the blanket to her chest.

She's wearing her leather trousers, too. Thank the fates. It's just the gown that's been replaced with this...tube of leather that barely covers everything it should.

Lorial keeps his eyes averted. Mostly. And she lets out an exaggerated sigh. "You might as well look. I'm your binding partner now."

He finds her eyes. "Nestraya—"

"What?"

As she waits for his response, she peers over the edge of the platform, and the world spins. This platform is really high. She tightens her grip on Lorial's hand and backs away from the edge, grateful for her plant magic to catch her if she falls.

"That's a long way down," Lorial says.

"It's just air. Air wielder."

He looks unconvinced, but he changes the subject. "I never meant for this to happen. I'm sorry."

She turns back to him, trying to pretend they aren't standing on a shelf of wood high above the forest floor. Despite her magic, it's unnerving. "I know you didn't. Forgive me for my...ire. I'll try to do better."

"Don't."

"What?"

"Here, you're just Nestraya. Everything you feel or don't feel—don't push it away. Just let it be. My...my light will fill your darkness. This is what my heart vowed when my words failed, is it not?"

She swallows. "Yes. When...when my light wanes, yours will guide me."

"Until my end of days."

"You know the words of the heartbinding?"

"I do now. I'm not sure how or why, but I do."

"They're etched on your heart."

Slowly, giving her the chance to pull away, he draws her hand to his chest over his heart, where a gaping wound and blood—so much blood—mar his beautiful skin in the real world. "Our two hearts beat as one. I bind myself to you until my end of days, Nestraya...Westaria."

"Wh-what did you call me?"

"Is that presumptuous of me? Forgive me. I—"

"The night Pera died, he told me—"

"You were meant for me?"

Her breathing grows shallow. Rapid. "He called me Nestraya Westaria. But he left before he could tell me why."

"He told me within the Tree of Memories that you and I together are better than we are apart."

Her breath catches. "You spoke of the tree."

"All secrets are laid bare in the heartlanding. I'll tell you everything I can. Soon."

She nods. Her thoughts swirl in a jumbled mess, leaving little more than confusion and numbness in its wake.

"Let's get you warm, all right? My *estrassa*." He gently tucks her hair behind her ear, and then he tugs her toward the stairs to see what's below. And she follows, clinging to his hand.

Because regardless of what her head tells her, her heart can't let go. Not anymore.

16

HEARTLANDING

As Lorial leads Nestraya down the spiral staircase, his thoughts jump around chaotically.

He almost died.

She...saved him. By binding with him.

And not just binding.

Heartbinding.

While Hothniel takes over Lorial's warrior bands and leads Lorial's people in a brutal and unnecessary battle.

After murdering Lorial's father.

But right here...right now...Nestraya.

She's...his. And she's not happy about it.

And none of this is fair to her.

What was he thinking, running into the middle of a battle like that? But it's done now. He can't undo this.

Not that he wants to.

But it wasn't supposed to happen like this.

And he can barely keep his eyes off her. She's enchanting. Alluring. His heart races just looking at her.

Whistling wind. Can she feel it? Their hearts are connected now, aren't they?

The thought is unsettling.

To his surprise, she clings to his hand as they descend into some sort of treehouse. It's a simple place, round, with enough windows to let in plenty of sunlight during the day. Yellow orb lights like he often makes dot the room now.

There's a table with two chairs. Cupboards. That must be the kitchen.

A rug and a couple of padded armchairs.

A bed. It's luxurious. Large enough for two people with thick moss and satin blankets.

He tears his eyes away from the bed to continue his perusal of the cozy space. A screen hides what must be some sort of water closet. He peers behind it to see all the expected fixtures, including a large tub, though where the water comes from is less clear.

And the food, for that matter. There's no door that he can see.

What sort of place is this?

"A wardrobe." Nestraya strides toward the enclosure built into the wall, tugging him along. She still clutches the blanket to herself with her other hand. He should have wrapped his covering around her before they left the platform.

Eyeing his hand and then the blanket, she huffs and glances at his face before tossing the blanket on one of the nearby chairs.

He does his best to focus on anything that's not her as she pulls open the wardrobe to reveal a few gowns and shirts. Leather and linen and satin.

"Here." She hands him a simple linen shirt and thumbs through the two satin gowns and warrior leathers in her size.

Nestraya is many things.

A wearer of satin gowns has never been one of them.

After scrunching her nose in the most adorable way, she pushes them aside and reaches for the leather.

She looks good in leather.

Then, to his surprise, she huffs again and shoves the leather away, grasping at a linen shirt like the one she handed him. He doesn't dare question her. If she wants to wear the clothes intended for him, he won't stop her.

Finally, she drops his hand and slips the linen over her head.

It's far too big for her, and as she rifles around in the wardrobe some more, one shoulder slides down over her arm.

He should put on his own shirt and stop gawking at her.

"Are you hungry?" he asks as he pulls the linen down over his chest.

Can you even get hungry in the heartlanding?

"No." She sighs and looks up at him as she tugs the shirt back onto her shoulder. "If you see a strap or ribbon or string, let me know." She lifts her long hair off her neck and twists it over her shoulder.

Ebony.

"You are so beautiful," he whispers before he can think better of it.

She starts to say something but stops and sighs before looking down at her hands. "Thank you."

"What would you like to do now?" he asks softly.

She gazes around the room. "I don't know. I don't understand this place at all. Are we supposed to stay locked in this tower until we wake in the real world?"

"I wish I knew."

She looks at him again. "My heart keeps racing, and every time, I wonder if it means something. If one of us is dying. It's unsettling."

He swallows and breathes out slowly. There are no secrets here. "I-I think it's me. You really are gorgeous."

For a moment, their eyes meet. What is she thinking now?

"I...see. I suppose...I suppose it's good you feel that way about me. Since you're stuck with me." Her eyes dart toward the bed before she turns away and rubs her brow.

She looks so lost.

"Is it me?" he asks softly.

"What?"

"It's obvious this arrangement distresses you. I'm just trying to understand."

"It's not—"

He lifts his brows, and she sighs.

"I just have never thought of you like that. I didn't realize that you...that you—"

"Have been in love with you for years?" The corner of his mouth ticks up, and her eyes widen.

"Years?"

"Yes, Nestraya. Years."

"You never said—"

"Can you blame me? You're everything. Strong. Brilliant. Gorgeous. Your magic puts mine to shame. I stand beside you, and I feel...unworthy."

She stares at him for a moment. "You spout nonsense. You're Lorial. King of Lostariel. You could have any woman you wanted. And your air magic is stronger than any powers I possess. You just need to practice more."

"Now you're speaking nonsense."

"You're stronger than you realize," she says softly. "When you're near, your air magic is overpowering. It seeps from your skin and the tips of your hair. When you breathe out, I can almost taste it. You may be even stronger than Pera."

Lorial shakes his head. Father was...it's not possible. She speaks madness.

"We just need to work on it." She glances at their surroundings again, and a thoughtful expression spreads across her face. "Maybe that's why we're here."

"What?"

"Maybe"—she finds his eyes again—"you're supposed to learn to fly."

"Fly. Like Zelovon? You really are mad, aren't you?"

She rolls her eyes, but before she can respond, a yawn tugs at her lips.

"We should sleep," he says. "Perhaps everything will be clearer in the morning. If we're still here come morning."

She glances uneasily at the bed and nods.

"Sleep, Nestraya. There's no rush. Perhaps with time, you'll come to see me in a different light."

"You need an heir."

Is that what she's stuck on? Elflings?

"Not right this minute, I don't. I'll sleep on the rug if it will put you at ease."

She eyes the bed again and sighs. "I'm your binding partner now. I won't make you sleep on the floor. Though if you touch me, I may douse you."

A smile spreads on his lips. "Fair enough."

"Just...give me time. To see you—the man. And not just...my closest friend. My own *estrasse*."

There's a vulnerability in her eyes as she gazes at him. She's never called him that.

"Take all the time you need. I'm not going anywhere."

"And I will give you that elfling. As far as it's within my power to do so. I swear it to you. When we return to the real world—"

He steps toward her and silences her with a finger to her lips. Her soft, full lips. "Let's just sleep, all right? Everything else can wait."

She nods, and after the slightest hesitation, he wraps his arms around her and draws her to his chest.

She stiffens at first, but then she slides her hands to his back and leans her head against his shoulder. "Lorial, your heart—"

"Is racing. I know. Just ignore it."

Laughter escapes her throat, and that makes it worse. She doesn't laugh enough. She never has. Not since they were elflings. She needs to laugh more—it's a beautiful sound.

As his heart pounds, she laughs harder, and soon, he's laughing, too.

When she pulls away, she's wiping away tears. "Oh, I needed that. Thank you."

"You're welcome. Let's get some sleep now, all right?"

She looks into his eyes and then lifts her chin and presses her lips to his cheek.

Whistling wind. This can't be good for his heart.

Another round of laughter bubbles from her throat, and he shakes his head as he tries unsuccessfully to maintain a straight face.

"Come on." He threads his fingers between hers and draws her toward the luxurious bed. "You need to sleep before you cave to delirium."

She breathes out between pursed lips as she shakes her head, and a sound that's half laugh, half sob escapes her throat. "I think you're right."

"I am. I know you well enough to tell, *estrassa*. Now, do you want to change before you sleep?"

"There wasn't a sleeping gown."

"Perhaps one of the other gowns?"

She glares at the suggestion as he leaves her by the bed and opens the wardrobe door. Perhaps something of his.

It's all different now, though. There are loose linen trousers for him and several sleeping gowns for her. Some offer more coverage than others. He pushes away images of her wearing the sheer one and reaches for the most modest gown of the three. It's cream and silky with long sleeves and a slightly rounded, wide neckline that should hang near her collarbone.

Even it's probably more risqué than anything she usually wears—he wouldn't know—but it will cover everything, and it should be more comfortable for her than sleeping in leather.

"Here. Go behind the screen and change."

She eyes the gown skeptically but doesn't argue. A few minutes later, she emerges, looking absolutely breathtaking with her ebony hair hanging loose over her shoulder.

His hands start to tingle with his fire magic, and he grabs the linen trousers and hurries to change before his heart takes wing and soars away completely, or he sets the whole place on fire.

By the time he returns, Nestraya has already crawled onto the mossy bed between the satin blankets. Her lips are slightly parted, and her arm rests on the pillow over her halo of black hair.

Her breath comes softly. Steadily. She really was tired.

As gingerly as possible, he lifts the covers on the other side of the enormous bed and slides in beside her.

He's heartbound to Nestraya. It's almost too difficult to believe.

Now he needs to win her heart.

17

DISTRACTED

Nestraya wakes with the sun, and it takes a moment for her to get her bearings.

The bed is so soft. And warm. And Lorial slumbers beside her.

She barely remembers lying down. She must have fallen asleep before he joined her.

And they're still here, in the heartlanding.

She should rise and dress while he's sleeping. It will be less awkward that way. She rolls toward the edge of the bed, but her head yanks back.

He's lying on her hair.

She gives her hair a gentle tug, but she's stuck.

Maybe she won't get up.

With a sigh, she nestles back into the warm spot where she was sleeping and stares at the ceiling. It looks as if it was constructed using plant magic, though the roof platform was made of planed wood.

The bed shifts beside her, and she steels herself for one of those awkward encounters she was hoping to avoid.

"Good morning," Lorial whispers in the most endearingly scratchy voice.

The thought catches her off guard, and she pushes it away.

"Good morning. I think you're lying on my hair."

The bed shifts again. "I seem to have tangled my hand in it."

She glances toward him. "Sorry. I usually braid it."

"I'm not complaining." He smiles at her as he frees himself. "Your hair is soft."

"It's going to be a tangled mess soon if I don't tie it back."

"I'll help you find something to fasten it with, though I like it when you wear it loose."

Their eyes meet before he looks back at what he's doing.

"I will keep that in mind," she says softly.

"There. You're free."

"Thank you."

"Would you like to try filling that tub with water? I'll warm it for you. I know how soothing water is to your magic."

Her mouth goes dry at the suggestion. "And...where would you be?"

"Looking for breakfast. Unless..."

"Unless?"

"You'd prefer the whole space to yourself. I could go up on the roof."

Compassion shines in his eyes. That was not the response she was expecting. Of course he's thoughtful like that, though. He's still Lorial. He's always been kind to her.

"A bath does sound wonderful," she admits. "But..."

"But?"

She sighs. "This is all so awkward."

"I know. I'm sorry. I'll go outside. Give you space."

He swings his legs over the side of the bed, and she sits up and reaches for his arm as if under some spell. "Don't go. Please. I...could use a friend."

He meets her eyes and nods. "Then I'll be a friend."

"Thank you."

He smiles, and something about his boyish grin does unexpected things to her belly. It's unsettling.

All of this is unsettling.

"Shall we see about that water?" he asks, and she nods, grateful for the distraction.

When he offers her a hand, she only hesitates for a moment before taking it and climbing from the bed. The wooden floor soothes her feet and her plant magic as she follows him around the screen to the tub.

It's big. Bigger than her private bath at Starhaven. It's big enough for both of them.

Her face warms at the thought.

"Do you sense water nearby?" he asks, interrupting her thoughts again. Thank the fates.

With her fingers still threaded between his, she closes her eyes. It's hard to sense anything but him right now. His air magic is even more overwhelming than usual. But it's familiar. And comforting.

"I don't know," she whispers. "Your magic is distracting me."

"It feels restless, as if the air outside is calling to it."

"Maybe we should go outside, then."

"Later. First, water for you, *estrassa*. Perhaps this will help." He tightens his grip on her hand as he vanishes. "Try now."

"I can't believe you used your magic to hide from me yesterday. I may never forgive you."

He laughs. Actually laughs. "You are so beautiful when you're angry."

"I wish I had water to douse you with." She almost leaps into his invisible arms when the tub beside them fills with water.

Neither of them speaks at first.

"This is a strange place," she eventually says.

"Perhaps we should wish for food next." He reappears beside her as she dips a hand into the tepid water. It feels so good. Exactly what she needs. He knows her too well.

If only it was warm.

"Next time, I should wish for hot water," she says.

"Where's the fun in that?" He grins as he leans close to hover his hand over the tub. "Is that warm enough?" he whispers near her ear.

Her breath hitches. It's definitely getting warmer in here. Warmer by the second.

"Y-yes. Thank you."

"You didn't even test it."

"Did I not?"

Why is she so flustered?

"No, you didn't. Am I distracting you again?"

He's doing that on purpose. Of course he is.

"You might be," she says breathlessly.

"Good." His breath tickles the sensitive skin on her ear, sending a shiver down her arm before he steps away. "I'll be in the kitchen, wishing for food."

She watches him go, not at all sure what just happened. As she slips out of the cream sleeping gown, she does her best to clear her thoughts.

And ignore the fact that Lorial is only a few feet away, separated from her by little more than a screen.

She quickly lowers herself into the tub as a sigh slips past her lips.

It's glorious. Soothing. Relaxing.

Just what she needed.

As he knew it would be.

Her sigh when she sank into the water nearly did him in.

Perhaps he should have gone outside.

For a while, Lorial stands near one of the windows, looking out over a sweeping forest. Their cozy treehouse sits atop the tallest tree for miles, and none of the others rise high enough to block the view. It's just blue sky and treetops as far as he can see.

The sound of water lapping at the side of the tub as Nestraya shifts draws him back to the woman bathing behind the screen. The gentle trickle of water as she hums. She must be washing her hair.

She always hums when she washes her hair, though how or why he knows that is a mystery. It's not as if he spies on her when she bathes.

Though he could.

He's never told her this, but he can see things in his mind with his air magic. The layout of a room. The people inside it. It's different from the way she senses people with her life magic. More physical.

And he should definitely keep his magic to himself right now.

Food. He promised her food.

To distract himself and keep his restless magic in check, he searches the handful of cupboards for something to eat, but apparently, the cupboards are just for show. There's no food to be found.

Perhaps he needs to wish for it first. Crossing his arms over his linen shirt, he stares at the largest of the cupboards.

Wish for it.

What would Nestraya want?

Tendrils of his magic seep out of him as she hums, and he pulls them back.

Berries with sweet almond cream. She loves that. He prefers his berries by themselves, but this isn't about him.

It's about her. Nestraya. His Nestraya. His binding partner. His queen. His First.

His...everything.

He pulls his magic back again.

Perhaps some venison steak, thinly sliced and fried. A side of quail eggs, over easy.

That's enough to start.

Tentatively, he opens the cupboard door.

Still empty.

Now what?

He stretches his neck and grasps at his magic again. Hopefully, she finishes soon.

The scent of fried venison wafts toward him, and he frowns as he checks the cupboard once more.

It's still empty.

Confused, he turns to find the table spread with an elaborate meal for two, just as he imagined it.

"Pear juice," he whispers, and two glasses appear on the table. "Spiced tea."

A teapot appears, along with two teacups and almond cream and sugar.

"What is that glorious smell?" Nestraya calls, and it takes all his willpower to keep his feet and his magic where they are.

"Breakfast. Whenever you're ready."

She groans. "I don't want to move. This is exactly what I needed."

He glances at the screen before looking back at the table. She probably wouldn't appreciate an offer to bring it to her.

He shakes his head. Of course she wouldn't.

"Lorial?"

"Yes?"

"I...need something to wear."

He exhales slowly and clutches his magic closer as he looks at the screen again and frowns. It goes to the ceiling. He can't exactly drape anything over it. What is she asking him to do?

"Can I bring you your leathers?"

"Do you mind?"

Does he mind? There's nothing about this he minds. But surely she isn't inviting him to...

His body heats at the thought. "How exactly—"

"Just keep your eyes closed."

Right. He can do that.

He steps toward the wardrobe. To his relief, her full warrior leathers hang inside, waiting for her, and he grabs everything the wardrobe offers, trying not to dwell on the clothing that clearly goes under the leather.

Whistling wind.

"Ready?" he asks.

"Yes. Are your eyes closed?"

He slides them shut. "Yes."

"Okay."

He steps around the screen, using his air magic to guide him, pulling it back when it brushes up against her bare feet.

"Lorial! I felt that!"

"I didn't want to trip."

"Can you see with your magic?" She sounds horrified.

He can't blame her.

"I...might be able to. I can see with my eyes, too, though, and I've been keeping both to myself."

She doesn't respond, and he resists the urge to glance at her.

"Your control is impressive, my king," she whispers.

He almost loses every ounce of control he wields. Every other time she's called him that, it's been distant as if she's pushing him away.

But this time...this time, it felt more like a caress.

Her damp fingers brush against his as she reaches for her clothes. Then her lips brush his cheek, and he stands still, frozen in place, as his fire magic threatens to burst forth.

"Thank you," she says softly, and he nods, his feet rooted to the floor. "You can go now."

It takes a moment for him to find his head, and as soon as he does, he hurries to the other side of the screen and keeps his magic close.

He definitely should have gone outside.

18
WARRIOR LEATHERS

Nestraya takes in the spread of food on the little table. "You wished for all this?"

Lorial nods. "I wished, and there it was. If you want something else, you can probably wish for it yourself."

"You already chose my favorite things," she says softly.

"Of course I did." He pulls out a chair for her, and their eyes meet.

"Thank you." She lowers herself to the chair as he pushes it in, and then he takes his own seat.

They've eaten together before. Many, many times. But this time feels different, somehow.

A tendril of his air magic slides along her leg, and she gasps.

"Sorry. That was not on purpose." His cheeks are pink, and he pulls his magic back.

"It's all right. Perhaps…for now, you can just…relax? Maybe…maybe if I don't have to hide here, you shouldn't either."

Whistling wind. Did she just give him permission to let his magic roam all over her?

His eyes grow so large she almost laughs at the comical expression.

"If you want to," she adds as she focuses on pouring a cup of tea.

"It's not usually this hard to control," he mumbles.

"You've never been heartbound. And you need to get outside. Find some release for all this magic pouring from you."

They fall into an awkward silence as they focus on their food. When tendrils of his magic find their way to her again, she doesn't gasp.

She plays with it. Loops her foot in it, wrapping it around her ankle. Brushes against it with her toes, which are still bare.

He struggles to hold back a grin across the table, and the corner of Nestraya's own mouth ticks up.

To his credit, he keeps his magic below her knees, but having something to do with the power he wields rather than locking it inside seems to relax him.

Which is good since he's supposed to be resting here while his body heals in the real world.

It's a sobering thought.

Lorial's magic fades, and he sets down his fork. "What's wrong?"

"What are we going to do? Assuming we ever wake up."

He leans back in his chair and sighs. "I don't know."

He doesn't need to worry here. He should be resting.

She forces a smile. "What should we do next here?" she asks as cheerily as she can manage.

"Anything, as long as I'm with you."

His heart is racing again. Unless that's her heart.

It's not her heart. Is it?

"I hope you don't tire of me," she says.

"Never." He gazes at her with an intensity that definitely makes her heart race.

It's Lorial, though. This side of him is jarring, and the urge to fight whatever is growing between them lingers.

But she chose this. Chose him. Promised him elflings, for goodness' sake.

As she meets his gaze, threads of his magic slide along her foot again. Her calf. Tickle the back of her knee.

Could she ever see him as more than *estrasse*? A brother? A friend?

"We need to get you outside," she breathes as his magic inches along her thigh toward her hip. "Teach you how to fly."

His reaction is as sharp as if she'd doused him with her water magic. "I thought you were joking."

A smile spreads on her lips. "I wasn't. Perhaps this is how you defeat Hothniel. Return as the new Dragon King. Prove that the blood of Zelovon flows through your veins."

"You have far more confidence in my abilities than I do."

"I want to see you fly, Lorial Westaria, King of Lostariel."

He eyes her for a few moments before leaning forward. "On one condition, my queen."

The way he says it—it's definitely her heart racing now.

"What's that?" she manages to ask.

"We're going to confront your demons. When we go back, I want my queen by my side. And I want her to own who she is. None of this nonsense about not being good enough. You are Nestraya Westaria, Queen of Lostariel, First among warriors, heart daughter of Restoval and Miravel, and you belong by my side."

She scoffs and looks away.

"Take it or leave it."

"And how do you propose we confront these demons, as you call them?"

"One at a time. Together. Until we slay them all. Probably just a lot of talking, though."

Before she can help herself, she laughs.

"Do we have a deal?" That boyish grin wends across his face, and she throws her hands up in defeat.

Let him try. She is what she is, regardless of what he says. But if it helps him master this magic of his, she can attempt to slay her demons, as he calls them.

She nods. "Deal. I want you in leather."

The words are out of her mouth before she can stop them, and his smile grows. "Your wish is my command, my queen."

He reaches over his head and grabs his linen shirt, tugging it off, and she leans back and crosses her arms.

"Am I supposed to swoon now?"

He strides toward her, and her heart speeds up again when he leans so close that his lips brush her ear. "Only if you want to, my queen."

Then his lips buss her jaw right in front of her ear, and she gasps. His air magic teases her hair and wraps around her waist.

When he leans away, her breathing is rapid and shallow, and if his smirk is any indication, he knows his nearness is affecting her.

"Leather?" he asks.

She shrugs and looks away. "If you want."

"Anything for you, Nestraya." Then he kisses her cheek and crosses the room to the wardrobe as her heart beats erratically.

Whistling wind.

Who is this man?

When Lorial emerges from behind the screen in warrior leathers, Nestraya looks him over from the corner of her eye.

He looks good in leather.

But this isn't what he wears in the real world. His jacket has been replaced by some sort of sleeveless vest that shows off his arms and shoulders to great effect.

Has he always been so muscular?

He's also secured his silver hair in long, thin braids from his temples past his ears, with a thicker braid running from his forehead over the crown of his head and down his back. The hair underneath hangs freely. It's darker there. She never noticed that.

He rarely dons warrior braids.

All he needs is korathite to line his eyes, and she might actually swoon.

Something tips over on the table in front of her, and she glances toward it. The food disappeared when Lorial rose, and now a little vial of the powdery black korathite lies on its side before her.

She eyes it for a moment before looking away.

Then it's in her hand.

Whistling wind, this is a strange and unsettling place.

"Fine, but I get hair ties. If he can braid his hair, so can I."

A strap of leather appears on the table next.

"Thank you."

"Are you talking to the heartlanding?" Lorial asks as he approaches her.

"I...may have been. Sit." She points to the table as she rises, and his forehead wrinkles, but he does as she instructs.

Breathing out slowly, she steps in front of him, between his knees, and his heart accelerates this time.

"What—"

"You are a warrior now, Lorial. A warrior paints his eyes before battle."

She twists the lid off the vial, and he looks at her with surprise written on his face.

"Hold still." She dips her smallest finger into the korathite and lines first his right eye and then his left with the dark substance.

Her heart skips a few beats as she looks at him.

"Your heart is racing," he whispers.

She chuckles and looks away. "Are we ready?"

"Maybe you should look your fill first. So you're not so distracted out there that I plummet to my death."

When she swings her eyes back toward him, he's grinning again. That lopsided, boyish grin of his.

"Like what you see?" he asks. "My queen?"

She opens her mouth and then closes it again.

"Speechless, Nestraya?"

He's enjoying this far too much.

Well, two can play this little game of his.

She sets the vial down and rests a hand on each of his knees where they flank her as she leans closer to him.

Now his heart is pounding again.

"What's wrong, my king?" she murmurs as she inches her hands higher along his legs. "You seem overcome."

His eyes dart to her hands. Her lips. His air magic winds around her, tugging at her hips, drawing her even closer.

Is it like an extension of himself? Can he feel with those tendrils of air currents the way he can feel with his hands? Because that air magic is getting very...personal...as it slides around her.

Whistling wind, what are they doing?

19

FLYING LESSONS

Nestraya pulls away, and Lorial lets her go. Turning from him, she gazes out the window as she attempts to regain her composure. Lorial. The man.

She said she'd try to see him as a man and not just her *estrasse*.

She definitely sees him now.

Tentatively, she glances over her shoulder at him. He's still sitting there. In those leathers, with his warrior braids and painted eyes.

Looking at her with a mixture of concern and guilt and...is that hope?

Neither of them speaks at first.

"Can you feel with your air magic?" She tries to maintain an aloofness with her voice.

The corner of his mouth ticks up. "Yes."

Whistling wind. He was running his magic all over her. She did tell him not to hold back, though, didn't she?

She turns back to the window and slowly breathes out as her heart rate—and his—returns to normal.

"I'm sorry," he says softly.

She shakes her head. "Don't be. I...see you now, Lorial."

There's a pause before he speaks. "And?"

"And I think you can figure out the rest for yourself. I need a few minutes alone. Do you mind?"

When she looks back at him, he's smiling again. Not his boyish grin that does strange things to her heart, but the smile of her *estrasse*. The comfortable, familiar smile that makes her feel safe and warm and...loved.

"Take as much time as you need. I'll be waiting above." He hops off the table and lightly climbs the stairs, and Nestraya exhales once more before striding toward the water closet.

"I wish for a basin of water." One appears before her on a ledge by the window. "And a small cloth."

She dips the cloth in the water and wrings it out before holding it over her face. For a few minutes, she just breathes in the soothing dampness. Then she runs it down her neck and along her collarbone. She lifts her hair and dabs at the back of her neck.

After setting the cloth aside, she braids her own tresses and lines her eyes with korathite.

It's time to become First Nestraya again. Her warrior king needs his First by his side.

Lorial gazes off into the distance as the memory of his air magic sliding over Nestraya warms him.

He probably shouldn't have done that. But she didn't seem upset. And she told him to let go earlier.

He definitely let go.

A gentle breeze swirls around him, and he closes his eyes and breathes it in.

Does she really think he can learn to fly? Not even Father mastered flying. An unbroken line of Westarian air wielders, and only two of them ever conquered the skill.

The Dragon King...and the Shadow King.

Lorial shivers, thinking of Polanis.

He was powerful. No one could argue with that.

He was also responsible for the deaths of hundreds of elves. The Years of Torment. When successive years of drought plagued the continent, and the high-born elves cut off the meager grain supply to the low born.

Elflings died.

But Lostariel survived.

As if that justified it.

The low-born elflings that were birthed during the Years of Torment—the ones that didn't die—were born with weaker magic.

No one speaks of it, but Lorial has wondered if Polanis caused the grain shortage himself. He was an air wielder with destruction magic—the ability to decay, decompose, and age prematurely. All it would take is an altering of the weather patterns—difficult but not impossible for a strong enough air wielder—and destruction of the crops that did grow.

And the low born suffered. Died. Lost some of their magic.

Became less of a threat.

And now, as the low borns regain some of their lost magic, Hothniel sends low-born warriors to die.

Even now, Lorial's stomach roils at the memory of what he witnessed on that battlefield.

Nestraya is right. It's time for Lorial to become more—to become the warrior his people need him to be. One who inspires an army of warriors to follow him rather than march to their deaths because that's just the way it is.

It starts with him becoming the new Dragon King. Reaching within himself to find a strength Nestraya swears is there.

And it starts with a low-born elf becoming Queen of Lostariel. Accepting that she belongs. That a low-born elf doesn't need to hide. To pretend to be less-than.

To be spat upon and reviled for daring to become more.

Together, they are Lostariel's hope. Just as Father claimed. Did he see this? See them? Did he know all along? From the time they were elflings? When elven warriors brought a frightened, low-born orphan before the king, Lorial's grandfather, and the king's own son took her in and gave her a home.

Lorial vaguely remembers the day Nestraya came to them. The fear in her eyes. The way she clutched her meager belongings to her chest as the water in a nearby fountain flowed around her to protect her.

The gasps at the power of such a young elfling. She couldn't have been more than six years old at the time—a year older than him.

And Father strode toward her. Lowered himself to the ground in front of her and her water magic. And used his own water magic to create shapes in the shield she had erected. Stars. Hearts. A leaf.

Then she laughed and accidentally drenched him.

He let it happen. It's obvious now. He was as skilled with his water magic as he was with his air magic.

But she looked at him in horror, and he smiled. Created a gust of wind around himself to dry the water off.

And then he took her hand and beckoned Lorial to follow. He led them to the private royal wing of Starhaven and said, "This is your home now. You'll be safe here."

Father couldn't protect her forever.

"Are we ready, my king?" Nestraya's voice interrupts Lorial's musings as she appears at the top of the stairs, looking like the fierce warrior elf she is now.

First Nestraya.

Did Father know back then?

"Lorial?"

He nods. "If you think I can do this—"

"I know you can."

He exhales slowly. "How do you plan to teach me? You're not an air wielder."

She steps closer to him. "Like this."

Before he can react, she shoves him off the platform.

The wind rushes past him as he flails. He grasps at the currents, but the air slips through his fingers. Fir boughs rush by, and he fumbles for them as needles rip at his palms.

What was she thinking? He's going to die here in the heartlanding.

Branches bang into him and slow his descent, and as the ground rushes toward him, vines wrap around his chest and his legs, stopping his fall.

He hangs suspended ten feet above the ground as his hands burn and his ribs ache.

Before long, Nestraya lightly drops to the forest floor and crosses her arms as she gazes up at him. "That was very poorly done."

"You pushed me! Are you trying to kill me?"

She waves his words away.

"I'm supposed to be recovering, not perishing from shock and terror! Or plunging to my death!"

A hint of remorse crosses her face. "Perhaps you have a point. Forgive me."

"Don't try to kill me again. Are you going to let me down?"

For a moment, she studies him, and a teasing gleam appears in her eyes. "I think I like this arrangement."

He glances down at himself where he hangs from her vines. He tugs at his arms and his legs, but she's restrained him.

"I can't move," he says.

"I am very much aware."

A vine slithers up his leg, wrapping itself around his thigh. This is...unexpected. When the vine slides beneath his vest, he gasps.

Is this her revenge for him using his air magic on her?

He clears his throat as the vine slithers along his chest. "Can you feel with your plant magic?"

She sighs. "Alas, no. I fear my magic isn't as nuanced as yours."

Should he be relieved? Or disappointed?

"So you're just going to leave me hanging here? I think I bruised a rib, you know."

"You poor thing."

He tugs against the vines again, but it does no good. "Nestraya!"

"What would the Dragon King do?"

He stares down at her. She is...so evil.

She wants to play? He can play.

As he reaches for his air magic, the tip of her braid flutters.

She glances down at it, a bored expression on her face. "Is that the best you can do?" Then she lifts her brows as she stares up at him.

Whistling wind—was that an invitation?

Tentatively, he threads tendrils of air around her waist. Her own vine continues its trail along his shoulder now.

When she doesn't pull away, he lets it wander down her hips. Around her legs.

Still, her bored expression doesn't change, though he could swear the tips of her perfectly pointed ears look a little pink.

When her vine slithers along his neck, trailing over his left ear, he loses his grip on his magic.

"You're not getting distracted, are you, my king?"

Whistling wind. What is she trying to do to him?

Gathering his air currents once more, he finds her own ear, and she jumps.

Her ears must be even more sensitive than most elves'. They feel perfect to him as he slides his magic over the pointed tips on both sides.

He doesn't need to learn how to fly, does he? They could find their way back to their cozy treehouse. Curl up on that enormous bed of the softest moss. He could slide his hand along the same path his magic takes now. Down the back of her ear. Along her neck. Past the dip at her collarbone toward—

Suddenly, he's falling again.

20
WARRIOR TRAINING

To say she's a little flustered would be an understatement. She didn't mean to let go of her plant magic.

But as Lorial hovers facedown six inches off the forest floor with his limbs spread and only his air magic keeping him aloft, Nestraya can't bring herself to regret it.

She clears her throat. "That was…well done."

He crashes to the dirt as she tries not to think about the way his magic roamed her body only moments ago.

Still on the ground, he groans. "You remember, if I die, you do, too, right?"

"I didn't let you die, did I?"

He looks up at her. "I suppose not. My ribs hurt, though. And my hands."

"Come here, and let me see."

With a whimper that he's probably overdoing for her sake, he pushes himself to his feet, and she lifts his hands to examine them.

She frowns at the shredded flesh. "You were supposed to use your air magic, not grab at branches on your way down."

"I was too focused on not dying to care how it happened."

Drawing on her water magic, she flushes the wounds before using her life magic to knit the skin back together. "What about your ribs?"

He gingerly places his hand on his left side, and she fumbles with the fastenings on his vest. She should have let him do this. He'd probably smirk if she backed off now, though.

As if she didn't just invite him to run his magic all over her.

"You seem to be struggling with the clasps," he teases, and she glances up at that boyish grin of his.

"I don't have to heal you."

His smile vanishes at her words. "Carry on."

That's what she thought.

Once she frees him from the leather vest, she grimaces at the purple mottling on his flesh. "Here." She does her best to reduce the swelling and mend the inflamed skin. At least nothing's broken.

"Thank you."

She nods as she looks up at him. Into those korathite-lined gray eyes of his. A shiver spreads from her neck along her spine as his eyes dart to her lips.

"Nestraya." His voice is low. Husky. Full of longing.

And like a fool, she backs away from him.

Toward him. She's supposed to be moving toward him. Not away.

"You should rest," she squeaks.

"I don't want to rest." He takes a step toward her.

"Then we should go back up and try again."

His entire expression changes. "I am not letting you push me off that platform again."

"Oh, really? How do you intend to stop me?"

At least he's not staring at her lips now.

He slashes his hands in an x across his body, and a barrier of air and fire magic forms between them.

She crosses her arms and encourages a vine to yank him off the ground from above.

"Nestraya!"

Then she drops him again.

This time, he catches himself sooner, and though his landing is far less than graceful, at least he's still upright.

"Your shield is worthless if it doesn't surround you completely. And even then, it could use some work."

He growls. Actually growls.

It's almost adorable.

He slashes with his hands and creates a new barrier. This one encircles him completely.

"Better!" she says.

Then a root grabs him by the ankle and sweeps him off his feet. He growls again, and she can't help the smile that slips across her face.

This time, the barrier surrounds him on all sides, including the ground beneath him.

"You're learning, my king. Well done!"

He relaxes, and a weak spot forms in his shield. Taking advantage of it, she wraps a new vine around his wrist. He closes the gap, and the vine slices off at the barrier as he shakes it from his arm.

She frowns. "If that was a musket ball—"

"I know. I know. I'd be on death's door with a queen who reluctantly heartbinded with me because I did something stupid." He glances at her, and she smiles again.

"Indeed."

He sighs. "I don't know if I can ever become what you want me to be. I'm not the Dragon King."

"You can do this. I know you can. We just need to keep practicing. Remember, if you have a weakness, your enemy will exploit it."

Slumping, he lets the shield drop. "I seem to have many weaknesses."

"Starting with letting your guard down."

Relentless, she hooks a vine around his arms and lifts him in the air again.

"Really, Nestraya? You are an awful person!"

She lets him go, and he lands in a crouch this time, flipping his warrior braids back over his head and down his shoulders as he looks up at her.

It's enough to make her heart skip a beat.

"See how you like it," he mutters.

The ground falls away as his air magic wraps around her, and she gasps. "What are you doing?"

"Don't give it if you can't take it."

Air currents encircle her arms and her waist, keeping her upright as she hovers ten feet off the forest floor.

She struggles against his hold, but Rafelis was right.

His air magic is stronger than her magic is.

Something else occurs to her, too, and she laughs. "Lorial!"

"Yes, my queen?"

"Lorial, I'm flying."

He almost drops her, but before she can ask the vines to catch her, he slows her fall and sets her lightly on her feet.

Then he stares at her.

With a hand to her mouth, she shakes her head in awe. "You did it. You made me fly."

"I suppose—"

But before he can finish, she runs to him and flings her arms around his neck. "I knew you could do it."

His eyes grow large, and when he hesitantly rests his hands on her waist, she stiffens.

What is she doing?

More to the point, what is he doing?

"Don't pull away," he whispers. "Please."

She gulps and takes a deep breath.

Toward him. Move toward him.

Her heart beats rapidly—unless that's his heart.

Perhaps both their hearts.

She slides her hands onto his bare chest between them but doesn't push him away.

"Perhaps..." she whispers.

"Perhaps what?"

His skin is warm, and his muscles are solid beneath her fingertips as she looks into his eyes.

"Perhaps I should jump off the platform next. Let you catch me."

His brows lower. "Don't you dare."

A breeze teases the end of her braid. Then it caresses her ear again, and her breath catches as Lorial slides his warm hands to her back and pulls her flush against him. Her hands and her warrior leathers are the only things separating them now as his magic wraps around both her ears, sending the most delightful shivers all the way to her toes.

She closes her eyes and leans into his magic as a small sigh escapes her lips. Does he know how sensitive her ears are? He's probably figured it out by now.

"Lorial," she whispers, though she has no idea what she was about to say.

"Yes?" He dips his forehead to meet hers.

As if propelled by someone or something else, her arms snake around his neck again, and he pulls her even closer.

"Do you see me now, my queen?" he asks, and her breath hitches again.

His magic continues playing with the tips of her ears, and she nods. "I see you."

"Good." He nuzzles her nose with his. His lips are so close.

She could close the distance between them. Press her lips to his.

She should. She's his now. And he's hers. And as his magic plays with her ears, it's hard to remember why she didn't want this.

Why she didn't want him.

I am what I am.

The words shoot through her, bringing every reason to the forefront of her mind.

She may have saved his life, but who will respect him with her for a queen? It's as if someone dropped a bucket of cold water on her head, and she tries to pull away, but his arms encircle her still.

"Nestraya—Nestraya, what is it? What's wrong?" He releases his hold on her, and her breaths come quickly as if she can't get enough air.

"I'm not good for you, Lorial. Can't you see that?"

"You're mine. Do you hear me? Mine. Whatever those voices in your head are telling you, it's not true."

She shakes her head as a sob catches in her throat.

And he wraps his arms around her again. This time not as a lover but as her *estrasse*, and she melts against his chest and sobs.

21
I AM WHO I AM

She has wounds you know little about.

Mother's words return to Lorial as he draws Nestraya to the base of the giant fir tree atop which their cozy treehouse sits. Her sobs choke her as she struggles to take a deep breath.

When he lowers himself to the ground, she curls up in a ball beside him, and he guides her head into his lap. Wisps of her hair have escaped from her braid, and he gently brushes them away from her face, being careful not to touch her ears.

This isn't the time for such things.

She cries until her eyes are puffy, and streaks of korathite line her tear-stained face. Her breath comes in shudders, and dampness coats his trousers where her tears have puddled.

It means little to him now.

"Tell me," he says softly.

She shakes her head and squeezes her eyes shut.

He holds back a sigh. "Shall I tell you about the Tree of Memories, then?"

With a shudder that shakes her whole body, she nods.

"It was incredible. One by one, each of my forebears appeared in the Council Chamber at Starhaven. Father was there, and Grandfather. Every King of Lostariel, all the way back to Zelovon."

She looks up at him in surprise. "You met Zelovon?"

Lorial chuckles. "I don't think he was impressed with me."

"Then he didn't truly see you." A hiccup interrupts her words, but she pushes them out.

"Perhaps. Polanis was also there."

She shivers against him. "The Shadow King."

"Indeed. His own father despised him and what he became." Lorial stares out across the forest as he shivers himself.

"And you spoke to them?"

"I did. Mostly about Father's memories. He had no recollection of his last moments. He said someone had blotted them out."

Nestraya's eyes close again, and Lorial regrets his words as a new series of sobs grip her and she curls in on herself.

He brushes back her hair as she weeps. When her tears slow once more, he runs his hand gently along her arm. "We spoke of you as well."

"Me?"

"Father called you the daughter of his heart. He regretted leaving you too soon. He meant to prepare you better for this."

Her eyes glisten like emeralds as she looks up at him. "Prepare me? For what?"

"He didn't elaborate, but he indicated that, through you and me, Lostariel would find peace. And you would become my queen. He...had visions."

"Is that why you suddenly—"

"It is. Nestraya, I have loved you since I was old enough to know what love is. But until that moment in the sacred tree, I thought you were out of reach. When Father insisted you and I were meant for each other, I"—he pauses to find the right words—"I knew I needed to win your heart. I gave myself permission to try."

For a moment, she looks up at him as he searches her emerald eyes. Then she turns her face away. "They killed him because of me."

Her voice is so quiet Lorial can barely hear her. "They what?"

"Hothniel and whoever helped him. They murdered Pera because of me. Don't you see that?"

Lorial shakes his head. "You speak nonsense."

"I speak the truth. I represent everything Hothniel hates. Everything he fears. Loss of power as the low born grow strong again. I think that's the real reason he foments war with the humans. If they slaughter the low-born warriors, Hothniel won't have to do it himself. The strongest low-born elves—they become warriors. It's tradition. Get rid of them, and who will be left to fight?"

Lorial's stomach turns at her words. Has that been Hothniel's plan all along? No better than the Shadow King, slaughtering the low born while lauding himself as a hero?

"You see the truth, don't you? When Pera took me in, he signed his own death sentence. He should have given me over to the elves who wished to cast stones at me."

Lorial's eyes snap toward her. "What? Who—?"

"I don't know. But I have vague memories of someone throwing stones before another warrior hid me away and brought me to Starhaven."

"I don't understand. Who would do such a thing?"

"I don't remember. My memories are...fuzzy. As if reflections in the water. I have often wondered if Pera had a healer blot them out. I barely remember my parents."

"You were young."

"Yes, but...I have the clearest memory of us going on a picnic together, and then it blurs. I see the stones as if through a haze. Hear muffled cries and a voice telling us to run as someone clutches me to his chest. And then, as clearly as if it happened yesterday, I see Pera kneeling before me to draw pictures in my water magic. It feels...unnatural."

Lorial lets her words sink in. Wounds he knows little about, indeed.

"Father dying—it wasn't your fault, and he would not have given you up to prevent it. He called you the daughter of his heart, remember? To the Council of Kings, you were known as the *estrassa*. Zelovon himself spoke of you as someone important. Someone who matters."

"Everyone I love dies because of me." New tears stream down her face as he gapes at her.

"What?"

"I think my first parents died to protect me."

"They died of old age—"

"That's the story Mera and Pera tell. The people I remember...they were aged, but not on death's door. 'Run. Take her and hide her!' I can hear my first pera's voice, garbled but strong."

"Nestraya, no. You were young. Your memories are confused. They—"

"Died to protect me. This...this is why I'm not good for you, Lorial. I may have saved you for now, but they'll come for you, too. I'm a harbinger of death and destruction. I—"

"You are Nestraya. Warrior Queen. You are mine. Do you hear me? Mine."

She rolls her head from side to side as her shoulders shake. "I am low born. Fae touched. Feared. Being near me will destroy you."

"Stop. I will not listen to such lies."

"Then you will die, too."

"Nestraya, stop. You promised to slay these demons."

"I can't. It's me. Don't you see? I am the demon. I am what I am."

"You are mine."

"I don't know why I'm so strong. I don't think my mother—they say she...with a fae...but she didn't. My father loved her, and she loved him. I...remember that."

So Hothniel's words about Nestraya being half-fae were untrue. Not that Lorial believed it. Nestraya's ears are too perfectly pointed for her to have the blood of the round-eared Lothlesi coursing through her veins.

Perhaps Hothniel would rather imagine her as a product of the Lothlesi than as a low-born elf with so much power of her own. She represents a future he fears.

Better to tear her down and make her less than. Make her out to be an anomaly born of infidelity so people will scorn her rather than admire her. And other low-born elves will hide their powers as Corivos and Third Derazyn were forced to do to ensure their own safety.

How many low borns have been hiding? Or slaughtered, as Nestraya insists her first parents were?

And then Father took a low-born elf with magic not seen in generations, if ever, and instead of getting rid of her, he elevated her. Made her a Princess of Lostariel, if not in name, then in practice. Clothed her in ayervadi leather and gave her all the training and opportunities that would normally be gifted to the daughter of the king.

How it must have rankled Hothniel and others like him, disgusting in their fear of being lowered. Of losing status. Power.

And he killed Father because of it.

"You see the truth now, don't you?" she whispers. "I read it in your eyes. I would run to keep you safe, but with the heartbinding, I can't leave you. Ever. I saved your life only to sentence you to—"

He lowers his finger to her lips to silence her. "You are who you are."

Her forehead creases, and she slides her eyes shut again.

"You, my queen, are exactly what Lostariel needs."

Her eyes flash open.

"You, Nestraya. You will change everything. Father died to ensure you get the chance. Do not let his sacrifice be in vain."

She shakes her head. "I don't—"

"Don't you see? You, Nestraya. You. A low-born elf who doesn't hide. Who became *estrassa*. First among warriors. Queen. You will bring elves like Corivos out of the shadows."

"No. I'll just get everyone I love killed. I—"

"You must battle your own shadows first. Why do you think the low-born warriors follow Hothniel to their deaths? Because they're afraid. Afraid for themselves—for their families. Their elflings. Afraid that if they resist, they'll lose everything. They die on that battlefield because, in their minds, a so-called hero's death is the only option that keeps their families safe. And they fear you because you challenge everything they've accepted their whole lives as true. That this is their lot in life. That they have no right to stand and be heard. That if they just go along with everything, all will be well. They need someone to fight for them, to empower them to fight for themselves. Someone to lead them. Someone who doesn't believe the lies. Someone like you."

She shakes her head. "Now you speak nonsense."

"I speak the truth. Search your heart, Nestraya. If you don't take a stand, who will? If now's not the time, then when will the right time be? How many more people need to die first? I can't do this without you. I tried, and look at what happened. I need you. All of Lostariel needs you."

Her emerald eyes study his gray ones.

Let her hear. Let her understand. Let her believe.

"I don't know if I can ever become what you want me to be," she whispers.

"You can. Don't you see? It's already who you are. You just need to let yourself believe it."

She takes a few moments to respond. "Will you help me?"

A half-strangled cry of relief flies from his throat as he clutches her to his chest. "Yes. Yes. Yes. Of course I'll help you. You're mine, Nestraya. Mine."

She wraps her arms around his neck again and chokes back a sob. "I hear you."

22

RECHARGING

When Nestraya lets go of Lorial, she's almost afraid to face him again, but she glances up at his eyes anyway, and he looks warmly down at her.

"What now?" she asks softly as she clears her throat and wipes at the tears on her face.

He gently runs his thumb along her cheek. "Perhaps lunch. Are you hungry?"

The question seems so mundane after their weighty conversation that a soft laugh bursts from her lips, and he smiles.

"How do we get back?" she asks. "I'm not sure I have enough magic in reserve to lift us to our treehouse after our practice session."

"You're worn out already?" He frowns, and she glances away.

"I told you I need to work on my endurance."

"You shouldn't tire that quickly, though."

"I am a low-born elf." She brushes at a bit of dirt on her trousers, and he lifts her chin.

"Don't ever be ashamed of that. We're going to slay your demons, remember?"

She nods hesitantly, and as he runs his fingers along her cheek, his eyes dart to her lips, but he looks away.

Thoughts of their embrace earlier warm her. She must look atrocious now, though. Not that she's ever felt the need to look her best around him. Of course, she didn't know he was looking before.

"Perhaps we could wish ourselves back," he suggests as he looks up.

"I suppose it's worth a try. Would you like to do the honors?"

"I wish to return to our treehouse."

Nothing happens, and Lorial sighs.

"I guess we're stuck here for a while," Nestraya says.

He studies her for a moment, and she shifts under his gaze.

"What?" she asks.

"How do you recharge your plant magic?"

Her brow wrinkles at the question. "I wait for it to recharge itself."

"That's it?"

She shrugs. "It's my weakest of the three. Pera tried helping me strengthen it, but he wasn't a plant wielder."

"And your personal trainers?"

She shrugs again. "Most powerful magic wielders don't tire as quickly as I do. I doubt they knew how to help me."

"Well, we'll figure it out. You and I, Nestraya. We're a team now."

A smile sneaks across her face. "Lorial and Nestraya against the world?"

"Mmm. I like the sound of that. Lorial and Nestraya." His boyish grin returns, and her heart flutters.

"Lorial and Nestraya," she whispers.

"Lorial and Nestraya."

She says it again.

"Louder this time," he urges.

"Lorial and Nestraya!"

"Louder. Own it. Make it yours. Make your heart believe it."

She gazes into his eyes. That's what he's doing. Slaying her demons. One at a time.

"I love you," she whispers, looking hesitantly up at him, and his eyes grow round.

"As...*estrasse*?"

"As you."

His eyes dart to her lips again, but as before, he doesn't act on whatever he's thinking.

And she's suddenly keenly aware of his bare chest. Breathing out slowly, she steadies herself.

Toward him. Run toward him. Slay her demons. Own the truth.

"As the only man I want," she whispers.

It's true, isn't it? Could there have ever been anyone else?

It's still new...and strange to think of him that way.

But she doesn't want anyone else. She wants him. At least, she wants to explore the idea. Ease into it. Let whatever they're building grow.

This time, she glances at his lips, and his heart speeds up.

But he holds back.

Uncertainty fills her, and her eyes drift to his chest again. His shoulder where the musket ball pierced his flesh. She lifts her fingers to the unmarred skin above his heart, and when she looks at his face, he nods. There's no mark here in the heartlanding, though there will almost certainly be a scar if he survives.

If they survive.

She gently runs her fingers along the dip between his muscles, up toward his shoulder. Over his upper arm. He flexes, and she smiles.

"Are you showing off, my king?"

His grin returns. "I might be."

She bites her lower lip and trails her fingers along his inner forearm, over the sensitive skin approaching his wrist. Onto his palm.

Then he threads his fingers with hers, and this time, she doesn't pull away.

He lifts his free hand to her ear, and she stills, bracing herself for his touch.

"May I?" he asks.

Her heart races as she nods.

Even more gentle than his air magic, his fingers connect with the tip of her ear, and she gasps. He trails the pad of his finger along the edge like a feathery caress, and she slides her eyes shut.

Whistling wind.

For a while, he just plays with her ear, and she leans her head against his chest and relaxes into his touch.

"I love you," she murmurs again. "And your hands. And your air magic."

"You sound overcome, my queen." He slides his thumb over the tip of her ear again, and she whimpers. "I want to try something, all right?"

When he pulls his hand away from her ear, the loss of his touch chills her, but she watches him curiously. What is he planning to do?

He reaches for a fallen maple leaf. From a bigleaf maple. Are there maple trees in this forest?

"I wished it here." He points, and sure enough, a maple tree stands nearby, clothed in the brilliant colors of autumn. Reds and oranges and yellows. Like the leaf in his hand. "Lie back," he says softly.

Her forehead wrinkles. "In the dirt?"

He lobs his teasing grin at her. "Across my lap."

Her face warms at his response, but she does what he says.

"Now close your eyes."

Hesitantly, she lowers her lashes, and the edge of the large floppy leaf tickles her cheek, and she twitches away. "Lorial!"

"Sorry. Let me try again." He rests the leaf over her face this time, and she struggles not to laugh at the ridiculousness of it.

"Why are we doing this?" she asks as the leaf sits on her face.

"Can you feel it?"

"The leaf sitting on my face? Yes. I can feel it."

"Nestraya," he laughs. "Not the leaf. The magic."

"Oh. Um. Yes. I feel it." She breathes in deeply, as she would with a wet cloth over her face. "It's soothing."

"Does it make you feel stronger?"

"A little? I can't bury myself in leaves when I get tired, though."

"We could weave plants through your hair. Attach them to your clothing."

She pulls the leaf away and opens her eyes. He has a faraway look on his face.

"Are you picturing me in a gown of nothing but leaves and flowers?"

He clears his throat. "What?"

"You heard me."

That smirk sweeps across his face. "Perhaps we should test such a thing now. For research purposes."

She smacks his face with the leaf, but it's harder to hold back her own smile than it should be. "I don't think I could fight in a gown of flowers."

He shrugs, and she smacks him again.

"What about eating plants?" he asks. "Does that revive you?"

"I have no intention of eating this leaf if that's what you're suggesting."

"Yes. Open wide." He grabs the leaf from her and dangles it near her lips, and she swats it away.

"Stop," she laughs. "You're ridiculous."

"Of course I didn't mean the leaf." He flaps it at her face, and she bats it away again. "I was thinking something you could carry with you. Dried berries. Nuts. You're always hungry after you work your plant magic."

He noticed that?

"You are observant, aren't you?"

"Maybe I just like observing you." He brushes her forehead with the leaf. Down her nose. Along her chin. Without thinking, she tips her head back, and he trails the leaf along her neck.

It all feels good. Every caress leaves her a little stronger. Wherever the leaf touches her skin, it recharges her magic. It's delightful.

Too bad her warrior leathers cover so much of her skin.

"I wish I was wearing the other leathers," she whispers without thinking.

They both still when the heartlanding grants her request.

Groaning, she covers her face with her hands. "I didn't mean it! Whistling wind. It can do that, but it can't take us back to our treehouse?"

"I'm not complaining."

When she peers around her hands at Lorial, he has that grin on his face again, and she shakes her head. "Of course you're not."

He attempts a straight face, but he's completely unsuccessful. "Would you like to borrow my shirt again?"

She groans and drops her head back onto his lap. "Just keep doing what you were doing. It was helping. Maybe this will restore my magic faster."

His grin disappears. "Really?"

"Stop talking before I change my mind."

She closes her eyes and tries not to think about anything. Just focus on the magic flowing toward her from the forest. From the leaf grazing her bare shoulders.

As Lorial paints her with it as if she were a canvas.

Whistling wind. Her heart is racing. Or his is. Probably both.

Still. It feels nice.

"You are exquisite," he whispers as he trails the leaf along her arm. He's probably not looking at her arm, though perhaps it's best if she doesn't open her eyes to check.

Less awkward that way.

"Open your mouth," he whispers.

"I am not eating that leaf."

He bops her nose with it, and she bats it away.

"Just do as you're told for once in your life," he laughs.

That elicits a smile. "Yes, my king."

Nervously, she opens her mouth, and he drops a berry onto her tongue. It's plump and juicy and sweet. So sweet.

"Where did you get that?" she asks as she gazes up at him.

"I wished for it. The heartlanding is very accommodating. When it wants to be."

"Yes, I noticed." She tugs her leather bodice higher.

"How do you feel?" he asks.

"Stronger. Feed me a few more of those berries, and I'll be ready."

"There's no rush. Take as long as you need." He tries unsuccessfully to hide that grin of his, but she grabs the leaf from his hand and smacks him with it.

"Just give me more berries, and keep your thoughts to yourself."

23

TO CLIMB A TREE

"So...how were you thinking to do this?" Lorial gazes up at the tree with Nestraya beside him. It must be at least two hundred feet tall.

"Well, I could climb it. I don't even need my magic for that."

He eyes her skeptically. "Do you often climb trees?"

"Don't you?" She somehow keeps her face devoid of emotion, and he shakes his head.

"I was there the day you fell and broke your arm. Don't forget."

She waves him off. "I was ten. It doesn't count."

"Uh-huh."

She tugs at her bodice and frowns. "I'm not dressed right for climbing trees."

"Do you want my vest?" he offers again, but she shakes her head.

"You only just put it back on. I've got this. I wish for my warrior leathers."

Nothing happens, and Lorial rubs the toe of his boot in the dirt as he tries not to smile.

"Not a word from you," she mutters as she points at him.

He lifts his hands. "I said nothing. Are you sure you don't want my—"

"No. I'll...manage. Though I'm not impressed!" She yells the last part. Then, without another word, she runs toward the tree trunk and launches herself against it for added height as she reaches for a low-hanging branch.

That was impressive.

"Are you coming?" she calls down to him.

He looks at the tree trunk and back up at her. "I don't think I can do that."

"Then fly."

He crosses his arms over his chest. "I just fed you a whole pile of berries and ran a leaf across you for the better part of an hour so you could help me climb this tree."

"Is that right? And here I thought you did it because you were enjoying yourself."

He was enjoying himself, in a tortured sort of way.

It's the only time in his life he's ever been jealous of a leaf.

"Have I rendered the King of Lostariel speechless?" She sits comfortably on that branch as her legs dangle.

"Just enjoying the view." He grins up at her, and she rolls her eyes.

"Good luck with that." She stands and hops toward the next branch, looping her leg around it to pull herself up.

He's enjoying the view a little too much.

With an exaggerated sigh, he strides toward the tree. "Fine. Don't let me die." Grumbling, he musters his air magic as he takes a running leap toward the branch.

It's a terrifying sensation as the air current sends him spinning upward, but he manages to catch the branch as his heart hammers within his chest.

"That was less than graceful," Nestraya says.

"Not another word," he huffs as he pulls himself onto the limb.

Only twenty more terrifying leaps to go.

By the time they pass the halfway point, the branches are close enough together that Lorial doesn't need his magic to reach each new limb.

And Nestraya only had to catch him four times.

Both their hearts are pounding from the exertion, and they pause to catch their breaths.

"Why can't we do this the easy way?" Lorial asks. "Use your magic."

She looks away, and he frowns.

"What's wrong?" he asks.

"I'm...scared I might drop you if my magic gives out. This is safer. I won't overextend myself this way."

"Maybe hug the tree or something first?"

She stares at him. "Hug the tree?"

He shrugs. "Do you want me to rub—"

"Let's keep going. And I'm not going to hug the tree."

"It was just an idea!" he calls to her, but she's already scaled the next two branches. She's in better shape than he is. Must be all her warrior training.

They make slow but steady progress, climbing another fifty feet before Lorial stops for a breath and groans at the blisters forming on his hands. "I wish we could be magically transported into our treehouse."

Suddenly, the branch below him disappears, and he's falling. He grasps at his magic, but moments later, he lands with a thud on the floor of their treehouse with Nestraya at his side.

"You can't be serious." She pounds her fists on the floor. The next words past her lips would have earned her a mouthful of soap as an elfling. "What is wrong with you?" she eventually spits out.

Hopefully, she's talking to the heartlanding and not to him.

"Maybe it only grants the wishes it thinks will help us...bond," he suggests, and she turns furious eyes his way as he gulps. "Or, you know. What you said."

For a moment, she stares at him. And then she laughs. That delirious laugh she exhibits when she's overwhelmed or tired. Or both.

"Do you want to take another bath?" he asks softly.

She just laughs harder.

It has been quite the day. It must be nearing late afternoon by now. She's probably hungry. And emotional from everything that's happened lately. Especially after their conversation earlier. She must be tired, too, after all that crying. Maybe food and a nap?

He silently wishes for a spread of all sorts of fruits and vegetables and leafy greens to replenish her plant magic. More fried venison, along with boiled quail eggs. And chamomile tea.

The laughter has subsided into tears as she rolls to her back on the floor.

Now what? Should he bring the food to her?

He asks the heartlanding to lay out the food beside them, and a blanket with candles appears along with all the food he wished for. He quickly snuffs out the candles and hides them behind a chair.

She probably isn't in the mood for romance.

He crawls closer to her and holds out an apple slice. "This will help."

She looks around in surprise and then lays her head back as she takes the apple from him. "Thank you. I'm...really hungry."

"I know. Let's get some food in you and then a bath and bed."

"Bed? It's not even dark."

"A nap, then."

"Maybe." She bites into the apple as she wipes at her eyes, and he pours her a cup of tea.

"Chamomile?" he offers.

She nods and gratefully takes it. For a while, they sit quietly and eat until they're both full.

"Let me look at your hands," she says softly as she pushes her plate away. She looks much calmer now.

After making quick work of his blisters, she traces the lines on his palm. His fingers.

"Are you ready for that bath?" he murmurs, reluctant to let her go. "I'll just be out here. Take your time. Let me know if you need anything."

"Thank you."

He nods and busies himself stacking the dishes, which will probably disappear as soon as she gets up.

"Are you worried about the fact that we're still here?" she asks.

Lorial stills at her question.

"It's been almost a full day," she continues. "Corivos sent warriors to find a healer, but they should have returned by now."

"If they had to go all the way back to Darlei, it would take time. We're still here. That means we're still alive. Hold on to that, all right?"

She nods and pushes herself off the floor, and he watches as she makes her way behind the screen.

He busies himself with the plates, but they vanish as her leathers hit the floor with a soft thwap.

Followed by a mouthful of obscenities.

He frowns at the screen. "Are you all right?"

"The water's cold. I asked for warm water, you…"

Lorial fights to hold back a grin at the new round of insults she lobs at the heartlanding. Should he offer to help? Or wait for her to ask?

Tentatively, he wanders to the edge of the screen, out of sight. "Do you want—"

"Yes. Just—not a word."

Doing his best to keep his eyes on the ground, he slips around the screen and quickly uses his fire magic to heat the water.

"Thank you," she says softly, and he glances up at her before he can stop himself. She's wrapped a towel around herself, and his throat goes dry.

Quickly, he turns away. "You're welcome. Do you need anything else? I might go sit on the platform for a while."

"I think I'm good."

With a nod, he hurries to the stairs and gulps in mouthfuls of fresh air once he reaches the platform.

Whistling wind. The heartlanding seems far too eager to torture them both.

24

YOU BELONG TO ME

B y the time Nestraya climbs the stairs to join Lorial, she's much more relaxed.

Lorial sits at the edge of the platform, leaning back against his hands. His legs dangle over the side as he watches the sun setting in the distance.

She must have lingered in the water longer than she realized.

"Are you warm enough?" she asks softly as she walks toward him, and he turns to look at her.

"I thought you were going to take a nap."

She breathes out slowly and smooths the satin sleeping gown she donned again after her soak.

Toward him.

"I don't know if it's this cursed place or...or more than that, but I...missed you."

Whistling wind. She sounds like one of those swooning high-born elves Lorial was supposed to bind with.

She glances at his face, expecting to see his teasing grin, but he looks steadily at her without censure. Just...warmth.

"Do you want me to come sit with you?" he asks.

"I thought maybe I could stay out here with you. The stars should be out soon. It's a little chilly, though."

"We can fix that."

As he pushes himself to his feet, a cozy nest of moss and blankets rivaling the bed below appears on the platform beside them, and Nestraya's heart speeds up.

"For the record, I wished for blankets," he says, and before Nestraya can stop herself, she laughs.

"I think the heartlanding is intent on throwing us together."

"It would seem so. Here." He grabs a blanket off the pile and sweeps it around her shoulders. "Better?"

"Much. Thank you." She pulls the blanket tight and gazes out over the forest. The sunset blazes above the autumn foliage in brilliant reds and yellows and oranges. The bigleaf maple Lorial asked for sits nearby, reflecting the sky in all its burnished glory.

"I missed you, too." Lorial tentatively glances her way.

The korathite lining his eyes has faded, but he still looks the part of the warrior king. Her stomach flutters just looking at him.

Toward him.

"You did?" she asks, and his boyish grin reappears, doing even more strange things to her stomach.

"I did. My magic missed you, too."

She struggles not to laugh. Or blush at the memory of his magic wrapping around her.

"Are you feeling better?" he asks, and she nods.

"Much. I'm sorry about all that earlier."

He shrugs and looks toward the western horizon again. "You're gorgeous when you're angry."

She shakes her head and resists the urge to smack his arm. His muscled arm that flexes as he folds it across his chest.

She drags her gaze back to the sunset, and neither of them says anything as the sky gradually darkens and the brilliant colors fade to pinks and grays and, eventually, black.

Nestraya eyes the nest of moss as the chill seeps through the blanket Lorial wrapped around her.

"Are you warm enough?" he asks.

"I'm a little cold. Aren't you?"

"You keep staring at my arms. I'd hate to deprive you of whatever pleasure you're deriving from doing so." He grins at her.

"I don't know what you're talking about."

"Uh-huh. In all truth, I am getting cold." He glances at the bedding as well.

Toward him. Run toward him.

"Do you want to lie down?" she asks. "Look at the stars? Help keep each other warm?" She pulls the blanket tighter as she awaits his response.

"If you think there's a scenario where I turn that down, you don't know me at all." His air magic teases her braid where it lies on her shoulder, sending shivers down her arm.

Both their hearts beat fast as they lower themselves to the mossy bed. Nestraya offers Lorial her blanket, and he drapes it on top of them along with the other blankets the heartlanding provided. Then he lies back beside her.

"Warm enough?" he asks.

Toward him.

Tentatively, she moves closer to him, curling against his side, and he wraps his arm around her.

"Now I'm warm enough," she whispers.

"Good. I suppose I should have made sure I don't stink first. I got warm climbing the tree."

Nestraya laughs. That was just what they needed to relieve some of the awkwardness and newness of...this.

After sniffing him, she nestles closer. "I've smelled worse in the barracks."

"You make a habit of curling up with sweaty men in the barracks?"

She stiffens. "That was not at all what I meant. I have never—"

Before she can finish, he bursts out laughing and then presses his lips to the top of her head.

"Be nice, or I'll push you off the platform again," she says.

"As long as you catch me at the bottom." His voice has grown husky, and she swallows.

"Always."

He tightens his hold on her, and she gazes up at the stars as they begin to dot the sky. Then she frowns. "These aren't our stars."

"Are they not?"

She turns her head to look at him. "Lorial Westaria, King of Lostariel, enthroned in Celesta, Master of Starhaven. No. These are not our stars."

A smile teases at the corners of his mouth. "Are you trying to convey something to me?"

"You of all people should recognize our stars!"

"Ah. I see. Well, that one right there"—he points, and she follows his finger to the brightest star in this unfamiliar sky—"is called Nestraya. It's part of the Warrior Queen constellation. See the way those stars are grouped? That's her with her bow in one hand and her water magic in the other."

Nestraya nestles against him again, biting her lip as she listens to him talk.

Who knew Lorial could be so romantic?

He lowers his hand again. "I like these stars."

"What else do you see?"

"Shall I name them all after you? Let's see...that one is First Nestraya. And that there is the Princess constellation."

"I've never been—"

"Hush. You wear ayervadi leather better than any elf I've ever met."

She warms at his words. And the way his finger traces circles on her arm.

"And that makes me a princess?"

"No. Father did that. The ayervadi leather just makes you nice to look at. Aside from its practicality for fighting, of course. Which is obviously the most important consideration."

Laughter bubbles up inside her, and he pulls her even closer.

"Slay your demons, my love," he whispers before he kisses her hair again.

My love? She stiffens. And heats and struggles against the voices raging in her head.

"What are you thinking?" he asks softly. "Tell me. We'll slay the demons together."

Slowly, she exhales. Together. He promised they'd do this together.

"You...you called me...and it just—"

How does she explain this to him? It barely makes sense to her.

"My love. My queen. My Nestraya," he whispers near her ear, and part of her wants to melt while the other part of her wants to dive off the platform.

"My head keeps telling me to push you away," she whispers.

"And what does your heart tell you?"

"To run toward you and never let go."

"This time, listen to your heart, my love."

"I feel like an imposter. As if I'm pretending to be someone I'm not. As if I don't belong here."

"You do belong here. By my side. Strong. My First. My queen. My Nestraya."

"Your Nestraya." She whispers the words. Could she ever believe them? Truly?

"My Nestraya." He says it like a caress, breathing life to a part of her deep within that begs for it to be true. For her to be his and him to be hers. For nothing else to matter.

Then he shifts beside her until he's looking down at her. "Slay your demons, my love. You belong to me."

The starry sky silhouettes him in the faint glow from an orb light that seems to exist just so she can look into his eyes.

"Nestraya Westaria," he whispers. "Queen of Lostariel. Enthroned in Celesta. Mistress of Starhaven. You...belong."

"I don't want to cry again." She chokes back a sob.

"Then kiss me, instead."

Her heart is racing now, as is his. Her eyes dart to his lips.

Run toward him.

"Lorial." She runs her fingers along his cheek. "My Lorial."

"Your Lorial. Always yours. There was never anyone but you. There never could be."

She trails her fingers onto his lips, tracing the dip of his upper lip. The fullness of his lower one.

"I'm so wrong for you," she murmurs.

"You're the only one for me. Only you, Nestraya. Slay your demons." He kisses her fingers. Nuzzles against them.

"Yours."

"Mine."

"There could never be anyone but you." She slides her hand behind his neck, threading her fingers through his silver hair as she pulls him toward her. For the briefest moment, he hovers there, so close she can taste him.

"Nestraya." The yearning in his voice feeds her own longing, and she closes the distance between them, pressing her lips to his.

25

A DIFFERENT KIND OF MOTIVATION

It ends far too soon, but when Nestraya pulls away, Lorial gives her space to process everything she's thinking and feeling.

Though it was a simple kiss, her lips were just as soft as he's always imagined they'd be.

"You taste good," she whispers, and he laughs.

"So do you."

Oh, he wants to pull her close again. Experience her in every way. Instead, he lowers himself to the bed beside her, and she nestles against his side as he wraps his arm around her. His hands have grown warm again, but that's not so bad given the chill of the night.

"That one is Lorial." She points to the star beside the one he named after her. "Lorial and Nestraya. They belong together forever. You can't separate them. Is that how the story goes?"

He can't help himself. He wraps both arms around her and squeezes her far too tightly. "Yes, my love. That's exactly how the story goes."

"Until he squeezed her to death, and they both died."

He bursts into laughter as he loosens his hold, though he doesn't let go.

"Be patient with me," she whispers.

"Always."

"You might have to remind me I'm yours all over again tomorrow."

"Every day for the rest of my life, if that's what it takes."

She snuggles closer, and eventually, she relaxes against him as her breathing slows and steadies. He doesn't let go even as sleep comes to claim him, too.

Birds sing, and the breeze caresses Lorial's cheek as the sun peeks over the horizon.

And Nestraya shivers beside him.

He wishes for another blanket, and one appears on top of them as he draws her closer.

"Mmm. You're warm," she whispers.

"And you're mine."

A contented little sigh slips past her lips, and he tightens his arm around her.

"I can't believe we're still here," she says.

"What shall we do today?"

"Fly."

"You are persistent, my love."

"That's why I'm your First."

"Not because you're warming my bed?"

Her eyes flash open. "I am warming your bed. Perhaps I should resign."

"I refuse to accept your resignation."

"Mmm. We can argue about it later."

He kisses her temple. "If you insist."

The sun continues its trek across the sky as Nestraya dozes off and on in his arms. Eventually, she yawns and stretches, and he reluctantly lets her go.

"Shall I warm some water for you?" he asks as she sits up beside him.

"Maybe later. We should get an early start on your flying lessons today in case we wake soon. We wasted a lot of time yesterday."

Lorial props himself up on his elbows. "Nothing we did yesterday was a waste. Everything mattered."

She glances down at him but doesn't argue. "In any case, we should get to work."

After Nestraya dresses in her full warrior leathers, they eat a quick breakfast and make their way back upstairs to the platform. Their makeshift bed has vanished, and Lorial stays as far from the edge as possible.

"I won't push you today. I promise," Nestraya says as Lorial eyes her warily.

"So what is your plan?"

"I thought you might jump."

"I'd rather not."

She crosses her arms over her chest. "Then how will you learn?"

He purses his lips as he thinks. "Perhaps we take smaller steps. I wish we were at the base of our tree."

The scene transforms around them, and Nestraya shakes her head. "Cheater."

"I submit myself to your punishment." He bows with a flourish, fully expecting a root to wrap around his ankle or a vine to lift him into the air, but nothing happens. When he looks up, she's studying him.

It's more than a little disconcerting.

"I wish I was falling," she says.

Lorial's heart pounds as she vanishes. Whistling wind.

He looks up, trying frantically to calm his panic as she rapidly approaches the forest floor.

Air. His magic. He grasps at it, sending currents toward her, but all he does is slow her down.

"Use your plant magic!" he yells.

But she doesn't, and he abandons his own feeble attempts to slow her descent with his magic and rushes to catch her instead. She slams into him, knocking them both down as the air whooshes from him. But he caught her. Sort of.

He coughs and wheezes, trying to fill his lungs, and she groans.

"That hurt."

"What"—he coughs again—"were you thinking? Why didn't you use your magic?"

"I knew you'd catch me one way or another."

He lays his head back and whimpers. "Please don't do that again. Ever."

"I felt your magic, but it wasn't controlled enough to do more than slow me down."

"You didn't even warn me! I had no time to prepare!"

"Do you think you'll always have time in the real world? Did you have time to stop that musket ball?"

He groans in frustration, and she climbs off him.

"Maybe you need a different kind of motivation," she says.

"As long as no one is in danger of dying."

She launches at the tree again, pulling herself onto the lowest branch. "Lift me from the tree, and set me on the ground."

"What part of this is supposed to be motivating?"

"The part where you wrap your air magic around me."

For a moment, he stares up at her as she smirks.

"I like this way," he says, and she leans back against the trunk of the tree and makes herself comfortable.

"I thought you might. Go ahead whenever you're ready."

He musters his air magic and wraps threads of it around her waist. Her legs. Her arms.

"You're supposed to be lifting me, not blowing air at me while you stand there grinning."

"I'm working on it." He narrows and strengthens the air currents, recalling how it felt to lift her yesterday. Tugging at his magic, he carefully raises her off the branch, an inch at a time.

She wobbles, and he hurries to wrap more air around her. To keep her steady. That's the only reason.

This way is better. So much better.

"See? You can do this," she calls down to him as she hovers in the air.

"Making you float isn't the same as making myself fly."

"Perhaps not, but it's a start. Try moving me toward the maple tree."

He'd rather pull her close, but he complies. She's altogether perfect in every way. The feeling of his magic wrapping itself around her is intoxicating.

As gently as he can manage, he uses his air currents to guide her to the maple tree, where he carefully sets her on a low branch.

"Well done! Try setting me on the ground now."

His heart pounds as he lifts her once more, but instead of settling her beneath the bigleaf maple, he carries her on air currents toward him, setting her down right in front of him as his air magic whips at their hair.

"Good. Now you just—"

Before she can finish, he slides his hands around her waist and pulls her closer as the wind swirls around them both.

"You seem distracted, my king."

He grins. "You are distracting."

"This is why I should tender my resignation. Kings rarely find their Firsts so alluring."

"No more talk of resigning."

He'd rather not talk at all.

"Focus, Lorial. Lostariel depends on it."

That's sobering. He lowers his magic and releases her. "Forgive me. It's easy to forget everything else when it's just you and me here together."

A pang of guilt stabs at him as thoughts of Mother and the low-born elves depending on him surface.

"It's all right," she says softly as she runs her fingers along his cheek. "The heartlanding makes us forget."

Exhaling slowly, he nods. "What now?"

"Now we keep practicing." She steps away. "Again."

For the rest of the morning and into the afternoon, she pushes him, challenging him to go farther and think faster. He lifts her and spins her and, by the time the sun begins its descent, he even manages to catch her with his magic. It's done clumsily, and he almost drops her, but when he sets her down safely, she runs toward him and throws her arms around his neck.

"You're doing so well. Pera would be so proud."

A sadness sweeps over Lorial. "He was just starting to train me in so many things. I feel robbed of so much."

"I know."

"Hothniel can't get away with this. With any of it. When we return, he'll wish he'd never set foot near either of us."

She clings to him, and he rests his cheek against her hair.

"We're stronger together," he whispers. "Lorial and Nestraya."

"Lorial and Nestraya."

"Say it louder."

She leans her head back and shouts it to the trees.

"And who are you?" he asks.

She tips her head forward to search his eyes. "What do you mean?"

"Who...are...you?"

"I'm Nestraya."

"Who?"

Her mouth twitches into a smile. "Nestraya."

"And who is Nestraya?"

She breathes out slowly. "I am who I am."

"And who is that?"

"I'm *estrassa*."

"And?"

"First among warriors."

He inclines his head and grins. "Go on."

"Queen of Lostariel."

"Mmm. Yes. I like that one. Say it louder."

She laughs and shouts it to the forest.

"And what else are you?" he whispers as he presses his forehead to hers.

"Yours?"

"Mine. And what am I, my love?" He circles his thumbs on her lower back, doing his best to keep his fire magic in check, and she twines her fingers in his hair.

"You're mine, Lorial." Then she finds his lips with her own.

26
WESTARIA

A week ago, it would have been unthinkable to consider kissing Lorial.

Right now, it's all Nestraya can think about.

Every step toward him changes the way she sees him a little more.

And the kiss last night?

Whistling wind. It was the shortest, simplest kiss imaginable. But she felt it so deeply. It was almost overwhelming.

This kiss, as she digs her fingers into his hair, is like fire. Sparks. Lights in the sky. Her heart pounds right along with his, and his hands on her back are warmer than they should be—hopefully, he doesn't set her on fire.

He presses her even closer, and she melts against him.

She pulled away so soon last night.

Not this time. This time, she gives in to the feeling. The overwhelm. The desire. Lets it crash over her as she clings to him like he's the only thing keeping her from drowning.

And when he tentatively deepens the kiss, she leans into it.

Lorial. It was always Lorial. It just took a musket ball and a diabolical heartlanding to make her see it.

This time, he pulls away first. "I'm worried I might set you on fire," he chuckles as he shakes his hands at his sides to cool them down. "Maybe we need to work on my fire magic next."

She laughs and tightens her arms around his neck, not wanting to let go. Soon, he rests his hands on her hips, and a soft gasp escapes her lips.

"Is this all right?" he asks, and she nods. Then he circles his thumbs over the soft flesh next to her hips. "Are you hungry? We didn't eat much lunch."

As if she could think about food while he does...that. It was one thing for his magic to trail along her body. His hands are another thing entirely.

She opens her mouth, but no words come out.

"Are you overcome, my queen? Shall I rub your ears next?"

She huffs a nervous laugh, and he moves his hands to her back again.

"Why don't we slow down a little?" he says softly. "Get some food. Maybe watch the sunset. Gaze at the stars again? Do you want to take another bath?" He sniffs himself. "Maybe I'm the one who needs a bath."

She loosens her hold on him so she can see his face. "How about you wash up, and I will see about dinner on the platform? Feel like eating while we watch the sunset? Assuming the heartlanding doesn't make us climb back up." She frowns, and he kisses the line between her brows.

"That sounds perfect. I wish we were in our treehouse."

The world transforms around them, and Nestraya sighs in relief.

"I'll be quick, all right?" He steals another kiss and then lets her go.

As he disappears behind the screen, she exhales slowly. She misses him already.

What in the Wildthorne Woods is wrong with her?

Shaking her head, she hurries up the stairs. Food. She promised him food.

Perhaps a romantic dinner for two as the sun sets in the background?

Romantic? Nestraya Cerianus isn't romantic.

Of course, she's legally entitled to the name Westaria now. If she wants it. Nestraya Westaria might be romantic.

Perhaps it doesn't matter what her name is or was. Perhaps she can be whatever she wants to be.

She wants to be a Westaria.

Not for Lorial, though. For Restoval.

For Pera.

He offered it to her when she began her warrior training. He wanted to make it legal, so everyone would know she was his.

And she turned him down.

Why did she refuse? Because she thought she wasn't worthy? That she would never belong to him the way Lorial did?

But she did belong to him. He proved it every day, day in and day out. He treated her like his elfling.

He gave her everything.

Why did she refuse his offer? Why did she push him away so much?

A sob catches in her throat. Did he know how much she loved him?

"Slay your demons, my love." Warm arms slip around her waist from behind, and she leans into Lorial.

"I...I pushed him away," she chokes out. "Why did I push him away?"

"Are we talking about Father?"

Nestraya nods, and Lorial tightens his arms around her.

"I loved him. Did he know I loved him?"

"He knew."

"But—"

Lorial turns her to face him. His hair is damp and loose, and he wears a casual linen shirt and trousers.

He takes her face in his hands and looks into her eyes. "He knew, Nestraya. He knew how much you loved him. And he loved you with the unconditional love of a father for his elfling. No matter what you did or said or didn't do or didn't say, none of it changed his love for you."

Sobs wrack her body, and he wraps his arms around her and pulls her against his chest.

"Westaria," she says through shuddering breaths.

"What, my love?"

"Westaria. My name is...Westaria. Because...because—"

"Because you're the daughter of Restoval Westaria. Because he gave his name to you."

She nods, and Lorial holds her close.

"Slay your demons, my love."

"My name is Nestraya Westaria."

"Say it louder."

"My name is Nestraya Westaria! And no one can take that from me."

"No one. You are *estrassa*. His *estrassa*."

His.

Nestraya wraps her arms around Lorial's neck—clings to him. And once again, he holds her until her tears are spent.

Then he gently wipes her wet cheeks and lets her go.

"I didn't get very far with the food," she says.

"It's all right. You were busy slaying demons." He sends her a soft smile, and she smiles in return.

"It was supposed to be romantic."

He crosses his arms and looks at her with that lopsided grin in place. "Romantic? You?"

She smacks his chest. It's wet with her tears, but he doesn't complain.

"I'm Nestraya Westaria. I can be whatever I want to be."

"Now that, I believe."

"I'm...trying."

"You're doing fine. Now, let's see. I wish for a table for two with candles and"—he turns to Nestraya—"Pear cider? Or berry cordial?"

"Both. Hard."

He grins. "Make that hard pear cider and the strong cordial like Grandmother used to hide in the cupboard in Grandfather's study."

"Perfect."

"What else?"

"Ruffed grouse with roasted turnips."

"This really is a romantic dinner, isn't it? What else?"

"Chocolate-covered strawberries."

"Like the humans serve?"

She shrugs, and he nods.

"What else?" he asks.

"Sugared plums."

A grin spreads across his face. "You and your sweet tooth."

She ignores him. "What do you want?"

"I have everything I want." He lifts her hand to his lips, and she shakes her head.

"Who knew there was such a romantic man hiding in there? I certainly had no idea."

"The Kings of Lostariel are known for their romantic ways."

She laughs. "I used to get so embarrassed when Pera would whisper in Mera's ear the way he did, and she practically melted. I always wondered what he said to her."

Lorial's smile fades as he looks intently into Nestraya's eyes, and her heart flutters.

"Star, shine so bright. For you alone can light up my night sky, where my shadows freely roam. For here, I'm safe. With you, I'm home."

"That's what he told her?" Nestraya whispers, her mouth dry.

Lorial nods. "I can steal words on the wind. That one, I regretted a little at the time, if I'm being honest. I was trying to figure out why we always got put to bed early on the nights he whispered in her ear."

Nestraya stares at him. Then she bursts out laughing. "When did you figure it out?"

"I'm done with this conversation." He rubs at his eyes and sucks in his cheeks as if to hide his own mirth.

She laughs harder. It feels so good to laugh. Really laugh. "I hope you didn't use your air magic to listen—"

"Stop. We're done."

"Lorial! Oh, I'm dying."

"Your grouse grows cold while you delight in my mortification."

When she looks up, candlelight flickers on Lorial's face, and her heart flutters again.

"We're dressed all wrong," she whispers.

"We could fix that."

Biting her lip, she nods. Hopefully, she doesn't end up in satin.

"I wish we were dressed for a formal dinner," he says, and in an instant, they're both transformed.

She looks down. Velvet. The softest black velvet gown. It falls from a high waist to drape across her body in a slim skirt that just grazes the floor.

"Wow."

She looks up at the sound of his voice as his eyes drink her in.

And she does some drinking in of her own. He wears a satin jacket over a formal vest with long, black trousers that glimmer in the candlelight.

"You look amazing," she whispers.

He steps toward her and slips his hand along her waist, never taking his eyes off hers. His palm is like fire through the velvet, and he frames her face with his other hand, warming her cheek as he presses his forehead to hers.

"Are you sure we need dinner?" he murmurs, and her heart speeds up.

Before she can respond, he steps away and offers his hand. It's hot as she places her fingers on his palm, and he leads her to a chair.

Everything on the table looks just as wonderful as she imagined.

"My love." He waits for her to sit and pushes her chair in before sitting across from her.

She's...nervous. She's never felt this way around Lorial. He's safe. Comfortable. Familiar.

Yet as he gazes at her as if he's starving for delights not on the plates in front of them, suddenly he's something akin to a stranger.

And it's as if she's meeting him for the first time.

27

BURNING

Her heart is racing. Lorial can feel it. Her hand trembles as she reaches for her glass of cordial.

Nestraya, nervous? Is it even possible?

Perhaps he came on too strong when he saw her in that dress. She looked so amazing, though. She still does.

His hands warm again as he studies her.

Whistling wind, he needs to get his fire magic under control. He's already coaxed air to spread the excess heat from his hands around the platform. It helped. A little.

"It's not as cold tonight," Nestraya says, and Lorial chokes on his bite of grouse.

"Sorry." He coughs and reaches for his cider.

"Are you all right?"

He nods. And then he shakes his head.

All secrets are laid bare here.

"I've been warming the air with my fire magic. I can't..." He scratches his brow and breathes out through pursed lips.

When he glances at her, her expression softens. "It's all right. We'll...figure it out."

He stills. What is she implying?

Suddenly, his fork burns his hand, and he drops it.

Did he just burn himself with his own magic? How in the Wildthorne Woods did he manage that?

A stifled giggle draws his gaze. Is she laughing at him?

"You think this is funny?"

She presses her lips together and shakes her head. Then she nods as laughter bursts from her. "Perhaps you should talk to Mera about how she manages her fire magic."

"You are an awful person." He struggles not to laugh himself. "Eat your dinner, and leave me be."

"Of course, my king." She takes a bite of her turnips as she attempts to hide her mirth, quite unsuccessfully.

He just shakes his head and carefully reaches for his fork again.

By the time they're both finished eating, Nestraya's nerves seem to have returned.

To no one's surprise, when they rise, the table and chairs vanish.

The stars are just appearing in the night sky, and Lorial raises his gaze to the light he named after her. The brightest star in the sky.

It's fitting. She's the brightest star in his sky.

"Are you warm enough?" he whispers, afraid to break whatever spell seems to have descended around them in the quiet of the forest since their laughter earlier.

"It is a little cold."

He could wish for blankets again.

That seems a bit forward, though. As if he's anticipating...

Whistling wind.

Instead, he wraps his arms around her. His hands have cooled some. As long as he occasionally swirls the air around his palms, he seems to be managing. More or less.

He hasn't burned himself again, at any rate.

"Better?" he whispers.

"Much." She nestles her head against his shoulder, and he just holds her. Her velvet gown is so soft. She rarely wears full dresses. It's not practical for a warrior.

Tonight, though. Tonight, she's not First Nestraya.

She's Queen Nestraya. All she needs is the gem-encrusted mahogany crown sitting in the vault at Starhaven to complete the picture.

He could wish for it.

But he won't. If she's not ready for that, the last thing he wants to do is push her. Especially since she already seems so nervous.

"What are you thinking?" he whispers.

"I...don't want to go back. I want to stay here with you forever. Where you're my Lorial, and I'm your Nestraya, and nothing else matters."

"We'll always have this place whenever we need it at night in our dreams. Besides, I thought you hated the heartlanding," he teases.

"It seems to have beaten me by accomplishing its goal. I'm ashamed to have been defeated so swiftly."

"And how has it defeated you, my queen?"

Nestraya pauses, and Lorial holds his breath, waiting for her response.

"It's made me fall wholly and completely in love with you," she eventually whispers.

One of their hearts is racing.

Perhaps both.

Before he can even begin to think of a response, she pulls away. "Can we take this slow still? I-I feel like we're careening toward...everything, and I don't want to look back and wonder if it was this place prodding us forward or us choosing each other."

She looks tentatively up at him, vulnerable and beautiful and the living incarnation of every desire he's ever had.

And it's the hardest and easiest answer all wrapped up in one package. Despite his longing and the aching in his chest when he looks at her, he doesn't even hesitate.

"I would wait forever for you, my love."

Then she kisses him. Passionately. Full of pent-up longing that brings the inferno under his skin to the surface as he tries not to touch her.

Either she delights in torturing him, or she has no idea what she's doing to him.

She wraps her arms around his neck as her fingers dig into his hair. When she grazes his ears, he hisses, and his hands tingle.

Whistling wind, he's going to light them both on fire.

With a low groan, he creates a fireball in each palm, keeping his hands straight out to the sides as he lobs the fireballs far above them, too high to catch the forest on fire. They'll burn out long before they fall.

The relief is immediate.

And Nestraya pulls away. "I am so sorry. I...lost myself for a moment. Did that help?"

"It did, actually." He flexes his hands and shakes them out before reaching for her and pulling her close again. "Now, where were we?"

"I think maybe we were getting carried away."

He rests his forehead against hers and wills the fire to stay away. And the rest of him to cool down. "All right, then. Shall we do some more stargazing? Or did you want to get some sleep?"

"How about both? I wish for a bed with plenty of blankets. And comfortable clothes for sleeping."

Her velvet transforms to satin beneath his hands—the sleeping gown she's been wearing—and a strange mixture of relief and disappointment fills him. His own linens are back, and the bed from last night has reappeared as well.

"Sounds perfect," he murmurs. He steals a soft kiss before letting her go, and soon, she's curling up against him beneath the blankets once more.

"When we return, if we return, and all of this is over...I'll give you your elfling," she says softly.

His heart speeds up right alongside hers, and he tightens his arm around her.

"Though I can't promise ebony hair and emerald eyes," she continues. "You might have to settle for silver and gray."

"I don't even care. I just want you."

When she leans over his chest and trails her fingers along his cheek, the desire to kiss her is overwhelming.

She tentatively sweeps her fingertips over his ear, and his fire roars back to life.

"Are you trying to torture me?" he murmurs.

She slides her hand along his jaw before snuggling against his side again. "Goodnight, my king."

He gently presses his lips to her temple. "Goodnight, my love. Sleep well."

The next day dawns bright and clear, and Nestraya barely gives Lorial time to wake before she wishes them both into their warrior leathers.

"Sit." She points, and he stifles a yawn as he lowers himself to the table inside their treehouse. He doesn't even register what she's planning until she climbs up behind him and twines her fingers in his hair.

"You'll be more confident in your abilities if you look the part," she says.

He doesn't argue. She grazes his ear, and he closes his eyes and grins.

She can play with his hair whenever she wants.

"There. Now your warrior paint." She hops off the table and steps between his knees to line his eyes the way she did their first morning here. His air magic isn't as restless after all the practicing they've been doing, but he lets it slide around her, anyway.

"Are you getting distracted, my king?"

"I admit I find my queen very distracting."

She finishes with the korathite and places her hands on his knees again. "It's not good for a warrior to be distracted."

As she slowly slides her hands along his legs over his warrior leathers, his palms warm. Along with other parts of him. He swirls his air magic more tightly around her, tugging her even closer.

She lifts her chin toward him. He can feel her breath on his lips. Just as he's about to press his mouth to hers, she whispers, "I wish we were falling."

And as the treehouse transforms into open air, his heart thunders, and he grasps at his air magic.

"Nestraya! You are an awful person!"

28

STANDING ON AIR

He isn't slowing.

With a sigh, Nestraya reaches for her plant magic to catch them both, when he spins. Then he flattens and rights himself.

He's doing it.

"Grab me," he grunts through clenched teeth as he struggles to reach her, and she clutches at his vest as branches whoosh past. She keeps her plant magic ready to intervene, but they've already slowed enough that she's not worried.

As the forest floor looms closer, she wraps her arms around his waist, and their downward momentum slows to a stop, leaving them to hover ten feet off the ground.

She'd kiss him if she wasn't afraid of interrupting his concentration.

"Nestraya," he whispers.

"I know. You're doing it. I knew you could do it."

"I'm afraid to move. It feels unstable."

"We're standing on air. I think that's a given."

He laughs, and they wobble, but he rights them. "I still think you're an awful person," he says, though it's impossible to miss the smile threatening to slip across his face.

"You seemed fond of me a minute ago."

He laughs at that, and they wobble again. "I'm not sure this counts as flying. It's more...hovering. I don't know how to move."

"It's a start. Can you set us down? It would be easier without me wrapped around you."

"Having you wrapped around me is the best part."

She laughs this time, but he gently lowers them to the ground, only wobbling once. The landing is rough, but he catches her with his hands on her hips when she stumbles.

"I think I'm steady now," she says. "You can let go."

"Do you want me to let go?"

She rests her hands against his chest and looks up at him. "I'm about to make you fall again."

His forehead creases. "You are relentless."

"So are your enemies. And so must you be."

He takes a deep breath and slowly exhales. Then he lets her go and steps back, shaking his arms at his sides to loosen up. "I wish I was falling."

He vanishes as her heart twists within her. Pera would be proud of him.

She steps back and searches the sky for him. He's falling fast, but he quickly rights himself this time. Then he slows. He's getting the hang of this.

"Well done!" she cups her hands around her mouth and calls to him where he hovers thirty feet off the ground.

They spend the rest of the morning practicing, and by midday, he's made so much progress that Nestraya just wants to wrap herself around him and not let go.

"I think you've earned a break, my love," she says as she saunters toward him.

His boyish grin lights up his face. "Could you say that again? I'm not sure I heard you."

"What? You've earned a break?" She crosses her wrists behind his neck, and he slides his hands around her lower back.

"Mmm, no. The other part."

"Oh. You've earned a break, my king." She sends him an impish smile, and he tugs her close to whisper in her ear.

"That is most definitely not what you said."

"Is it not?"

"Don't play innocent with me, *estrassa*. I've known you far too long to fall for it." He teases his lower lip along the edge of her ear, and her knees almost betray her. "You seem overcome, my queen."

"My love," she whispers.

"That's the one." His hands on her back warm her through her leathers.

"After lunch, we work on your fire magic."

He removes his hands, a guttural groan of frustration lodging in his throat.

"Here." She holds her hands toward his. "Trust me."

Reluctantly, he rests his palms against hers, and she dampens them with her water magic.

"Now blow air on them."

The air around them shifts, and he sighs. "Thank you."

"You're welcome, my love. Now, lunch and then target practice. We'll see if you can keep up."

"With you? Very funny."

She runs her hand down his chest and shrugs as she turns toward the picnic lunch she's already imagined nearby, but he grabs her hand and pulls her back.

"Thank you. I couldn't have done any of this without you."

"I'm First Nestraya. It's a First's job to make sure her warriors are fit for battle."

"And you didn't want to be my First." He loops his arm around her waist again.

"I didn't want to be a lot of things."

"And now?" His eyes are intense as he gazes down at her.

"And now, I realize I was wrong. About everything. Let's eat, all right?"

He slides his free hand behind her neck and pulls her into a slow, lingering kiss.

Never has she been so happy to be proved wrong.

"No matter what I do, you just douse my fire magic!" Lorial complains as he wipes his wet face with the back of his hand. His bare chest glistens in the late afternoon sun as rivulets of water trail over his muscles.

"I'm not the only water wielder you're going to meet out there. You need to figure out how to deal with it. What did Pera teach you to do?"

Lorial exhales through pursed lips. "I got wet a lot."

Nestraya does her best not to laugh. He's pretty wet now.

"You watched Mera and Pera spar. How did she manage his water magic?"

"I don't know. You tell me. I clearly haven't been paying enough attention." He turns away and rubs his eyes. Korathite streams down his face, making him look almost sinister. It's such a startling contrast to who he really is.

"She would use her soil magic to block as much of his water source as possible first."

"I'm not a soil wielder."

"No, but you're an air wielder. Use that to your advantage. What happens when you heat the air strategically?"

"The air gets warm."

She pulls his hands away from his face so he can see her. "You're not thinking big enough."

"If you're suggesting I should create lightning storms like Zelovon—"

"That's exactly what I'm suggesting."

He stares at her. And then he laughs.

"Fine, we'll start smaller. Where am I drawing my water from?"

"That creek you wished into existence, which is cheating, by the way."

"So use your air and fire magic to hold back the water with one of your shields."

"You mean the one that couldn't stop a musket ball?"

"We just need to practice more—"

He groans.

"I spent years training to join the warrior bands." Nestraya pokes his chest. "You are not going to master this in a few days."

He throws his hands out to the sides. "I only have a few days. We could wake up any minute just to face down an army whose leader wants me dead. I don't have years."

"So you won't even try? You didn't think you could fly, either."

He takes a deep breath and slowly breathes out. "All right. So I need to cut off your source of water? I can dry the air out easily enough. But damming the creek? You could just pull water from farther upstream."

He's right.

She sighs. "I don't know what else to suggest. We usually train as teams in the warrior bands."

"Perhaps it doesn't need to be this complicated. Let's try something else. Come at me with your water magic again."

She swallows, trying to wet her cottony throat, but nods. While she coaxes the water from the creek to respond to her, the most blinding light shines from Lorial's hands, and a few colorful words slip past her lips as she turns away from him, the water forgotten.

"Huh. I didn't think that would work," he says.

"Whistling wind, Lorial!" She blinks a few times. Her eyes would water if she weren't so close to her limit with her water magic. "I've never seen a fire-wielder bend light the way you can. Are you sure that's fire magic?"

For a moment, as he directed the light her way, she caught a faint whiff with her life magic of...something unfamiliar. Fire magic is easy to sense. At least most fire magic is—Lorial's is usually blotted out by his air magic. There's a warm, faint smoky feeling to fire magic that hangs heavy in the hair.

But this...was totally different. It was warm, like fire magic, but clear, like air magic.

He frowns. "What else would it be?"

"I don't know. I can't see anything now, though. That will probably work. But we're going to practice your barriers and heating air currents, too. I just need—"

She sways, and he rushes toward her.

"I wish we were in our treehouse with a warm bath," he quickly says.

"Yes. That. I need that."

The forest transforms into their cozy home in the trees, and Lorial carries her behind the screen. "Why in the Wildthorne Woods didn't you say something sooner?"

"We need to practice. We don't have time for me to be weak."

"Forgive me," he murmurs, and she squints at him around the spots she's still seeing.

"What—"

"I wish her leathers were gone."

"Lorial!"

The heartlanding, diabolical place that it is, kindly grants his request, leaving only her small clothes, and she groans as he gently lowers her into the tub.

As soon as the water hits her skin, it offers the most satisfying relief imaginable, and she almost forgives Lorial.

"Will you be all right if I let go?" he asks softly as he focuses on her face. His arms still brace her in the water.

She nods. "My throat is so dry."

He carefully releases her and mumbles something under his breath. Soon, a glass of cool, clear water hovers at her lips. "Here, my love."

She gulps it down gratefully. "Thank you."

"More?"

She nods, and he soon offers her the refilled glass.

"Better?" he asks.

"Yes. Thank you."

"I'm going to go now. Yell if you need me, all right? I'll be on the other side of the screen."

She nods, and he presses his lips to her forehead before leaving. With a quiet groan, she ducks under the water and tries to pretend none of that just happened.

29

SPARKS AND WATERFALLS

It takes every ounce of willpower Lorial can muster not to use his air magic to check on Nestraya.

She keeps muttering under her breath, and his magic itches to listen more closely, but he resists that as well. He caught a few of her words with his ears, though. For a full minute, she berated and cursed the heartlanding. She wasn't quiet about that.

Then she murmured something about Pera, but Lorial caught little else.

Now, she seems to be expressing her frustration with herself.

He knew she struggled with her endurance, but she's done such a good job of hiding it most of the time that he didn't realize until they arrived here at the heartlanding how quickly she drains her magic reserves.

And beyond feeding her berries and painting her with a leaf and getting her to water, he has no idea how to help her. Perhaps the Tree of Memories will offer insight.

If they ever wake. It's been nearly three days since they arrived here. Surely Corivos has located a healer by now. Unless there are no loyal healers left.

"Lorial?"

He stands from his perch on the bed. "I'm here. Do you need something?"

"The water is growing cold, and this fates-forsaken place won't warm it for me."

He swallows. "I see. Shall I help, or do you want to get out?"

"Will you warm it?"

"Of course." He steps around the screen, doing his best to keep his eyes averted as he focuses on the tub and not the woman in the tub. He hovers his hand over the water near her feet, pushing his heat into it. "How's that?"

"Perfect. Thank you. Will you...sit with me?"

He finds her green eyes gazing up at him, and his own throat feels suddenly dry. "If you want me to stay, I'll stay."

"I do."

She hasn't asked him to avert his eyes, but she hasn't invited him to look, either. He won't take advantage of her vulnerable state. It was one thing to help her into the water when she was near fainting. Sitting beside her to keep her company is something else entirely.

Gingerly, he lowers himself to the floor, leaning his back against the side of the tub. If he turns his head, he can see her face and shoulders, but that's it.

"Is the water helping?" he asks softly.

"Yes. It's perfect. Thank you."

"What does it feel like? When your magic reserves run low?"

Her brows knit. "Don't you experience it yourself?"

He shakes his head. "I've never used enough of my magic at once to run out. I have the opposite problem. So much magic, it gets away from me."

"You've never run out of magic?"

"I don't think so."

"Even Pera ran out of magic at times."

"I guess I don't use my magic enough." He looks at his hands, still coated with dried streaks of dirty water from their practice session.

"It's different depending on the magic being drained," she says softly, and he turns his attention to her again. "With my water magic, I grow dehydrated. My throat dries, and my eyes sting. I become faint. My plant magic is similar. I get hungry instead of thirsty, though."

"And cranky." He grins at her, and she chuckles.

"Yes."

"And your life magic?"

She traces her fingers along the surface of the water as she responds. "I grow nauseated. Weak. I look like death. Pale and sunken. I have larger reserves for my life magic, though."

"How do you replenish it?"

She leans her head back and looks at the ceiling. "Touch. That's the fastest way."

"As in…a hug?"

"That's one way. Any skin-to-skin contact helps."

"A kiss?"

She glances at him with the hint of a smile tugging at her lips. "Do you really want me to answer that?"

He leans his arm along the side of the tub and rests his chin on it. "I'm not naïve enough to imagine you've never kissed anyone else."

She sighs. "I wish I hadn't. It was…not something we need to discuss."

"When you say it like that, it makes me think we should talk about it."

She glances at him again before covering her eyes with her arm, and he frowns.

"Now I definitely think we should talk about it."

"It was all a cruel joke that taught me a very important lesson about how the world sees me. Let's leave it at that. Please."

"Nestraya."

"If you start talking about slaying my demons, I'm going to douse you."

"I am filthy."

She lifts her arm to see him and laughs. "You are. You should look in the mirror."

"I'd rather look at you."

Her smile fades. He shouldn't have said that. Not right now, anyway.

"I was new at the barracks." She doesn't meet his eyes as she speaks. "We had an extended training session, and I could only use my life magic that day. It's one of the few times I've ever drained it so completely. And one of the other new warriors told me a kiss was the best way to replenish life magic."

"And you believed him?"

"I'm not as naïve as I once was. I overcame that quickly."

"What happened?"

She plays with the water's surface again. "I let him kiss me. It helped my magic, but any flesh contact would have. I know that now. It didn't have to be a kiss. And when it was done, he told me he'd drawn the short straw among the other recruits to determine if I really tasted like fae slops. Which, according to him, I did."

Lorial's fire magic crackles beneath the surface.

"So…that's what happened," she continues, "and now we don't need to discuss it again."

"Who was he?"

She turns her emerald eyes his way. "I can fight my own battles, my king. Besides, it happened years ago. No need to dwell on it now."

"It's not true."

"What?"

"You usually taste like berries. Especially if you've been using your plant magic."

Her brow creases. "And my water magic?"

"I'd have to test it." He lobs a teasing grin her way, and she smiles.

"You would, huh?"

He nods against his arm.

"All right." She shifts to face him as water drips from her ears, and his grin grows.

He slides his hand along her jaw and draws her closer. Her lips are wet against his, and he quickly deepens the kiss. If he's supposed to be tasting her, he'd better do a proper job of it.

When she eventually pulls away, the vulnerability in her eyes catches him off guard, though it probably shouldn't. She's not as tough as she portrays herself to the world.

"What's the verdict?" she asks.

He runs his thumb along her ear, and her swift intake of air makes him smile. "Imagine a waterfall—the mist as the water droplets spray off the rocks and the surface of the pool below. You taste like the mist from a waterfall."

She doesn't respond. She just slides her eyes closed and leans into his touch. He shifts so he can reach her other ear, and she utters another delightful little gasp.

Then he kisses her again as he plays with her ears.

"You taste like sparks today," she whispers against his lips. "I don't know how else to describe it."

He nuzzles her nose with his own. "And the rest of the time?"

"Your air magic has a slight saltiness to it. Like ocean air."

"I want to taste your life magic," he whispers.

"All right." The vulnerable note has returned to her voice. After a few moments, she whispers, "Try now."

He pulls her into another deep kiss, his tongue tracing her lips and her teeth. Tangling up with hers. "Life is sweet," he murmurs against her. "It's a lot like your plant magic, but sweeter. Like candy and sweet almond cream and sugared plums. Not overwhelming, though. Just...perfect."

Then she pulls him toward her, into the tub, and he barely hesitates.

"I wish his leathers were gone," she whispers before finding his lips again.

30

NOT ASHAMED

Lorial can barely think straight as the water engulfs him. "Nestraya—"

"Just kiss me. I just want you to kiss me."

So he kisses her. His fire is less overwhelming after using it so much earlier, and the water tempers his magic, keeping his heat manageable as he braces his hands against the tub on either side of her.

All too soon, she pulls away, leaving him hovering over her in the warm water. Her eyes are large, and her breathing is shallow.

"How are you feeling?" he asks, unsure where to rest his limbs without touching her. Is he supposed to be touching her?

"Better. Much better."

"Are you ready to get out?"

She opens her mouth and then closes it again.

"It's hard not to brush against you," he says softly. "I'm not sure what you want me to do now."

She clears her throat. "Right. Maybe we should get out."

"All right."

"Wait. Your fire magic. How are you doing?"

"The water helps. As did our practice earlier. It took the edge off."

"Good. I'm...glad."

"So am I. I don't have to worry about catching you on fire."

She nods. "We should try to avoid that."

"Yes." He studies her face, and her cheeks grow pink under his scrutiny. "You seem flustered, my love."

"Do I?"

"A bit."

"I've never done this before." Her heart is racing now. He can feel it.

"And what exactly are we doing?"

"I have no idea. We seem to be bathing...together."

"Yes. It was unexpected for me."

"Me, as well."

He drops his head and laughs. "You pulled me in!"

"I know." She covers her face and groans. "I think I got carried away again."

"Yes. You keep doing that. I keep not minding."

After a moment, she laughs, too, and he grins.

"When you kiss me, I lose my head," she says.

"I see. So this is my fault?"

"It must be." She trails her fingers along his cheek. "At least let me wash the korathite off your face."

"You're welcome to wash any part of me you desire."

She flicks water at him. "So generous of you."

"I thought so."

After wishing for a small towel, she dips the cloth into the warm water and gently scrubs at his cheeks, being especially tender with the soft flesh around his eyes.

When her foot brushes his calf under the water, she reddens. She's blushed more in the past three days than he's ever seen her blush in her life.

"Now what?" she asks.

"Dinner on the platform? Stargazing? Unless you want me to kiss you more."

She flicks water at him again, and he grins. He probably deserved that.

"Dinner sounds lovely."

He nods. "I'll get out first. Take your time, all right? I love you." He presses a kiss to her forehead before awkwardly climbing out of the tub around her. His own face heats with the way his small clothes cling to him, but he grabs a towel and moves behind the screen to give her privacy.

After spending the next morning practicing with his air magic, Lorial pulls Nestraya close and twines his fingers together behind her lower back.

"I think this afternoon should be about you," he says softly.

She growls. Actually growls. "I've slain all my demons."

"Have you?" He can barely hold back a smile at the murderous look she sends him.

"Yes."

"All right. What I was going to suggest was working on your endurance."

She eyes him warily. "Not slaying demons?"

He shrugs.

"What about your fire magic?" she asks.

"We can do both at the same time. I'll use my fire magic when you need a sparring partner, but we'll focus on you." He circles his thumbs over her warrior leathers, and she grudgingly nods.

"I'm not sure what good it will do. Pera tried to help me. I just don't seem to have deep magic reserves. I am a low-born elf, remember?"

"Are you? I'd completely forgotten."

She smacks his chest, and he steals a kiss.

"All right, First Nestraya. Explain to me how you hide your limitations so well. I've been oblivious to many things in the past, but I think I would have noticed how quickly you tire."

She shrugs. "We sparred little after we came into our full magic as adolescents."

"Because Father wouldn't let us. Did he ever explain to you why?"

Nestraya feigns a sudden interest in the fastenings on his vest.

"You know, don't you?" he asks. "Tell me?"

"He said he never wanted us to compare our magic. That we both needed to grow into our strengths on our own before we could be strong together. That we were to become a team and not competitors."

"Become a team. As we're doing now?"

She looks up at him. "Just as we're doing now."

"We're better together," he says softly as he rests his forehead against hers. "I'd kiss you, but then we'd probably waste the entire afternoon being distracted by each other."

"Is that not what we're doing now?"

"Is it?" He grins, and with a quick kiss, he lets her go. "So, how do you hide it?"

"Little tricks I learned. If I have a practice session scheduled using water magic, I drink a lot of water ahead of time. That helps. And if I can, I stand in puddles or creeks. Or offer to spar in the rain when no one else wants to."

He nods. "What about your plant magic?"

"I try to avoid sparring with plant magic."

"But you're one of the most skilled plant wielders I've seen."

She shrugs. "I pretend not to be."

"You what?"

"I let other warriors beat me. Pretend my plant magic is weak. Let people imagine my third affinity is so worthless it hardly counts. Only skilled life wielders could sense the truth."

Lorial gapes at her.

"Don't look at me like that. I'm a warrior. Warriors do what's necessary to survive."

"Did Pera know?"

"No. Because he would have reacted just as you are now. You don't understand. How could you?"

"Oh, I understand. You need to slay your—"

"Do not say it." She practically snarls at him.

"When we return, this ends, Nestraya. You are who you are. And you are a plant wielder. One of the strongest plant wielders in the warrior bands. Whistling wind, you're probably one of the strongest plant wielders in all of Lostariel. Don't hide that. Don't let one more person make you feel ashamed of who you are."

"When we return, that's all anyone will see. The low-born elf who wormed her way into becoming the Queen of Lostariel."

"Who are you? Say it."

"What?"
"Your name. Tell me your name."
"I'm Nestraya," she whispers.
"Nestraya what?"
"Nestraya Westaria."
"Louder."
"My name is Nestraya Westaria."
"Louder!"
She yells the words this time.
"And who are you?"
"I...I am who I am."
"And who is that?"
"First Nestraya?"
He nods. "Who else?"
"I'm the Queen of Lostariel," she whispers.
"Say it louder. Make it yours."
"I'm the Queen of Lostariel." Her voice catches, but she pushes out the words.
"And why are you the queen?"
"Because I saved you?"
"Because you, a low-born elf, saved the life of a king. What are you?"
She shakes her head.
"Are you a low-born elf?"
She nods.
"Say it, Nestraya."
"I'm a low-born elf." She wipes away a tear.
"And is that something to be ashamed of?"
She shakes her head. "I'm a low-born elf. And I'm Nestraya Westaria, Queen of Lostariel. And I am not ashamed."
"Say that last part again. Louder."
"I am not ashamed!"
"And what else are you?" he asks softly.
She looks into his eyes, and he nods.
"I'm yours," she whispers.

He closes the distance between them. "You're mine. And you, Nestraya Westaria, Queen of Lostariel, are the strongest plant wielder I know."

She wraps her arms around his neck and clings to him. "I'm tired of slaying demons."

"I know, my love."

"If I use the full strength of my plant magic, it won't last long."

He pulls away to look into her eyes. "Have you been holding back from me?"

With a lingering shudder, she nods.

"Whistling wind. How is that possible?"

"The less I use, the longer it lasts."

He steps back. "Show me."

"Right now?"

"Wait. I wish for a bowl full of berries, nuts, and seeds."

One appears on the ground beside him, and he hands it to her. "Eat your fill first."

She hesitantly takes the bowl and starts nibbling.

"And I wish for"—he tilts his head as he looks at her—"jasmine and almond oil."

Her chewing slows. "What in the Wildthorne Woods are you planning to do with that?"

As he picks up the corked bottle at his feet, he tries not to smile. "We're going to slather it on you to see if it helps."

Her eyes narrow. "Why jasmine?"

"I believe it assists with alertness."

"And it's rumored to be an aphrodisiac, Lorial. I have some training as a healer, remember?"

He shrugs. "I like the way it smells. Now keep eating. When you're done, wish for your other leathers."

Horror crosses her face. "You want to slather me in jasmine oil while I'm wearing that...that thing?"

He grins. "I do. Now eat up."

31

STARHAVEN

Nestraya eyes Lorial and the bottle of oil in his hand.

"I have no intention of rubbing that on myself. Have you considered what would happen if you got too close to me with your fire magic? And how am I supposed to absorb water if you've coated me in oil?"

He purses his lips. "Perhaps just a little? I'm open to suggestions. What could we put on you that would help?"

"If you suggest a gown made of flowers, I will douse you."

He grins at her, and she throws a berry at him.

"All right, so we'll save the oil for after if you need it."

She scowls at him but doesn't argue. It's not the worst idea, though he doesn't need to hear that.

She takes another handful of the berry mixture and then sets the bowl aside. "What do you want me to do?"

"Well, I know you can control vines and roots to great effect. And I've seen you construct small things. Could you build something bigger?"

She brushes off her hands. "How big are we talking?"

His lopsided grin makes a reappearance. "A bed?"

"Please. I could grow something that size when I was five."

"A really big bed?" His teasing eyes draw out her smile.

"You seem to be stuck on this bed idea, my love."

"As long as I'm stuck there with you."

Something in her chest tightens. "I thought we agreed—"

His expression turns serious. "We did. Forgive me. I was teasing."

With a gulp, she nods. "What about a whole house?"

"A whole house? It takes most plant wielders hours to construct one room without assistance."

"As you seem intent on proving, I am not most plant wielders, my love."

"No, you're not." He gestures to a flat area near the base of a large cedar. "Show me your magic."

"Right." She takes a deep breath and slowly exhales before closing her eyes and reaching out with her magic. First, she finds the cedar tree's roots and coaxes them to grow for her. Then she pictures the house in her head like the spokes of a wheel branching off from a central hub. The entertaining wing with its grand hall. The private family rooms. The guest section. The Council Chamber at the center with its dais and long table.

She guides the roots to grow and take shape and become the vision in her head.

"Nestraya, what are you—"

"Hush."

The walls lace together, stretching from the smooth wooden floor to connect in domed roofs covered with leaves—cedar fronds, in this case. The real thing is constructed of oak.

As she's about to put the finishing touches on everything, she sways.

"Nestraya, that's good enough, my love."

"But I'm almost—" she staggers and opens her eyes to Lorial hovering over her as he lowers her to the forest floor.

"I wasn't...done. Let...go." She tries to push him away, but he takes hold of her hands.

"You're done for now. Finish later."

"Stop...hovering." The edges of her vision darken, and her stomach gnaws at her.

"I can't believe you reconstructed Starhaven as if it was nothing. I didn't mean for you to kill yourself."

She'd argue, but the effort that would take...

Is it getting dark already?

"I wish for her other leathers," he murmurs.

"What...what are—"

Then he's rubbing something on her. The jasmine oil? It feels good, whatever it is. Soothing.

"Stay with me, my love," he whispers. The panic in his voice is confusing. Where does he think she'd go?

But when she attempts to reassure him, her muscles refuse to cooperate.

So tired.

"I wish for almond milk," he says.

A moment later, liquid dribbles into her mouth, nearly choking her.

"Drink, Nestraya," he pleads, and she manages to swallow a tiny bit.

He rubs more oil over her arms. Along her shoulders and neck. Then he turns her onto her side, and she tries to protest, but her tongue refuses to cooperate.

Cool air hits her bare back, followed by his warm hands. When he pulls her onto his lap, more liquid drips into her mouth, and this time she swallows a little more.

"Yes, my love. That's it. Drink." He continues slathering every bit of her exposed skin with the oil, and it takes her a moment to realize he removed the leather bodice completely. The only thing covering her upper half is the thin linen of her small clothes.

"Lorial," she whispers.

"You look stronger. Please tell me it's working."

She musters her strength to nod, and he clutches her to his chest. They'll both be coated in oil at this rate.

"Hungry," she whispers, blinking up at him, and he loosens his hold enough to reach the bowl of nuts and berries.

He carefully feeds her, little by little, until the aching gnaw in her stomach abates.

"How do you feel?" he asks.

"Tired." She chuckles. As she eyes her tree-grown imitation of Starhaven, she frowns. "It's not to scale. You'll hit your head on the ceiling."

"Do you think I care about that? You almost killed yourself. No wonder you weaken so quickly. Magic flows through you like a surging flood. No one could hold enough in reserve to manage that."

"You do," she whispers, her throat raspy, and he offers her another sip of the almond milk.

"I thought we weren't supposed to compare."

She manages a weak laugh in response.

"Did Father know how strong your plant magic is?" he asks.

"I don't know."

"Are you sure it's your weakest affinity?"

"Healer Cadowyn told me it was."

Lorial shakes his head. "Nestraya, you are...you're...amazing."

She chuckles. "Third Rafelis said your air magic slightly blunted his sense of my magic."

"I am inclined to think he was lying." Lorial hugs her with her back to his chest as he wraps his arms around her middle.

She relaxes her head against his shoulder, trying not to dwell on how underdressed she is. Somehow, she keeps ending up inadequately clothed here in the heartlanding.

"I'm so tired," she whispers.

"Then sleep. I've got you, my love."

"Your air magic is stronger than you realize," she whispers. "My Dragon King."

"Shh, my love. Sleep. I'll be here when you wake."

When Nestraya stirs, orb lights dot the otherwise dark room surrounding her, where she lies on her side on a bed of the most luxurious moss imaginable. Her back presses up against something solid and warm as a heavy weight rests over her waist.

The press of lips to her neck draws her from her drowsy state, and she twines her fingers with Lorial's where they rest against her bare stomach.

"Where are we?" she murmurs. "This isn't our treehouse."

"You don't recognize it?"

She shakes her head.

"You built it. Well, most of it. The heartlanding helped me furnish it while you slept."

She studies the room again. The desk against the wall. The plush chairs by the hearth. The round bed they lie upon.

It's been years since she last visited Lorial's rooms at Starhaven. She's rarely been home to Celesta at all since she joined the warrior bands.

"Did I get it right?" she asks. "I don't remember adding a bed."

"The heartlanding was more than happy to oblige with that."

"I imagine so." She shuffles onto her back so she can see him as he gazes down at her. "Thank you."

"For what, my love?"

"For helping me regain my strength."

"Aside from the part where I thought you were dying, it wasn't an unpleasant experience for me." He grins, and she laughs and shakes her head.

"Why bring me here? Why not the treehouse?" she asks as she trails her finger along his jaw.

He shrugs. "I guess I wanted to bring my queen home."

"Home." She slides her finger across his lower lip. "To your bed?"

He catches her finger with a kiss. "Just home. We're supposed to be taking this slowly." There's no censure in his gray eyes as he looks at her.

"Thank you."

"I meant what I said, Nestraya. There's no rush."

"Though I did promise you an elfling." She brushes back a wisp of silver hair that escaped his braids.

"Yes, but not here. I doubt it works here."

She laughs. "No, I imagine not."

"How are you feeling?"

"Better. Oily."

"You smell good." He grins.

"I'll probably smell like jasmine for days. If we're here for days." Her brows draw together. "How long have we been here? I'm starting to lose track."

"Counting the night we arrived, this is our fifth night. I think."

"What if we never wake up? What if we're stuck here forever?"

"I think that's unlikely, but if this is our afterlife, I won't complain about spending it with you."

He leans down to kiss her, that faint saltiness tickling her taste buds.

"You've been using your air magic," she murmurs.

"And you taste like berries." He presses into the kiss as she frames his face with her hands. His own hand blazes against the soft flesh at her waist.

"Don't catch me on fire," she whispers, and he groans as he pulls away.

"I didn't use my fire magic enough today. It's a little...eager."

She laughs and traces the edges of his ears before letting him go. He rolls to his back beside her, and she snuggles against him as he wraps his arm around her.

"I have no idea what to do once we return. Say what you want, Nestraya. I'm no Dragon King."

She traces her finger along the fastenings of his vest. "Perhaps you're more like a phoenix, rising from the ashes. The Dragon King reborn."

He gazes at her. "A phoenix?"

"The rise of the Phoenix King. He rides on the wind, commanding the light and fire of the sun."

"The Phoenix King? I don't know, Nestraya."

"Maybe I'm not the only one with demons to slay, my love."

He sighs. "Perhaps."

"We'll figure it out. For Pera. For Mera. For every low-born elf who deserves better. We have to."

32

UNWRITTEN RULES

"You can do better than that!" Nestraya says the next afternoon as she pushes her water magic toward Lorial. She stands barefoot in the creek this time, and it's helping her endurance.

"You try doing this while you're flying," he yells as he pushes against her water with his air magic. He hovers fifteen feet off the ground, only wobbling a little as he moves to his left to avoid her stream of water.

"Well done. Try to cut off my water supply."

He whimpers, but he doesn't argue.

He's so strong. And he has no idea. She's sparred with many elves during her time in the warrior bands—low and high born alike.

Never has an elf given her as much of a challenge as Lorial does when he embraces his air magic. Not even Pera.

Lorial turns his hands in a circular motion, and by the time Nestraya realizes he's cutting her off from the water rather than the other way around, he's already caught her in a cyclone of wind. She reaches for any source of water she can find, but the air he whips around her is warm and dry.

He's using his fire magic, too. Her smile grows as she struggles to free herself from his grip. She reaches out with her plant magic instead, but the air currents are too strong for her to get a sense of the surrounding plants. Every thread of magic she extends just whips back toward her.

She hovers at eye level with him now, and the circling wind makes her eyes water as she tries to glimpse him through the swirling currents. But what she manages to catch sight of thrills something deep within her.

He looks...fierce. His eyes shine like silver orbs while he channels the wind as if it's part of him—as if nature itself is bound to obey his command. His braids whip in the air, and the muscles of his bare arms flex with each rotation of his hands. Those hands. So strong and yet so gentle when he touches her.

Plant magic. She was reaching for her plant magic.

She'd rather reach for him. Whistling wind, she wants him.

"Are you all right?" he calls out over the wind circling her. "I don't feel your magic."

"Sorry." She pushes against him more, but it's no use. She may slaughter him when he's limited to his fire magic, but when he commands the air itself, he overpowers her. Every time.

As he draws her closer, she stops struggling, and the wind dies down. When she's close enough to touch, he reaches for her, and she wraps her arms around his neck.

"You're all right?" he asks softly. The brightness in his eyes has faded a little, but they still shine with the power of the air flowing through him.

"I think we should practice maintaining your concentration." Then she kisses him. Passionately. Urgently. With nothing held back. Her fingers dig into his hair, and he groans as he presses his hands into her lower back, drawing her even closer.

They wobble when she slides her thumbs along his ears, but he quickly rights them where they float on air currents high above the ground.

He runs a trail of kisses along her jaw, down her neck, sending thrills to her fingertips.

"And you thought you couldn't fly," she murmurs as she nuzzles his ear with her nose.

His hands slide to her hips, his heat warming her flesh through her full warrior leathers.

Then, he sighs and rests his forehead against hers as his air magic swirls around them both, keeping them aloft. "I don't think I expended enough fire magic today to be doing this. Whatever this is."

What is this? Does she even know? It felt as though it went beyond a kiss—the start of something...more.

"I'm sorry," she whispers. "I think I got carried away again."

He looks into her eyes as the silver light swirls in his irises to match the air currents surrounding them. "It's all right for the answer to be yes, my love."

"The answer? To what question?"

"The one you keep asking yourself."

She swallows. "And what question is that?"

Before responding, he leans near her ear. "The one where you ask yourself if you want this. If you want everything. There's no wrong answer. Fast or slow or now or later. Whatever you want, Nestraya. If you want to get carried away, let's get carried away. If you want to slow down, we'll slow down. But here, where it's just you and me? There's no guilt. No shame. Just us. Lorial and Nestraya."

Shivers race through her at his words.

But would it be real? If it happened here first?

Would it matter if it was or wasn't?

"Take your time, my love." He sets them on their feet on the forest floor. "But don't let your fear decide for you."

"When did you grow so full of wisdom?" she whispers.

"I'm not. But I know my Nestraya." He presses his lips to hers again. "Let's get you some water. Maybe a bath, all right? Refresh your water magic. Your lips are dry."

She licks them self-consciously.

Then he leans close to her ear again. "My fire magic burns hotter when you get like this, but I don't want you dehydrated."

Her eyes snap to his. "What?"

He shrugs. "You smell good when you use your magic enough to run low. You taste good, too." That boyish grin teases her, and a smile sneaks unbidden across her parched lips.

He's right. She could use a drink. And a bath. Should she ask him to join her again?

Perhaps she should use the time to think.

As if reading her thoughts, he says, "Let's get you taken care of, all right? I don't want you to decide anything while you're tired. You soak in the tub while I visit the platform. Believe it or not, I feel a slight twinge in my lungs telling me I need air."

She shakes her head. "I am so jealous of you and your endless magic reserves."

"Nearly endless, apparently. And there's no jealousy here. Lorial and Nestraya against the world. We're a team, remember?"

She sighs. "I remember. And let me just say, I am beyond glad you're on my team."

He drapes his arm over her shoulders and kisses her temple. "So am I, my love. So am I."

By the time Nestraya joins Lorial on the platform, she's no closer to knowing what she wants than she was before.

Maybe it doesn't matter. It doesn't have to be this big thing, does it? She could just stop pulling back the next time she feels herself getting carried away.

And yet, the reality of their situation niggles at her.

If Lorial had chosen someone the Council of Elders approved of, his forthcoming binding would have been announced throughout Lostariel, and a time of separation would have ensued. A time for both binding partners to search their hearts and commit to the binding process.

At the end of the separation, they would have reunited and spent time in conversation where either elf could express a desire to halt the binding proceedings. And if they both chose to move forward, the ceremony would take place the next day, with only the parents of the participants standing as witnesses. A binding ceremony is a private thing. The fact that Nestraya and Lorial's binding took place in front of Lorial's elite warrior band is scandalous in itself.

After the ceremony, the couple would be left to their own devices—presumably to complete the binding by consummating the relationship. The joining, as it's called.

But nothing about this is normal, starting with the fact that it's an unwritten law that a high-born elf may not tryst with a low-born elf.

It happens, of course. But in secret. And no life wielder would sanction such a match by overseeing an official binding between such a couple. No, these trysts happen in dark corners—hidden chambers. Any elfling conceived is ostracized. Never allowed to bind themselves lest their tainted blood dilute the lines of the high born or strengthen the magic of the low born.

But a king has never sought to flout the unwritten rules.

Until now.

The thought of joining with the King of Lostariel—of consummating this binding irrevocably—brings back all her doubts about herself.

But when she's in his arms? Whistling wind, she couldn't care less.

"You look as though you've been wrestling demons," Lorial says softly to her as she steps onto the platform, and she sighs.

"I suppose I have."

He draws her close and presses his forehead to hers. "Tell me? Perhaps I can help."

She hesitates, but his hand circles gently on her lower back over the silken sleeping gown she donned following her bath, and the intimacy of his touch, or maybe it's the heartbinding itself, takes away any desire for secrecy she might have otherwise entertained.

"High-born elves..." she begins slowly.

"What about them, my love?"

"Are not allowed to tryst with low-born elves."

He stiffens. "If you tell me this is why you keep pulling away—"

"Not the only reason, no. Not even the primary reason. But it's there in my mind—"

He lets go of her and starts pacing the platform as he glances back at her. "There is no law."

"No. But—"

"And haven't we already established that you and I are going to change these archaic constructs that do nothing but cause division and unfairly devalue an entire segment of Lostarien society?"

"Yes, but—"

He returns to her and clasps her hand. "Show everyone that the world is changing. That the old ways are ending. That—"

She places a finger over his lips. "That a new way forward starts with us?" Her voice is less confident than she might wish, but she pushes out the words, trying to own them—to believe them for herself.

To slay these demons that haunt her.

He crushes her to his chest. "Yes, my love."

"You know our elflings may be scorned. It may be difficult to find elves willing to bind with them."

Lorial grins. "Will there be many of these elflings?"

She shrugs, trying to hide a smile. "Perhaps, if we wish to belabor the point."

"I think we do."

Her smile wins out at his response before her mirth fades, and she searches his eyes. "Do we destine our elflings to lives of being ostracized and scorned because of the choices we make?"

He looks at her steadily. "We do what's right to make the world a better place, not only for our elflings but for the elflings of every low-born family to follow. And we show our elflings by our actions that some things are worth fighting for, even when it's hard."

She breathes out slowly and nods. He sounds so much like Pera right now.

"Our elflings will be strong, Nestraya. With you for a mother, how could they not be?"

"That's assuming we live long enough to retake your throne. And that we wake someday."

"Yes." He sighs as he loosens his hold on her. "But with every day that passes, we grow stronger. I refuse to give up hope. And you're not allowed to either."

"I will try, my king."

"Are you hungry?" He traces his fingers down her cheek, and she closes her eyes and leans into his touch.

"Perhaps a little."

"Would you rather sleep?"

Something subtle changes in the surrounding air, and it takes Nestraya a moment to realize the crackling energy is coming from Lorial. Her eyes flash open to find him lighting a ball of fire in his free hand before shooting it high in the sky.

He's trying to drain his fire magic.

33

BECOME THE WIND

"Sorry," Lorial says when he sees the surprise in Nestraya's eyes. "I just—"

"Want to be ready in case we decide to get carried away?" Her surprise has given way to amusement, and he chuckles before wrapping his arms around her again.

"Something like that." His face warms. "That may have been presumptuous of me."

"Or practical. As your First, I can appreciate your desire to be prepared for anything. Well done, warrior."

He looks into her emerald eyes…which are full of mirth. "I get the feeling you're mocking me, my queen."

"I would never do that."

He pokes her ribs. "That is a bald lie."

Laughter flows from her throat, and he grins in return.

"Let's get something to eat, all right?" he says softly, and she nods as they descend the stairs together.

Lorial watches Nestraya around the screen as she trails a wet cloth across her forehead. It relaxes her—the water on her face. On her neck.

He almost offered to do it for her, but the last thing he wants is for her to read more into his actions than he intends.

As if he's pressuring her.

Somehow, their conversation earlier has made everything awkward now as the air between them sits heavy with questions neither of them seems to know how to ask or answer.

"Do you want to sleep inside our treehouse tonight?" he manages. Last night, they slept at her version of Starhaven, but it got chilly with no windows to keep out the night air on the coldest night they've experienced since they arrived here.

Not that he minded when she nestled closer to him in her sleep.

She glances at his reflection in the mirror. "It is warmer in here."

"It is."

She sighs and turns to face him. "Why is everything awkward again? We were doing so well."

"It's not quite like it was before. You don't hate me. I don't think."

She throws the wet cloth at him, and he catches it before it hits his face.

"I never hated you. I was angry at you. There is a difference. And it was well-deserved."

A grin slips across his face as he drapes the cloth over the side of the tub. "Perhaps." When he straightens, he steps toward her and reaches for her hands. "Tell me what you're thinking?"

"Honestly? I don't even know. My head is such a jumbled mess."

He lifts her knuckles to his lips, never taking his eyes off hers. "Do we need to slay more demons?"

She huffs in frustration. "I don't know. Maybe? I'm so tired of—"

"Slaying demons. I know. Let's just sleep tonight, all right?" He does his best to keep any hint of disappointment from his voice, while a mixture of relief and frustration fills her own eyes.

She nods. "Thank you."

"You don't have to thank me, my love. I'm the one who should be thanking you. For the rest of my life, I owe everything to you."

She wraps her arms around his neck, and on a whim, he scoops her up and carries her toward the bed, where he drops her gently on the soft moss before crawling up beside her.

"Lorial," she laughs. "What are you doing?"

"Going to bed." He reaches out to steal all the light from the orb lights scattered throughout the room, plunging them into inky darkness.

"That was dramatic," she whispers, and he laughs.

"According to you, I'm the Phoenix King. I'm supposed to be dramatic."

"Well, you're off to a good start."

He slips beneath the covers, draping the warm blankets over both of them. "Come here," he says softly, and once she's nestled with her back against his chest, he wraps his arm around her waist and holds her close. "Is this all right?"

"Mmm. Yes," she murmurs. "Perfect."

With a soft smile, he presses his lips to her hair. "Goodnight, my love. Sleep well."

"Lorial. Lorial, wake up."

Lorial groans as Nestraya pushes against his chest in the darkness.

"What's wrong?"

"Listen."

He rubs his eyes and tries to focus on whatever she thinks she hears. The soothing whisper of rain pelting their treehouse and the surrounding forest is the only sound he can pick out.

It's the first time it's rained since they arrived, but surely she didn't wake him in the middle of the night just for that.

"It's raining," she breathes.

Or perhaps she did.

"Is there a reason we're awake talking about it instead of sleeping?" He stifles a yawn.

"I wish we were falling."

Lorial's eyes flash open as the bed drops away, replaced by nothing but air and water droplets pelting his linen sleeping shirt and trousers.

"Nestraya!" he growls as he tries to wake up enough to grasp at his air magic. It's harder to control with the water swirling around him.

She really is evil.

"Lorial, what are you waiting for?" she cries, and he stretches an air current toward the sound of her voice, tugging her into his arms as he finds the wind between his feet and the swiftly approaching ground.

It's a rough slowing of their momentum, but they land gently enough. He immediately lets her go and tosses out a set of orb lights to illuminate the dark woods around them.

Just as he's about to turn to her and inquire after her sanity, the soft sound of her laughter gives him pause.

She's spinning—happily—as the water droplets wet her ebony hair and run in rivulets onto her cream sleeping gown.

For a moment, he stares at her as he struggles to find his voice. He knew she loved the rain, just as Father did, but this is...well, it's a little odd.

Especially for her.

"Nestraya," he finally says. "I find myself catapulted from my warm bed into a rainstorm in the middle of the night, and I wonder if you could enlighten me about the thoughts going through your head that led to this unexpected situation."

"It's raining, Lorial."

"Yes. We established that."

"This is what I long to do every time it rains, but I always stop myself. I'm always so afraid. Afraid of what people will think. How they'll judge me. And I heard the rain, and I thought..." Her voice trails off as she sighs. "I'm sorry."

Her shoulders rise and fall, and she turns away as he gapes at her, the rain plastering his linens against him like a second skin.

She's slaying her demons.

In a rush, his sense returns to him, and he runs toward her and throws his arms around her waist, lifting her from behind and spinning her in the air.

"Lorial!" she laughs.

"Dance, my love. Dance in the rain. Just let go and be yourself. Be Nestraya. There's no judgment here."

She turns in his arms to face him, and he spins her around again as her laughter rises above the drone of the rain. Soon they're both soaked and breathless and shivering as wide smiles stretch across their lips.

Nestraya brushes back the tendrils of soggy hair that cling to her face as she looks up at him. "Thank you. I'm sorry I didn't warn you."

He slips his hands around her waist and sways from side to side. "That would have been appreciated."

"You managed despite the rain. That was impressive."

"I thought so."

She leans her head back and laughs, and he nuzzles her neck as he brushes her wet skin with his lips. He's tried not to ogle her, but her gown clings to her in the most alluring way—it's impossible to overlook while she's wrapped up in his arms.

When she lifts her head to look at him, it's like a ball of fire bursting into being, and his breathing grows shallow as his heart races.

"Your hands aren't burning me," she says.

She's right—he barely noticed. It must be the rain dampening his fire magic.

"Our platform," she whispers, a faint hint of vulnerability in her eyes, and his heart beats even faster.

Right alongside hers.

"I wish—" she begins, but he presses his finger to her lips.

"Let me."

Mustering his air magic, he pulls her even closer as they lift off the forest floor. It's harder to control in the rain, but he manages. Higher and higher, as she clings to him and looks around in wonder.

"Wish for whatever you want to find waiting for us on the platform," he whispers near her ear, and she nods as her lips barely move.

The higher they rise, the harder it is to push enough air beneath them to stay afloat, and he feels the bounds of his magic. Not like a limit but a wall, waiting for him to tear it down—to reach a new level of control, of mastery.

With a low growl, he presses against it, grasping at the air currents keeping them aloft.

Then, with a crack, the boundary falls away, and air flows through him, becoming one with him, as if it's an extension of himself. And not just here and now as he lifts Nestraya toward their platform, but beyond. Everywhere his air currents fly, he feels it. Senses it as if his fingers were brushing against the trees and the distant mountains. The creeks and the river a few miles away.

It's all there for him to reach out and touch. Experience.

When he opens his eyes, Nestraya gasps.

"You've mastered the wind," she breathes. Then she shakes her head. "No, you've become the wind."

It courses through him, empowering him, as they shoot toward their treehouse—and the bed she wished for just as he hoped she would.

He gently steps from the air to the platform, lowering her to the soft—though somewhat soggy—moss. She reaches for him when he crawls up beside her.

"Let's get carried away, my love," she murmurs.

His lips find her jaw. Her neck. Pulling away, he peels the linen shirt from his body and tosses it aside before finding her again. "Are you warm enough?"

"You're giving off the most delightful heat." She runs her chilled hands along his chest.

"Not too hot?" he whispers as he nuzzles her ear, and the most enchanting sigh slips past her lips.

"Absolutely perfect, my love."

"Good. Tell me if you want to slow down."

She shakes her head and pulls him closer. "I don't want to slow down. I want you, Lorial. In every way, I want you."

He opens his mouth to respond, but his words are cut off.

Then there's pain. Searing, burning, raw pain. Right above his heart.

And everything goes dark.

34

SLAY YOUR DEMONS

"He's waking. Hold him steady." The voice drifts to Nestraya through a fog.

"They both are."

That's Corivos.

What just happened? Where's Lorial? He was there, his weight pressing on her as he kissed her.

Then he was gone.

She bolts up, but the room—or is it a cave? A copse of trees? Whatever it is, it spins around her as gentle hands coax her back down.

"Lie still, Nestraya. According to Healer Cadowyn, the dizziness will pass soon."

Nestraya blinks, trying to focus on the woman behind the voice. "Mera?"

"I'm here, my darling."

"Lorial. Where's—"

"He's here, too. Healer Cadowyn is working on him."

"Is he all right? Please tell me he's all right. I tried to save him, but he was dying, and—"

"And you did save him, my elfling." Mera brushes back her hair.

"Healer Cadowyn said no one else's magic could have sustained the heartbinding with such a critical loss of blood," Corivos says.

The heartbinding.

Nestraya shrinks as she looks up at Mera. "I binded with Lorial. To save him."

Mera smiles down at her in the dim light. Whether it's sunrise or sunset or something else entirely, Nestraya has no idea.

"You did bind with him, my elfling. I believe that makes you the new Queen of Lostariel."

Nestraya's breath comes heavily at Mera's words.

Slay your demons.

Then Lorial's tortured cry rends the air.

"Can't you do something for the pain?" Corivos asks.

"I just did. Hold that light steady, young man."

That must be Healer Cadowyn.

Nestraya tries to rise again, but Mera holds her back. "You need to let them work. I will not lose both my elflings in one day."

"Do you feel up to hearing a report on the battle and the situation with Hothniel, my First? Or rather, my queen?" Corivos asks quietly, and Nestraya stares at him.

"It's still going? I don't even know what day it is. What took you so long to find a healer?"

Corivos and Mera exchange a glance.

"It's only been eight hours, my queen," Corivos says.

"Eight hours? We were in the heartlanding for—" Her words lodge in her throat, and she closes her eyes.

She can't discuss the heartlanding.

"Perhaps we should give her a little more time to get her bearings," Mera suggests.

"You shouldn't be here, Mera. It isn't safe."

"A daughter needs her mother on her binding day."

Nestraya fights back the sob that threatens to choke her. She's First Nestraya. There's no time for tears.

"Did I do the right thing, Mera? You know this will only make life harder for him."

Mera smiles as she brushes back Nestraya's hair some more. "He would have died without you, my darling. And he loves you. A mother knows these things."

The memory of Lorial's face as he looked down at her, his eyes lit by the air magic flowing through his body, flashes across Nestraya's mind. The desire on his face. The gentleness with which he touched her before they were whisked away.

Should she laugh or cry at the ridiculous timing of it all?

She tries to catch a glimpse of him, but her view is blocked by the other elves hovering around them both.

Mera leans closer. "If I am not mistaken, there's a new light in those green eyes of yours as well."

Nestraya's lip quivers as she fights to steady herself. "I-I love him, Mera. Desperately. The heartlanding—"

"Helped you see him more clearly?" Mera's lips tip into a smile.

"But I'm low born. I—"

"You are exactly who your father and I raised you to be."

Slay your demons.

"You're not upset that I...that we—"

"The only thing I am troubled over is the fact that I wasn't present to see you join your heart to his. And that your pera didn't live to see his vision of you come true."

"Is that why he took me in?"

Mera smiles. "No, my elfling. That vision came later. He took you in because his heart told him you were ours the moment he first saw you."

Nestraya glances at Corivos, who seems to be trying not to listen to their private conversation. He meets her eyes and reads the question on her mind before shaking his head.

They didn't tell her.

They left that for Nestraya to do.

After slowly exhaling, Nestraya turns back to Mera. "I need to tell you something that will...that will be hard to hear."

A familiar resoluteness fills Mera's eyes. "I am strong, young one. Speak."

"Pera wasn't killed by humans. He was murdered...by Hothniel."

Mera breathes in and out slowly and swallows, yet her strength never wavers. "The man who steals my son's throne?"

Nestraya nods.

"The man who sends low-born elves to be slaughtered?"

"Yes, Mera. I think...I think it's because of me. He killed—"

"Hush. You will not say such things. Restoval would have gladly died a thousand deaths to protect you. You will not blame yourself for the actions of a traitorous monster."

Nestraya nods as she pushes against the emotion that threatens to swallow her.

"What you will do," Mera continues, "is fight by Lorial's side to slay this demon. That is what your pera would have wanted."

Slay your demons.

This is one demon she will gladly slay.

A burning ache in her chest calls out for Lorial. She can feel him—his powerful magic. He's alive, and every minute he grows stronger.

And with every moment that passes, it becomes clear that her longing for him is real. As real as the dirt beneath her fingernails and the blood coating her hands. Lorial's blood.

She loves him. Really, truly loves him. Not just in the heartlanding but here, surrounded by healers and warrior elves and Mera, it's him her eyes long to see. His voice she longs to hear. The scent of his air magic as the wind engulfs them. The salty taste of his kiss.

His touch.

Now isn't the time for such things—for lovemaking and talk of elflings.

Soon, though. If they survive this.

"Nestraya." Lorial's voice is weak but urgent and slightly panicked. "I need...Nestraya. Where—"

"I'm here." She pushes everyone away and squeezes her eyes shut at the dizziness that assaults her when she shifts to her knees. But she keeps going, crawling toward the sound of his voice as a wave of nausea sweeps over her.

They've lifted him onto some sort of makeshift table, and Corivos is there to help her stand as the room spins.

Healer Cadowyn turns to Mera. "My queen, I've—"

"Address yourself to our queen Nestraya," Mera calmly says as she rises.

But all Nestraya cares about are those gray eyes gazing weakly up at her as she chokes back a sob. The flesh over Lorial's heart has been knit, but a scar remains. She doesn't dare touch it.

"My love," he whispers. "That...was the worst timing."

A laugh that's part sob bursts from her throat.

"I hope you will soon give me another chance," he says softly.

"Of all the things to be concerned with right now, you oaf of a man."

He laughs weakly. "Is that a yes?"

"Of course it is. Soon, all right?"

Healer Cadowyn clears his throat. "First Nestraya—"

"Queen Nestraya," Lorial murmurs.

Healer Cadowyn exhales slowly. "Of course. Forgive the slip, my king. Queen Nestraya, a word?"

With Corivos's help, she reluctantly lets Lorial go and turns to Healer Cadowyn as Mera takes her place. "Please forgive my...family. They are relentless."

Healer Cadowyn smiles. "I meant no disrespect. You were one of my brightest students, my queen. Your change in status, though—it won't go over well among many of the high-born elves."

"No. It won't. I am grateful to you for not abandoning your king when so many others have."

"There are many of us who were loyal to our king Restoval who continue to be loyal to his son. Do not think you are abandoned."

"Thank you, Healer. Tell me what you wish to report." Nestraya sways, and Corivos steadies her.

"Our king is weak, but he should make a full recovery. Thanks to you. It was a very dangerous thing you did, heartbinding when he was so near death."

"It was the only option."

"Yes. And I'm prepared to testify as much should anyone question your actions here today."

She nods. "Thank you. When will he be ready to fight again?"

Healer Cadowyn shakes his head. "Our king is not a warrior, which I think he proved today—"

"I need him ready to fight. How long?"

Healer Cadowyn rubs the back of his neck and shrugs. "A week with frequent infusions of life magic. But it's better to let him heal at his own speed, as you well know."

"He doesn't have a week. There are elves dying right now who will continue to be sacrificed until Hothniel is brought to account. I need my king by my side."

Healer Cadowyn sighs. "He's young and strong, but even my life magic can't do the impossible."

Nestraya glances back at Lorial, where Mera hovers over him. "What about mine?"

"My queen, you're not a fully trained healer. You don't—"

"Would my life magic be enough to get him on his feet tonight?"

"Tonight? You ask for the impossible—"

"Can Starhaven be regrown in a day?"

Corivos frowns at her, and Healer Cadowyn shakes his head.

"An hour?"

"Of course not, my queen."

"I can do it in five minutes," she says under her breath, surprised the magic let her speak the words. "Now, you told me once that my plant magic was my weakest affinity. Is that still true?"

He breathes out through pursed lips. "Our king's air magic blunts everything but you at the moment. That said, I stand by my prior assessment. Your life magic is your strongest affinity, though all three of your affinities are fairly close in strength."

Corivos leans close to her. "How long have you been lying about your plant magic?"

"We'll talk later, Second."

He looks amused, but he nods. "Of course, my queen."

"Regardless, you are a warrior-class healer, my queen," Healer Cadowyn says. "You're not qualified to do the type of magic required to accelerate our king's healing to this degree. And if you overextend yourself, you put both your lives at risk. Your heart beats for both of you now, my queen. Do not forget."

Tendrils of air magic drift closer as Healer Cadowyn speaks, and Nestraya turns toward Lorial.

"No." He looks straight at her. "I will not allow you to—"

"Whistling wind, Lorial! You weren't invited to be part of this conversation. As your First, I recommend you bugger off and let me assess our options so I can properly advise you when the time comes."

35

MAGIC AND PROMISES

Everyone stills at Nestraya's tirade, and she clears her throat. That was perhaps a bit...much.

After a moment, Lorial grins. "Bravo, my love."

She scratches her brow and looks down as her face heats.

Corivos shakes beside her with silent laughter. "How long were you in the heartlanding?"

"Long enough. Now let's refocus."

"Perhaps we should include our king in this conversation," Healer Cadowyn says.

"He's still listening," Nestraya mutters.

Healer Cadowyn's brow furrows. "You can sense his magic with that much nuance?"

Nestraya tilts her head. "Is that unusual?"

"Extremely. I can't sense anything other than the power of his magic. And yours."

A different sort of air magic wraps around her leg, and she slides her eyes shut. Now he's playing games with her.

"It is a bit breezy in here," Corivos says, and Nestraya shakes her head.

"That would be our king. His air magic is restless."

Apparently, using it in the heartlanding has had little effect on his stores in the real world.

Unless he's toying with her.

"Excuse me for one moment." She strides toward Lorial, and he grins up at her. Then she leans close to him. "That is incredibly distracting."

"So are you," he murmurs.

"Save it for later, my love. After we reclaim your throne."

That sobers him. "I'm sorry. It's just so...restless. I've grown accustomed to using my air magic, and this bottling up of it has me itching to let it out. I don't know how I lived like this before."

Mera smiles from nearby. She probably heard some of that. Not the part about using his magic in the heartlanding—that part he whispered so only Nestraya could hear.

But the rest?

Whistling wind, this will take time to grow used to.

"Let's give our king and queen some privacy," Mera says as she instructs everyone to turn away. Then she leans closer to Lorial while Nestraya endeavors not to die from mortification. "Let it out for a few minutes to take the edge off. Then you'll be able to focus better. That's what your father—"

Lorial holds up a hand. "We get the idea. Thank you."

Soon, they're alone in the middle of a circle of elves with their backs turned.

"Focus on me, my love," he whispers. "It's just us right now."

"And your entire band of elite warriors. Plus healers and Mera—"

He presses his finger to her lips to silence her. "I'm just going to let my magic wrap around this table. Unless you want me to wrap it around you. Either way, I need to get it out so I can focus."

"No flying," she warns. "Healer's orders."

He grins. "I didn't hear Healer Cadowyn say that."

"I'm saying it."

"Understood, my queen. You are magnificent, as I knew you would be."

"Yes, well, it's probably best if your queen refrains from yelling at you in front of all your warriors in the future. Forgive me for that."

He laughs, and a smile tugs at her lips.

"Just let it go, my love," she whispers. "I could use some of your magic to get me through this night."

"You make me long to wrap you in my arms rather than my magic."

"Now that would be awkward. It's been millennia since elven royalty had their first joining witnessed as a matter of course."

"I don't see anyone watching."

Thank the fates for that. His magic has already encircled her waist.

"People are waiting, my love. Perhaps you could speed this up a bit."

His grin grows as he wraps his magic all around her, enveloping her in a cloud of air. She relaxes into it, letting it carry her completely.

It's not the first time he's wrapped his magic around her like this, but it's the first time he's done it in the real world. The intimacy of it warms her cheeks.

After a few minutes, he lets her go, and she smiles down at him. "Better, my love?"

"My air magic is sated for now. Other appetites are not."

Whistling wind. He didn't even whisper it. Her cheeks warm again as she glances around. A few members of their entourage shift, and one elf clears his throat.

"Lorial," she hisses.

"You're mine, Nestraya Westaria," he says a little more softly. "Let every elf from here to Celesta know it." Using his good arm, he draws her hand to his lips.

"You may romance me later, my king. For now, we need to discuss getting you back on your feet."

His expression darkens. "I will not put you at risk. You are my binding partner now, Nestraya. The Queen of Lostariel. You are not expendable."

"Lostariel needs her king—"

"And her queen. We're a team, remember?" He lowers his voice. "You almost died by overextending your plant magic. I never want to witness such a thing again."

"I'll be more careful this time. What choice do we have? We can't wait a week for your strength to return."

He looks so torn that her heart softens.

He loves her. She won't fault him for that. Not anymore.

"I need you by my side, my love," she says. "You with all your hidden strength. Lorial and Nestraya against the world, remember? Let me do this for us. For those elflings you desire and for all our people who need us to fight for them. And when my life magic is spent, I'll need your help to replenish it."

She brushes back his silver hair, caked with dirt and flecks of blood. It's shorter here than in the heartlanding. Then she continues trailing her fingers through his hair until she grazes his ear as he stares up at her.

"We're better together," he whispers.

When she leans down to kiss him, he meets her lips with a gentleness full of all the tender love he's shown her these past few days. He slides his good hand along her jaw, his flesh heated against hers.

"You burn hot tonight, my love," she whispers.

He quickly reclaims his hand.

"It's a good thing you're bound to a water wielder," she murmurs as she cools his hand with her own magic.

"I knew we were perfect for each other." With a sigh, he meets her gaze again. "You'll be careful? I can't live without you, Nestraya. Literally."

A smile slips across her lips at his words. "I promise. I won't overextend myself this time."

He breathes out slowly and nods, and she straightens, turning to the line of elves encircling them. "Healer Cadowyn? Teach me what to do."

Mera and Corivos wait nearby, along with Healer Cadowyn and Third Rafelis.

Second Quilian stands at the ready with several elite warriors, as he's done all day, according to Corivos.

Guarding his king and queen with his life.

There's something fatherly about the man that reminds Nestraya of a wisp of a memory she can't quite grasp—a memory of a feeling, perhaps. He wields water magic, as Pera did, and the thought tugs at her heart.

And he's strong. Stronger than most low borns.

He looks right at her as she studies him, and she frowns. His eyes. She's seen those eyes before.

Every time she looks in the mirror.

Images like a reflection flood her, and she wobbles.

"My queen?" he says softly.

"I know you," she breathes. "'Run. Take her and hide her.' You were there."

He glances at the elves standing nearby and eventually nods. "I was, my queen."

Before she can say anything else, Healer Cadowyn speaks to her. "Whenever you're ready, my queen. Just as we discussed."

Lorial frowns up at her. "You look shaken, my love. What is it?"

He must not have heard her conversation with Second Quilian.

Focus. She needs to focus.

"I will continue to guard you, Nestraya," Second Quilian says so quietly that surely no one else could have heard. "As I have watched over you all your life. I only wish I could have protected you from everything."

She shakes her head, trying to make sense of his words.

"Nestraya?" Lorial says again. Threads of his magic wrap around her protectively, and she tears her attention away from Second Quilian.

"I'm all right. It's just…been a long day." She pushes her questions and unsettling thoughts aside to focus on Lorial. "I'm ready."

She discarded her leather gown with its long sleeves for a simple, loose linen shirt someone handed her a few minutes ago. All the elves turned their backs again so she could change.

Whistling wind, that was awkward. Especially with Lorial lying there trying not to grin at her. He and Healer Cadowyn both insisted they need easier access to her bare skin in case she overextends her life magic.

Which she has no intention of doing. Putting her own life in danger won't do Lorial any favors.

Nestraya places her hands on Lorial's chest, one over his sternum and the other gently on the scar over his heart. He grimaces, and Corivos hands him a stick to bite down on.

Unfortunately, all but the minor pain reduction Healer Cadowyn already worked will slow Nestraya's healing efforts.

"Forgive me, my love," she whispers. Then she closes her eyes and lets the magic flow through her, just as Healer Cadowyn instructed.

Lorial whimpers and reflexively jerks away, but several warriors hold him down.

Nestraya almost pulls back. She knew it would be unpleasant, but watching him in so much pain, knowing she's the one causing it, roils her stomach.

"Keep going, my queen," Healer Cadowyn says softly as he holds his own hand over Lorial's shoulder to monitor her efforts.

She pushes forward, feeling the magic pouring from her and into him, knitting flesh and muscles completely, accelerating the regrowth and rebinding of his own body. Forcing his body to replenish his lost blood, as she was attempting to do after he was shot. With Healer Cadowyn's instruction, she knows what she was doing wrong before and does it right this time.

"Slow down, my queen," Healer Cadowyn murmurs. "His body can't keep up."

She pulls back slightly as the beginnings of her own fatigue settle in.

"Your power is remarkable," Healer Cadowyn breathes. "I mourned when you chose to train as a warrior rather than join the Healer's Circle."

Lorial breathes heavily as he bites down on the stick, his chest rising and falling beneath her hands.

Something drips down Nestraya's cheek, and only when Mera wipes it away does Nestraya realize it was a tear. A wave of nausea sweeps over her, but she pushes past it as her knees wobble.

"Almost done," Healer Cadowyn murmurs. "Don't overexert yourself."

She's so close. His labored breathing slows as she continues, the edges of her vision growing dark.

She needs to pull back.

Lorial looks up at her and spits the stick out. "Nestraya. Nestraya, stop!"

"Almost—"

"Now. Stop now. You've done enough. You promised!"

Strong hands grasp her from behind, and she pulls back on her magic. "I'm fine. Just a little weak."

When her knees buckle, the elf behind her catches her, and Lorial jumps off the table before anyone can stop him.

"You're not supposed to get up yet," she murmurs.

"Put her here," Lorial says, and Nestraya looks up into Second Quilian's eyes as he lays her on the table and takes one of her hands, pushing up her sleeve and rubbing her arm.

"So like your father," he says under his breath. "Both of them. Giving everything for the one you love."

Before Nestraya can ponder his words, her vision wavers, plunging her into darkness.

36

LIFE MAGIC

Lorial stares at Second Quilian. What did he say?

Mother has copied Second Quilian's actions with Nestraya's other arm, attempting to rub life back into her. Her heart beats steadily. Lorial can feel it. But she lies limp, her eyes closed and her face like death.

She promised.

"Turn her to her side," Healer Cadowyn says, and Third Rafelis is there with a knife to cut open her shirt and small clothes, exposing her back completely.

"Lorial," Mother whispers.

It's enough to kick him into action as Third Rafelis moves out of the way so Lorial can climb on the table with Nestraya and press his chest to her back.

She's so cold. Hopefully, he doesn't burn her. Not that his fire magic burns hot at the moment.

His shoulder aches, but other than a slight weariness, he feels fine. Ready to pour his life back into Nestraya's limp form. He wraps his arms around her waist beneath the shirt that lies loosely against her as he tries to make as much contact with her skin as possible.

Mother and Second Quilian continue rubbing her arms, and Lorial presses his cheek to hers. "Stay with me, my love."

He glances up at Healer Cadowyn, and to Lorial's complete and utter relief, the healer nods. "She stopped soon enough. Just keep doing what you're doing. You, especially, my king."

As if Lorial has any intention of letting her go.

Ever.

They continue their ministrations, and soon Nestraya's skin begins to warm.

When she stiffens, he nearly cries in relief.

"It's all right, my love. I've got you," he says softly in her ear, and she relaxes against him.

"Lorial? How are you feeling?"

"How am I feeling? You scared me half to death again. How are you feeling?"

"Nauseated. And weak."

"You should have pulled back sooner."

"I know. I'm sorry. It all happened so fast." She shifts slightly, and he adjusts to match. "Mera?"

"I'm here, young one."

"Quilian?" she whispers. "Is that you?"

Lorial follows her gaze to the man pressing his forearm to hers.

"I'm here as well, my queen. Perhaps, when this is all over, we can talk."

Nestraya nods, and Lorial swallows the questions that swirl in his head about the man as he focuses his attention back on Nestraya.

"Corivos?" Nestraya says weakly.

When Nestraya's shirt was cut, Corivos stepped back to give her privacy, but he approaches again at her call. "I'm here, my queen."

"Your report. I'm ready to hear it."

Lorial frowns. "Right now?"

"As soon as I regain my strength, we need to act. Go ahead, Corivos."

"Very well. The fighting continued after we fled. Not long after you binded with our king, I ordered our retreat to a safer distance to ensure we weren't discovered, and our king's elite warriors carried you both here behind this mound of soil where I could more easily protect you."

Nestraya nods. "And the fighting?"

"Our primary scout, Third Rafelis, hasn't left your side, but I recently sent two of our other warriors to observe and report back. They have yet to return."

"How long ago?" Nestraya shifts again, but this time Lorial pulls her back.

"Stay put, my queen. I'm not done with you yet."

She huffs but doesn't argue.

"I sent them right before you awoke, my queen," Corivos says. "Approximately two hours ago. I expect them to return at any time."

"Two hours? How far are we from the fighting?"

"Several miles, my queen. We carried you a great distance to ensure your safety."

Lorial looks around in surprise. These warriors carried them for miles?

"It seems your elite band of warriors is quite loyal to you, my king," Nestraya says over her shoulder.

"And to you, my queen," Third Rafelis says. "To the rest of us, you represent a better future for our elflings. One we will fight, and if need be, die for."

The slightest tremble sweeps over Nestraya, and Lorial tightens his hold on her.

"Let's hope it doesn't come to that," she whispers, clearly overcome. "Have any of you slept?"

"No, my queen," Corivos says.

"We take it in shifts. I want half our warriors to sleep now for a short time. The other half, including you, will take the next shift once I'm on my feet again."

Corivos looks as though he wants to argue, but he nods instead. "Yes, my queen."

He steps away to relay her orders, and Nestraya turns to Mother. "I think I'm doing well enough with Lorial's help now. Perhaps—"

"Of course, young one. We will give you some privacy."

With Healer Cadowyn's approval, Lorial and Nestraya are left to themselves, and when Nestraya tries to shift again, Lorial holds her tight.

"Not yet," he says with a hint of quiet laughter. "Just let me hold you for a little longer."

"Shall I explain how mortified I am now? It hasn't escaped my notice that nothing lies between your skin and mine."

He kisses her neck. "Is that a problem?"

"It is when we're surrounded by others."

"It was to save you, my love. I promise your modesty has been protected as much as possible given the circumstances."

She sighs. "I'm just glad you're all right. You are all right, aren't you?"

"I am now. I almost lost my head when you passed out, though."

"My life magic flows faster than my plant magic. I'm sorry for the pain I caused you. It was...hard to watch. Harder to do."

"It was necessary, my love."

"Did I finish healing you?"

"My shoulder aches, and I'm tired, but I'm ready to do what needs to be done."

She turns to look at him, and this time he doesn't stop her. "Shall I finish—"

"No. You shall not. Now come back here." He settles her against his chest again. "How is your nausea?"

"Better."

"Good."

"Lorial, your hand is growing warmer."

He thought it might be. The longer he lies here with her like this, the more his fire magic prods at him.

"Do you want me to move it?"

"Not yet."

He kisses her neck again and leaves his hand on the soft flesh around her navel.

"Are you ready to rise from the ashes, my love?" she asks.

"As ready as I'll ever be. Something happened in the heartlanding, right at the end, before..."

"Before we failed to get carried away?" There's a smile in her voice, and he chuckles.

"Yes."

"You became the wind. I saw it in your eyes. They glowed like storm clouds as you looked at me."

"My eyes glowed?"

She nods. "It wasn't the first time, but it was the most striking. Tell me what you felt?"

"I felt everything. The trees. The creek. A nearby river. Even the mountains in the distance."

"When the time comes, remember that feeling, my love. Become the wind."

"I'm not sure I was focusing on the wind when it happened," he murmurs near her ear.

Before he nuzzles it.

"Lorial," she half-hisses, half-whimpers. "I'm not sure now is—"

Corivos clears his throat nearby as a smile ghosts across his face. "Forgive my intrusion. Our scouts have returned. A temporary ceasefire fell sometime this afternoon while both sides tend to their wounded, and an uneasy stalemate now exists. The human prince seems reluctant to continue this bloodbath, but Hothniel plans to push forward as soon as the, forgive me, 'the dreck' can be cleared and new warriors brought in from the Outerlands. Apparently, they were summoned days ago and should arrive soon."

"I think I'm going to be sick," Nestraya mumbles as she veers to the edge of the table. Lorial draws her hair back just in time for her to lose mostly bile on the forest floor.

"Forgive me," she whispers.

"There's nothing to forgive, my love," Lorial says as he holds her hair and shirt in place.

Without so much as a grimace, Corivos uses his magic to cover the sick with a layer of soil.

"Did he really call them dreck?" Nestraya whispers.

"Yes." A blood vessel twitches at Corivos's temple, and Lorial frowns. "By 'dreck'—"

"The bodies of the low-born elves who gave their lives to protect the high borns," Nestraya whispers.

Lorial might be sick himself.

"Corivos, we need to cut off the advancing warrior bands," Nestraya says. "Convince them to fight for us."

"I was about to suggest the same. I'll take Second Quilian and Third Rafelis—"

Nestraya shakes her head as she tries to sit up. "Us. Lorial and me. It needs to be us."

She sways, and Lorial wraps his arms around her to keep her from falling off the table. "You need to rest." He pulls her back against his chest, and she whimpers in frustration.

"Perhaps she's right, Lorial," Corivos says. "I'm not sure these warrior bands have even received word of your father's death. They need to know who they're fighting for. And why."

"They need to know Lostariel has a new queen. A queen who is one of them—a low born from the Outerlands," a new voice says.

Lorial looks up into the eyes of Second Quilian.

"I'm from the Outerlands?" Nestraya asks.

"Yes, my queen. You don't remember because...because I blotted those memories from you when I carried you to our king Restoval."

37

QUEEN OF LOSTARIEL

Nestraya stares up at Quilian. "Lorial, would you cloak yourself? Just for a moment?"

Lorial frowns, but he does as she asks.

Her dizziness grows as she sends out feelers with her life magic. Quilian's water magic is powerful. But if she digs deeper, the hint of sweetness is there. Hidden, unless you know to look for it.

"You wield life magic."

Quilian nods. "I do. All the elves born in the last two generations to the House Thariosi of the Outerlands do. You and I are all that remain."

She frowns. "Thariosi? My family name—"

"Your first father's name was Cerian Thariosi, and you were born Nestraya Thariosi. I...gave you a new name to keep you safe—Cerianus, after your first father, my older brother. Though Westaria suits you now, my queen."

The dark forest around them spins, and Nestraya grasps at Lorial, searching for him behind his cloak until he reappears.

"I'm here. I'm here, my love."

She tries to put words to the questions forming on her lips as she gazes up into the eyes of this man who claims to be...her uncle? Nothing comes out, though.

"What happened?" Lorial angles her back against his chest again, his arm wrapped around her to steady her.

Quilian rubs his eyes and breathes out through pursed lips. "The Outerlands...it's a different sort of existence than what you're used to here, my king. Harsher. We depend on each other for survival as we live in caves, battling against the elements."

"I am aware of the conditions for those who make their homes in the far north," Lorial says softly. "It's a difficult life."

"It can be, my king. But it's a rich one, full of companionship and kin. We take care of each other in the Outerlands."

Nestraya hears his words, but they barely register as she tries to process everything he's said.

"The Years of Torment were...difficult for our people. The Shadow King abandoned us completely. If not for the Lothlesi taking pity on us, we all would have died."

"The fae?" Nestraya says softly.

"They don't like to be called that, but yes."

"You've had contact with them?" Lorial asks. "It's been centuries since they've held parley with Lostarien kings."

"Blame Polanis for that, my king. They offered their help, despite their general distrust of others. He refused."

Lorial stiffens behind Nestraya. "He refused? While elflings died?"

"He did. So the Lothlesi offered what little they could to those far outside the eyes of the Shadow King, who feasted happily in Celesta while his people starved."

"Your lands border New Valderi," Lorial says. "The Lothlesi stronghold under the mountains."

"Indeed, my king. We share water resources. Our caves border their underground cities. Their magic seeps into our dwellings. Our food."

Nestraya's eyes grow wide at his words. "Strengthening your magic."

"Our magic, my queen. Every generation is born stronger than the last. It's a gift and a curse. For centuries, we managed to hide our increasing strength. Then Cerian was born with dual affinities."

"My...father?"

"Yes. One strong affinity. One weak, easily concealed. His strength was life magic, like yours, my queen. His water magic was weaker."

"I don't understand," Nestraya whispers. "What happened?"

"You were born, Nestraya. My queen. Stronger than any Outerlander elf since the Years of Torment."

"And Cerian...he really was my father?"

Quilian's eyes darken. "The venom these people spew—that a fae lord impregnated your mother. Lies, all of them. That's all they ever were. Lies meant to fit inside their tidy narrative, to justify their treatment of you. You are every ounce the daughter of Cerian Thariosi. I see him in your eyes. Your hair. Your face. No one could doubt it."

Nestraya fights the prickle in her eyes, and when a soft hand lands on her shoulder, she jumps.

It's Mera.

"Did you know?" Nestraya whispers.

"We knew some. Not all. We knew you were from the Outerlands. That your first parents were old. Quilian told us they died of old age. We could find no record of the House Cerianus, but records in the Outerlands are sparse. No one would give more than vague answers to the elves Restoval sent to the Outerlands to learn more about where you came from. Eventually, he gave up. You were ours. That was all that mattered. We didn't know Quilian was more than your protector."

"For Nestraya's benefit. My entire purpose since mercenaries murdered the House Thariosi has been to protect you, my queen. Forgive me for not doing enough. For letting Hothniel snatch you. By the time I found you, our king and Second Corivos had already intervened."

Nestraya digs her fingernails into Lorial's arm, grasping at something to steady herself.

"Murdered?" Lorial's voice is dark as he takes her hand in his own.

"We couldn't hide Nestraya from the mercenaries. She was...too strong."

Her breaths come rapidly at his words.

Her fault. It was her fault. Just as she feared.

Then Lorial is in front of her, his hands on either side of her face. "Not your fault. You've slain these demons. Do not give them a new foothold to weaken you, my queen. My love."

"But it was my fault."

"No, Nestraya," Quilian says. "You were an elfling. It was not your fault. It was the fault of the evil that infects these lands. Elves like Hothniel. I don't know who sent the mercenaries, but I wouldn't be surprised if it was him. He knows far too much about your past. Far more than he should."

"What mercenaries do you speak of, Second Quilian?" Mera asks.

"The Outerlands are frequently patrolled, my queen Miravel. On whose orders, I cannot say. Rewards are given for anyone who turns over traitors."

Lorial's eyes burn as he turns. "Of what traitors do you speak?"

"The low born whose power grows, my king."

"This is not sanctioned by the Crown," Mera says. "Restoval would never—"

"No. We know that. We are loyal to the House Westaria in the Outerlands. Polanis may have betrayed us, but your great-grandfather, my king. He sought to offer restitution for his own grandfather's evils. He provided the Outerlands with grain and economic recompense. And as the stories go, he lowered himself to the ground before my own grandfather and begged forgiveness. Made the Vow of Trulesya. That any wish my grandfather or my grandfather's descendants made that was within his power or the power of his own descendants to grant, it would be done."

Nestraya gapes at Quilian. "That is heavy life magic to wield."

"Indeed. As the rumor goes, he sacrificed a number of his own remaining years to make the vow."

"Was the favor ever called upon?" Lorial asks.

"It was. When I fled with Nestraya, I used my meager life magic to access the promise etched in my blood. That Nestraya would find a home—"

"With Restoval," Mera says softly.

"My magic was not that specific, my queen Miravel. I merely begged for a haven for her where she would be safe. A position in the kitchens or a home with a lesser noble under the protection of the king. When the Crown Prince of Lostariel himself stepped forward, I...I was not expecting that."

"He would have loved her, vow or not." Mera squeezes Nestraya's shoulder. "It's who he was."

"This I don't doubt, my queen Miravel," Quilian says. "I saw the love he held for her with my own eyes, over and over again. The love of a father."

"And the elves of the Outerlands remain loyal? Even after being...hunted?" Nestraya manages through the catch in her throat.

"The elves of the Outerlands would have given their lives for Restoval, my queen. They hoped he would eventually be the one to free them from the tyranny of the high born."

"Why him?" Lorial asks.

"Isn't it obvious, my king? As I said, the Outerlanders are extremely loyal people. We protect our own. And when Restoval stepped into the place of Cerian Thariosi—became the devoted second father of young Nestraya Thariosi—he became kin. The bond of chosen family is even more highly revered among Outerlanders than it is here. He became *estrasse*."

"He was trying to change things," Mera says with a slight catch in her voice. "Nothing ever changes quickly, though. He thought he'd have more time."

"We all did," Nestraya whispers as thoughts of all the things left unsaid between her and the man who loved her like a daughter threaten to slay her.

"I fear Hothniel means to use the loyalty of the Outerlander warrior bands to his advantage," Corivos says quietly.

"Indeed," Quilian says. "All he need tell them is that humans killed our king Restoval, and they will fight to the death to avenge him."

Nestraya shakes her head. "We have to stop them. Bring them over to our side before Hothniel murders them all."

"They will fight for you, my queen," Quilian murmurs. "You are one of them, and they have protected your secret your entire life. First, the truth of your magic. Then the truth of your past. Their loyalty to the daughter of Cerian Thariosi and Restoval Westaria knows no limit."

The weight of his words rests heavy on her chest as Lorial turns to her again.

Taking her face in his hands once more, he leans down until their eyes are level. "Will you believe me now, my love? You were born to be the Queen of Lostariel."

She exhales slowly as she gazes into his eyes. "I am who I am."

"And who are you?"

She glances at the others, but Lorial draws her gaze back to him.

"I'm Nestraya," she whispers.

"And who is Nestraya?"

"I'm the Queen of Lostariel."

He presses his lips to her forehead and nods. "And who else are you?"

"I'm yours, Lorial. Until the beating of our hearts fades."

Then he kisses her. Right there in front of everyone. His hands warm against her cheeks, his undeniable yearning for her bringing his fire magic to life once more.

When he pulls back and rests his forehead against hers, she banishes her embarrassment at his display of affection to a distant corner of her mind.

She's the other half of his heart. Let the world know they belong to each other.

Let the world know Lostariel has a new queen. Wholly and completely devoted to this man. She's his strength. At times, his weakness.

Always his.

"We need to suit up, my love," she whispers. "The Phoenix King rises tonight with his queen by his side."

"No, my love. You rise—I'll be the wind that holds you aloft. But it's the Queen of Lostariel who flies this night."

38

PRACTICE SESSIONS

Lorial fingers his warrior leathers, examining the hole from the musket ball and the jagged cut someone made to remove his jacket.

"I'm not sure this is wearable," he says to Nestraya where she stands beside him, holding her own ayervadi leathers once again. Hers is covered in blood just as his is—his blood.

She frowns. "If it were a plant-based material, I might be able to mend it, but leather—I doubt it would answer to my life magic."

"I don't want you using your life magic until you need to. Had I known that's what you were doing with Quilian earlier, I would have stopped you." He eyes the leather again. "I'll just have to make do."

Gingerly, he slips his aching arm into it, trying not to let Nestraya see how sore he still is. Healer Cadowyn cleared him to fight with his magic. That's all that matters.

As he slides his other arm in place, she studies him. "You know, the torn leather just makes you look more impressive."

The corners of his mouth tilt up as he frees his hair. "More impressive, my queen?"

"Mmm. Yes. Very impressive. Give me a moment, and I'll braid your hair and paint your eyes."

Their elf band has turned their backs once again to give their queen her privacy. The smooth flesh of her back lies exposed as her borrowed shirt and small clothes gape around her.

She's moving more slowly than he would expect.

"Are you still weak?" he asks softly so only she can hear. She looks more or less like her normal self again.

"Perhaps a little."

"Do you need help?" He gently presses his hand to her back.

"I...I need to get dressed," she whispers.

Then understanding dawns. She changed into the shirt in front of him earlier...but her small clothes remained intact at the time.

"Do you need this?" He fingers the cut cloth she normally fastens around her chest. "Does it serve a purpose other than to torment me?"

She glares at him, as he knew she would. "Not everything is about you, my king."

He's about to return a witty jab when he catches sight of a red mark running along her side. It looks inflamed. "What is this?"

She winces at his touch. "A knife wound. I did a poor job healing it in the dark stone enclosure."

Drawing his brows together, he pushes the shirt aside to follow it around her ribcage. "They did this to you?"

"I'm sorry. I know it will leave a scar. Perhaps—"

Lorial's eyes snap to hers. "You think I care about such things? It looks infected. How did I miss it when you changed earlier?"

She pushes her shirt back down. "I'm pretty sure your eyes were trained elsewhere."

Admittedly, he may have been a little distracted.

"Healer Cadowyn," Lorial calls out.

"I'm fine, Lorial."

The older man steps toward them. "What is it, my king?"

Lorial lifts the hem of her shirt again, and Healer Cadowyn hisses through his teeth.

"You didn't clean this properly before you healed it, my queen."

"I know. I couldn't see what I was doing."

"Sit so I can deal with this before you become ill."

Lorial lifts his brows at her, and she glares back at him.

"You heard the man, my love. Sit."

Her expression makes her displeasure more than obvious, but she does as instructed.

While the healer is occupied, Lorial leans near Nestraya's ear. "May I?"

When she nods hesitantly, he reaches beneath her shirt to tug the torn band away from where it hangs around her torso and shoulders.

"Lorial!" she hisses.

"Hold still, my queen," Healer Cadowyn says.

Lorial fiddles with the cloth. It's in pieces now, but it looks like one continuous strip that she binds herself with. Which is what he guessed based on the few times he's seen it on her.

"It's fine," she says. "I'll make do without it."

"It's linen. Flax. Could you mend it?"

"All done, my queen," Healer Cadowyn says. "Try not to do the same again. I trained you better than that."

"Thank you," she says as he steps away. Then she turns to Lorial. "I should save my magic for something more important. Let me see the longest piece."

He hands it to her, and she bites her lip as she examines it. Then she slips it beneath her shirt, where she slides the strip of cloth around herself under the cover of the linen. After knotting it, she nods. "That will have to do."

Lorial's hands suddenly feel like fire.

Whistling wind.

There are too many trees to launch a fireball overhead to let some of the heat out.

When his palms tingle, he huffs in frustration and drops the remaining strips of cloth so he can shake his hands and try to cool them.

Nestraya's movement catches his eye, and he looks up in time to see her sliding her leather gown over her head.

Fire spews from his left hand before he can contain it, and a colorful word flies from his lips. He stomps at the ground to put out the spark before he lights the entire forest on fire.

Then Nestraya is there, taking his burning hands in hers and cooling them with her water magic.

"Perhaps we don't speak of this," he mumbles as she grins up at him.

"Whatever you say, my king."

To his surprise, she kisses him, not letting go of his hands. Or her water magic, thank the fates.

"Soon, my love," she whispers when she pulls away. "Shall we braid your hair and paint your eyes?"

He grins. "Are those my only options?"

"For now. Sit."

With his smile still in place, he lowers himself to the table, and she climbs up behind him as she tears strips from the linen he dropped.

She's going to tie his hair with the remnants of her small clothes? She's either evil, or she's the most wonderful woman he's ever met.

Perhaps both.

"Your hair is short here." Sadness clouds her voice. "I like it long."

"I will keep that in mind, my love."

A few of their warriors shift in the circle surrounding them.

What's come over her? Nestraya's sudden public embrace of the affection and attraction growing between them is as startling as it is welcome.

As is the way her fingers deftly plait his hair.

When she grazes his left ear for the third time, he exhales slowly and circles his air magic around his hands. "I'm beginning to think you're doing that on purpose."

"What's that, my love?"

He smiles when she does it again.

"There. Does anyone have korathite?" she asks.

A vial is soon procured, and Nestraya steps between his knees where they hang at the edge of the table. His hands itch to draw her closer, but he'd probably catch the woods on fire.

He'd send up a few orb lights, but that doesn't relieve his heat the way fire does. He tried in the heartlanding. It didn't help.

Instead, he sits still, trying not to focus on what she's doing.

After finishing both eyes, she leans closer to examine her work.

Whistling wind, this is maddening. He can barely touch her without worrying about burning her right now. And with the way her mouth keeps twitching up at the corners, she knows it.

Then she plants her hands on his knees. "What's wrong, my king? You seem overcome."

"You are evil, my—"

But she cuts him off with a kiss.

Air. If he swirls the air around his hands...

Someone nearby clears his throat. "You must have had quite the time in the heartlanding."

Corivos.

Nestraya steps away, looking embarrassed. "I thought I told you to rest."

"You may have done that."

"And?"

"I'm clearly not resting."

Lorial sucks in his cheeks to hold back a smile. "What is it, Corivos?"

"As soon as our second shift wakes from their sleep, we'll be ready to head out. I've sent Second Quilian ahead with his band to scout out the approaching Outerlanders. He refused to rest. He almost refused to leave you, my queen."

Nestraya nods. "Thank you. We'll be ready when everyone else is."

After Corivos steps away, Nestraya lowers herself to the table beside Lorial, and he puts his arm around her shoulders. She leans against him, resting her hand on his leg. The action seems casual as if she doesn't realize what she's doing.

As if she's growing comfortable with casual touch between them.

"Are you all right?" he asks softly.

"Yes. I'm Nestraya. And I need to be strong, especially tonight."

He can't argue with that. Now's the time to be strong. There will be time to process everything later. Hopefully.

"You seem more affectionate than usual," he says.

As she shifts beside him, she nods. "I'm practicing. For when I have to convince the entire kingdom that you and I..."

Confusion knits his brows as his stomach tightens. "We what?"

She shrugs. "There aren't words to describe it. We just...are."

"So...this is all an act?"

"What?" She turns startled eyes toward him. "Of course not."

That's a relief. His stomach relaxes as he twirls a wisp of her hair around his finger. At least his fire has cooled. "You are confusing at times."

She leans against him again, but not before he sees her attempt to hold back a smile.

"What are you practicing?" he asks when she volunteers no further information. "And why?"

"I'm practicing being the binding partner of the King of Lostariel. Slaying my demons. Owning my role—becoming the person so many people need me to be. They need to see us together. Loving each other. They need to know they can trust you with everything, the way I trust you with everything."

A warmth seeps around his heart—not the heat from his fire magic. Something deeper. Something…more.

Before he can respond, she continues. "I'm giving myself permission to be me. To not care what the world thinks. If I want to kiss you, I'm going to kiss you. If anyone is offended, they can gouge out their eyes."

He barely represses a grin. "Sounds reasonable."

"If the King of Lostariel can win the heart of a low-born Outerlander, and she can…she can win his devotion in return…then anything is possible. Right? We might really be able to change things."

His fire returns at her words. "We'd better do a good job showing the world how much we love each other, then."

She pats his leg. "Exactly. Within reason. There are certain bounds of propriety that—" Her words cut off in a soft moan as he feathers his air magic over her ear.

"Too much?" he whispers.

Her eyes slide closed, but she doesn't ask him to stop. "We're going to scandalize Lostariel, my king."

"I hope we do."

39

APPROACHING MAGIC

Their small band of warriors advances quietly through the woods toward the northeast—toward the Outerlands. Nestraya keeps threads of her life magic active in every direction, wary of anyone whose path they might cross, despite Lorial's protests.

His air magic is distracting, though he contains it. It's like standing in a crowded room, trying to hear unfamiliar voices over the din of the ordinary conversations surrounding her.

"You keep sending cross looks my way, my queen," Lorial murmurs. "I thought we were trying to convince Lostariel we love each other."

"At the moment, I'm trying to keep you alive. Your air magic is blinding."

"I thought my fire magic was blinding."

She glares at him.

"Not the right time for teasing?" he asks.

"No. Be good, or I'll make you walk with Mera." She juts her chin back to where Mera walks surrounded by six warriors tasked with protecting her. If Nestraya didn't know how powerful Lorial truly is, she would have insisted on guarding him as well.

"I promise to be good," he quickly says.

Thank the fates for that.

"Shall I cloak myself to make this easier for you?" he asks more seriously.

That would help. And he wouldn't broadcast his presence like a beacon to anyone within a three-mile radius.

She nods, and he soon disappears from view.

"If you do anything heroic when I can't see you, though, I will kill you myself," she warns.

"Understood, my First."

She jumps when something brushes her hand. "What are you doing?"

He twines his invisible fingers with hers. "I don't want you to fatigue yourself. If you can make demands, so can I. You will hold my hand while you're scouting with your life magic so I can keep you strong."

The urge to argue fills her, but she doesn't. It's probably a good idea. Plus, if she's holding his hand, he won't be running off and getting himself shot or something equally terrifying.

She focuses on her magic again, pushing past the sensations of their small cluster of warriors. And Mera. At least Mera's magical signature isn't as overwhelming as Lorial's.

A faint snatch of water magic hits her, and she holds up a fist.

"What is it, my queen?" Corivos asks as their troops halt and Mera's guards splay in a defensive position around her. Corivos gazes around wildly. "Where's our king?"

"Here." Lorial lifts Nestraya's hand, but she ignores them both as she tries to pick out how many elves approach.

There's plant magic in addition to the water magic, though it's fainter. A soil wielder. The others are harder to identify, but she senses their essences. Five total.

"Does Quilian have a plant and soil wielder with him?"

"Yes Two plant wielders as well as a fire wielder."

Pushing her magic, she picks out the second plant wielder in the group. The faint sense of smoke joins them.

"They're approaching," Nestraya says. "Quickly, but not at a pace to indicate danger."

Corivos nods.

"Let's keep going. This way." She tugs Lorial slightly more northward, and the others follow.

Keeping tabs on Quilian's band, she scans the rest of the woods with her magic. A buzzing of sorts teases the edges of her senses, but it's too far off to identify. The advancing Outerlander warriors, perhaps?

Quilian's water magic grows stronger as their paths draw closer, and eventually, she picks up faint threads of his life magic scouting the woods just as she's doing. It seems almost hesitant, as if he's searching for something in particular. Either her or Lorial, probably.

Soon, Quilian steps out of the trees ahead, the lights from their lanterns illuminating his face. His eyes dart around, but before Nestraya can assure him Lorial is fine, Lorial speaks up.

"I'm here, Second Quilian. Cloaked to hide my magic, which I'm told is overwhelming."

A look of relief crosses Quilian's face. "It is…loud at times, my king."

Nestraya almost laughs at his understatement. "What can you report?"

"The Outerlanders approach as our scouts indicated—approximately five miles to the north. And it's not just the warrior bands. Judging by the numbers, it's nearly every able-bodied Outerlander."

"All of them?" Nestraya asks. "I don't even remember the last time the warrior bands from the Outerlands marched this far south, let alone all of them."

"I can only speculate, my queen, but if Hothniel summoned them in our king Restoval's name, every available elf would have answered his call."

"How many?" Lorial asks.

"My guess is two hundred. Perhaps three."

Against Hothniel's warrior bands? Will it be enough? With Lorial wielding his combined air and fire magic, it might be. It will have to be.

Hopefully, there are more loyal elves among Hothniel's numbers than stayed behind yesterday. *Was that only yesterday?*

"The Outerlanders are fierce, my queen," Quilian says as if reading her thoughts. "They have to be."

She sighs. "I have no doubt. Lead the way to intercept them, Second."

With a nod, Quilian turns in the direction his band of warriors came from, toward the buzzing that tickles the edges of Nestraya's life magic. It must be the magic of the Outerlanders she senses.

The kin of her birth.

Lorial squeezes her hand, and she steels herself.

"Move out!" she calls, and they continue their trek through the Wildthorne Woods.

The closer they get, the louder the buzzing feels. Individual affinities stand out to Nestraya. A lot of water magic and, surprisingly, or maybe not since they're cave dwellers, stone magic.

"I thought stone magic was rare," Nestraya says to Quilian.

"It is rare everywhere but in the Outerlands, my queen. I think such knowledge irks Hothniel. He likes to pretend he's special."

"I'm sure he does," Nestraya mutters.

The other surprising thing is how strong some of the Outerlanders' magic is. No wonder certain high borns feel so threatened by them.

Perhaps not as surprising is the noise. Long before the elite band catches their first glimpse of the Outerlanders, Nestraya hears them.

"Those are the loudest elves I've ever heard," Lorial whispers to her.

"They aren't forest dwellers."

"No. I suppose not. We won't be sneaking up on Hothniel, though."

"We don't need to. He believes the Outerlanders will fight for him. Die for him. All he has to do is tell them humans killed not one but two of their Westarian kings, and they'll rally to his cause. He won't be wary of them."

"Right. This is why you're First, and I'm just following your orders. I'm still not a warrior, despite my new training."

"Keep your head when it's time to prove yourself, and I'll be satisfied."

"Do you mean that figuratively...or literally?"

Nestraya resists the urge to smile as she carefully avoids a stick in her path. "Both."

"Understood. A clear head that's still connected to my body."

"Precisely." She lifts her hand again to halt their troops. "Corivos, you remain here. Quilian and I will continue alone."

"And me," Lorial says firmly.

"I suppose we need you. Just don't get yourself killed."

"I see the rest of my life playing out before me with my queen constantly reminding me I once did a stupid thing and almost died."

"Yes."

"That's it? Yes?"

She shrugs and turns toward him, though, of course, she can't see him. She doesn't dare have him reveal himself now, though. Every strong life wielder nearby would sense him within seconds.

"I need you to be serious now, my love. People will live or die based on our actions this night."

"I know. I am."

"You are their king, Lorial. The Phoenix King. They will look to you for guidance. For strength."

His invisible fingers cup her face. "And to you, my love." Then, without warning, he kisses her. With their entire warrior band watching. Well, watching her, at least.

Toward him. Run toward him.

"I'm Queen Nestraya," she whispers against his lips. "And I am not ashamed."

"And you, my love, are unequivocally mine." Then he kisses her again, and she closes her eyes and clings to him. When he pulls away, he whispers in her ear, "Now, my queen, let's go change the world."

40

THE OUTERLANDERS

Nestraya tightens her grasp on Lorial's hand as they draw closer to the Outerlanders. The buzzing is deafening now, and the elves themselves aren't much quieter.

She pushes against the overwhelming magic of their numbers to make out a few approaching individuals. Do they sense her magic? Did they send a small band to investigate?

"We're not alone," Nestraya whispers. She can feel their presence as she searches the woods for some sign of them.

Then, like lightning, a small band of elves surrounds them—warriors, judging by the newcomers' defensive stances.

Instead of leathers, they wear shaggy furs, their hair completely captured in braids. At least it looked that way from the brief glimpse Nestraya managed before Lorial uncloaked and wrapped himself around her.

"I thought I told you to keep your head," she whispers.

"I'm protecting you."

"I'm your First. I protect you."

"An air wielder," one of the Outerlanders says. Nestraya sensed the man's life magic before Lorial's air magic blunted everything.

"And the woman? Is this our—"

"Yes," Quilian says.

Nestraya pushes Lorial away as hushed whispers rise at Quilian's words.

One man steps forward. "Quilian? Is it really you?"

"It's good to see you, Deridyn."

The two men embrace like old friends, and all the other elves drop their defensive stances and regard Lorial with something akin to awe.

"And does she know?" Deridyn asks Quilian.

"She does now."

After releasing Quilian, Deridyn drops to one knee before Nestraya, and the other elves soon follow. "My princess."

Whistling wind. They weren't looking at Lorial. They were looking at her.

"Princess?" she says with as much strength as she can muster.

"Are you not the *estrassa* of our king Restoval? His daughter by choice?" Deridyn asks.

"Yes," Lorial says before Nestraya can form a response.

The Outerlanders consider her a princess?

"Our king honors us by sending you and his son to greet us."

She exchanges a glance with Lorial. It was as they suspected. The Outerlanders don't know Pera is dead.

Lorial opens his mouth, but Nestraya lays a hand on his arm to stop him.

These are her people. She should tell them. Taking a breath, she reaches deep within. She is who she is.

She's Nestraya Thariosi Westaria—a daughter of two worlds.

And she is not ashamed.

"My kin," she says softly. "I bear tidings that will fill your hearts with dismay. Our king Restoval, my...father, has passed from the light. He has taken his place in the Tree of Memories."

Gasps arise, followed by a growl from Deridyn. "Our king has fallen? Who has done this, my princess?"

"Hothniel," she says. "My father's elite warrior betrayed him. He betrays us all."

"Hothniel." Deridyn, along with the other warriors, spits on the dirt at their feet. "Who sits on the throne at Starhaven now? This Hothniel?"

"I fear that is his goal," Nestraya says. "Right now, he provokes war with the humans, sending low-born elves to be slaughtered by human weapons. We must stop this. Retake the throne of Lostariel and avenge the deaths of my fathers, Restoval and Cerian, and every low-born elf that has died at Hothniel's hand. I'm asking you to fight with us, to take back what's ours."

"Our magic and our essences are yours to command, my princess." Deridyn lifts his head to look at Lorial. "Does the sacred tree honor your right to take on your father's mantle, my prince?"

"It does," Lorial says.

"And are you of the same mind as our king Restoval and our princess Nestraya? Will you be a king to us all?"

Lorial clears his throat. "Let this be my answer, and judge me as you will. I have flouted the unwritten laws of our forebears and made your princess my queen." Lorial wraps his arm around Nestraya and draws her to his side. She doesn't resist.

Deridyn staggers. "Is this true, my...queen? A Westarian king has openly binded with an Outerlander?"

"It is," Quilian says. "Not just a binding. A heartbinding. Their hearts beat as one."

That garners a few more whispers.

"An Outerlander queen?" Deridyn shakes his head in disbelief. "My heart quakes at such a thing."

"Someday, a descendant of Cerian Thariosi will sit on the throne of Lostariel," Nestraya says. "But for that to happen, we must defeat Hothniel."

She pauses to gather her thoughts. She can do this. She is who she is.

"As the Outerlander Queen of Lostariel," she continues, "and the king's First among warriors, I am asking you to fight at my binding partner's side. To trust him as I trust him. When we swore our hearts to each other, we became one. By the power of the heartbinding, Lorial Westaria has become an elf of the House Thariosi."

Solemn, Deridyn straightens and steps toward Lorial. "Quilian, as the head of the House Thariosi, do you accept the essence of Lorial of the House Westaria into your clan?"

"I do."

"Then today we are kin, Lorial of the Houses Thariosi and Westaria. We vow our magic and our essences to your cause and your protection."

Nestraya breathes out in relief. That was easier than she feared it would be.

Then, to her surprise, Lorial lowers himself to his knees before Deridyn and Quilian and the other Outerlanders. "May I bring honor to the House Thariosi and to all Outerlanders."

Deridyn swallows back his own surprise, but not before Nestraya glimpses it written in his eyes as he speaks. "May it be so."

"May it be so," Nestraya echoes with the other elves.

"Rise, young Lorial of Lostariel," Deridyn says. "The Outerlanders stand with you."

As Lorial finds his feet again, one of the elves hands Deridyn a knife, and Nestraya's stomach tightens. *What's that for?*

"For our king Restoval!" Deridyn fists his hand around his warrior braids, and with a swift slash of the knife, he slices them off just past his shoulders.

Without hesitating, the other elves copy their leader, each one laying their shorn braids at Lorial and Nestraya's feet.

Lorial fumbles for her hand, clearly trying to be strong, and she squeezes it tightly. "The time to mourn will come," he says in a stronger voice than she suspected him capable of at the moment. "Tonight, we march!"

"Take us to the rest of our people," Nestraya says.

"Yes, my queen. My king." Deridyn bows his head and then turns toward the buzzing that's been softened by Lorial's air magic.

"You were magnificent," Lorial whispers near her ear as they follow Deridyn through the dark woods.

"I was terrified."

"So was I." He squeezes her hand. "Stronger together, my love."

"Yes. Stronger together."

Soon, lantern light dots the woods ahead as dozens of elves in furs come into view. Men and women of all ages with not only their eyes painted for battle but their entire faces. Streaks of korathite in various patterns. She hadn't noticed the battle paint on Deridyn and his warriors in the shadows of the woods. It's impossible to miss now with the dozens of lanterns casting flickering yellow light on the dark forest.

"Quilian," she whispers, "the face paint—what does it signify?"

"The elves' Houses. Each House has its own pattern."

She hands him the vial of korathite from her pocket. "Paint Lorial with the markings for the House Thariosi."

Quilian quickly does her bidding as Deridyn approaches the other Outerlanders.

"Now you, my queen," Quilian says. As he finishes with her, a line of elves approach them.

A young elf, not much older than her and Lorial, stops before them. "For our king Restoval." Then he slices off his warrior braids and drops them at Lorial's feet.

One by one, men and women, young and old, follow his lead.

The Outerlanders, for all their noise, know how to spread word quietly and quickly, it seems.

"Are you really our queen now?" a young woman asks Nestraya as she lays her braids at Nestraya's feet.

Nestraya glances at Lorial, but he's focused on the elf in front of him, and she turns back to the woman, who's little more than an elfling. "I am. My heart belongs to the King of Lostariel."

"And he chose you?"

"He did." Lorial joins their conversation. "For this Lostarien king, there could never be anyone but Nestraya Thariosi Westaria." Then he kisses her as if to prove his point.

It's a short, chaste kiss, and when he pulls away, Deridyn stands nearby, studying them with Quilian at his side. "I'm told your binding ceremony was today, my king and queen. In the Outerlands, we have a tradition after the couple emerges from the joining."

"And what is that, my Second?" Lorial asks, and Deridyn shakes his head.

"I am an Outerlander, my king. Low born. A Third."

"I ask again, my Second Deridyn—of what tradition do you speak?"

A rousing cheer rises around them, and Lorial drapes his arm over Nestraya's shoulders as Deridyn raises his hands in acknowledgment. "An honor, my king. Thank you."

"Well deserved, I have no doubt," Nestraya says.

Another round of whoops and hollers sounds, and Deridyn waits for the cheers to die down. "You honor me, as well, my queen."

"What of this tradition?" Lorial asks again.

He's sure determined.

"After the binding ceremony and the joining—" Deridyn is interrupted by yet another round of cheers, and Nestraya wills her cheeks not to flame. Especially when Lorial pumps his fist in the air.

Whistling wind. Can they get to the fighting and reclaiming a throne part yet?

Hopefully, no one asks about the joining, which, strictly speaking...hasn't happened yet.

"After the joining, the people need to see a kiss," Deridyn says over the cries of his people. Their people.

"Isn't that what we just did?" Nestraya asks.

Deridyn shakes his head, and the people boo. It's such an odd thing to be discussing with the mound of braids lying before them, but this scene seems to be improving morale.

And as First, keeping up morale is one of Nestraya's concerns.

Besides, Lorial's clearly bonding with the Outerlanders, however mortifying this whole ordeal might be.

"Show us you love each other!" someone shouts.

Whistling wind.

She glances at Quilian, and he shrugs in acknowledgment.

"Before we do this, I need all my water wielders at the ready," Lorial says. "My fire magic gets antsy when my queen is in my arms."

And...there's another round of cheers. Which Lorial joins.

"You are enjoying this far too much," Nestraya whispers as he slips his hands around her waist.

"Maybe. Weren't you the one who said our people need to know how much we love each other?"

"It's possible I said such a thing." She slides her hands along his leathers and behind his neck.

"Then let's show them."

That boyish grin of his makes her stomach flip. And then he claims her lips in a salty kiss full of sparks that could leave little doubt in anyone's mind that the King of Lostariel is extremely fond of his low-born queen. Hoots and hollers surround them as Lorial's hands heat her flesh through her leathers.

When he pulls away, he rests his forehead against hers. "I think I could live forever on the sweet taste of your life magic, Nestraya," he whispers.

She gently traces her fingers along his jaw. "Don't tell them we haven't completed the joining, or I will kill you, my love." She speaks quietly so only he can hear, and he leans his head back and laughs.

But, to her relief, he keeps that bit of information to himself.

41

THE HOPE OF LOSTARIEL

Lorial does his best to follow the swift conversation of his First and Seconds as they discuss their battle plans while their warriors rest. It's all warrior-speak, though, and his mind keeps drifting to what's expected of him.

Of course, neither he nor Nestraya could elaborate on Lorial's...talents.

If he can even manage any of it in the real world. Just because he mastered the wind in the heartlanding doesn't mean he can do it here.

"Will you excuse us? I need a private word with our king," Nestraya says, and Lorial looks up in surprise.

"Of course, my queen," Corivos says, and as the others file back toward the makeshift camp, Nestraya grabs Corivos's leathers at his chest.

"If you do not rest, I will douse you. And then demote you. And douse you again."

Lorial struggles not to grin as the corner of Corivos's mouth ticks up. "Understood, my queen."

"I mean it. You'll be useless to us if you're too exhausted to think straight."

He nods, and she lets him go. Once he's out of sight, Lorial reaches for the edges of Nestraya's skirt where it splits high over her perfect legs and tugs her closer. "What do you want to talk about?"

She looks up at him with that same expression she used in the heartlanding right before she flung him from the platform, and he stiffens.

"I don't like that look."

"Noted. Show me your magic."

"The kind that wraps around you and makes you go weak at the knees?"

She lifts her brows in an unamused expression, and he shrugs.

That's what he figured.

"You're doubting yourself, Lorial. If the moment comes, and these doubts get the best of you, all of this will be for naught. People could die. I need you ready to fight. I need to know you believe you can do this."

"What if I can't do this? What if all of it—everything we did in the heartlanding—was just a product of our imaginations with no bearing on this world?"

"Let's find out. Show me your magic, warrior."

"You want me to fly? Here?"

She sets her hand on his chest and looks up into his eyes. "I want a great many things from you, Lorial of Lostariel. For now, flying will suffice. You can do this, my love. You just need to prove it to yourself."

He takes a deep breath and breathes out slowly before letting her go and putting a few feet between them. Shaking his limbs to loosen up, he reaches for his air magic. It answers, restless and eager. Familiar, as in the heartlanding.

Then with a thought, he lifts from the ground as air currents hold him aloft. It feels like it did in the heartlanding.

A vine slithers from the dark and wraps around his wrist, but he makes quick work of it with a spark of his fire magic.

"Well done, my love. How do you feel?" Nestraya calls to him.

How does he feel?

He leans into his magic, letting it flow through him. "I feel...like myself. Free."

"Good. Are you ready to become the Phoenix King?"

He gently lowers himself to the ground. "I don't know if I am or not. I'm ready to be your king, though."

She takes a step toward him, and his fire magic stirs at the light in her eyes. Another step. Then another. When she's close enough to touch, she rests her hands on his chest and slowly slides them behind his neck. "I think you're ready."

"I'm ready for a great many things, Nestraya of Lostariel. All of which involve you."

"Mmm. How about a kiss?"

He slips his hands to her lower back and pulls her close. "That's a good start."

"You won't catch the forest on fire, will you?"

He grins. "I make no promises. It's a good thing I'm bound to a water wielder."

"Hmm. Yes. How convenient." Then her lips find his with a passion that surprises him.

When her hands slip beneath his leather jacket, his fire magic takes on a mind of its own. His palms tingle, and he lets go of her to cool them with his air magic.

Then she takes his hands in hers, and the tingling abates.

"I...got carried away," she whispers. "Forgive me."

He leans his forehead against hers and slowly breathes out. "Normally, I wouldn't mind, but right now—"

"I know." She kisses him more softly this time before wrapping her arms around him and resting her head against his shoulder. He clings to her, and for a while, they just stand together, waiting for the morning.

For the battle to come.

"I'm sure Hothniel has spies in these woods," Nestraya says to Lorial as their group breaks camp in the shadowy twilight of dawn. "I want you to cloak yourself. Let him think you're dead until the last minute."

Lorial nods.

"And don't do anything heroic until I tell you to," she adds.

"I make no promises, my love."

"If you get shot again, I'm planning to let you die." She manages a straight face, but the gleam in her eyes gives her away.

Ignoring the bustle around them, he tugs her close. "You remember our hearts are connected, right?"

"Minor technicality."

"Uh-huh."

"We're ready to move out on your order," Corivos says. A hint of a smile ghosts across his face.

Nestraya's flirtatious expression morphs into her warrior mien as she pulls away. "And you rested, Corivos?"

"I did. Briefly."

She eyes him skeptically but nods. "Give the order to move out. Lorial is going to cloak himself until the last minute, so alert our other Seconds not to be alarmed at his disappearance."

Corivos hurries to convey their orders, and at a touch on Lorial's shoulder, Lorial turns to find Mother looking at them.

"I'm proud of both of you." She draws him and Nestraya close. "Your father would be proud as well."

"I hope so," Nestraya murmurs, and Mother pulls back to look into Nestraya's eyes.

"I know so. Now, you both will argue with me, but I plan to join you."

Lorial opens his mouth to protest, but she shushes them both.

"I am neither helpless nor old, despite being your mother. I will march, and I will fight until we either defeat the man who stole my love from me or I die trying."

Lorial opens his mouth again, but Mother eyes him so sternly that he swallows his protests.

Woe to any warrior she meets on the battlefield.

"If you insist on joining us, I want you in the garb of the Outerlanders," Nestraya says. "You will be less of a target. As First, I command the warrior bands, and my word is law on the battlefield."

Mother's mouth twitches in a faint smile, but she inclines her head. "Very well, First Nestraya."

Nestraya calls a few of the Outerlander women to assist Mother, and soon, they stand ready to move out.

"You should say something inspirational," Nestraya whispers to Lorial.

"Me? Why not you? They'd rather hear from their queen than lowly Lorial."

"Lowly Lorial? Really?" She rolls her eyes. "Fine. Lift me so they can see me."

"With my arms or my magic?"

She thinks for a moment. "Your arms. Let's save your big reveal for the battlefield. Just boost me up onto your shoulders. And try not to set anything on fire."

With a grin, he dips to his knees, and she straddles him as he grasps one of her legs with each hand. Then he pushes himself to his feet as she sits on his shoulders. She takes a moment to gather her thoughts, but soon, she speaks.

"Warriors of Lostariel!" Nestraya calls out, and the surrounding conversation dies down as everyone turns toward her. "You came for Restoval. You honor his memory with your loyalty. He was stolen from us. Taken before his time. But together, your new king and queen represent everything that mattered most to him. Kin. Family. The one you're born with or the one you choose—he didn't care. His heart was big. His love strong. He would have made a good Outerlander."

Several cheers ring out at that, and Lorial's heart swells at the words flowing from Nestraya's lips.

"My king Lorial and I are a picture of the future we want for Lostariel—a future where birth doesn't matter. Where elves are elves. Where fear doesn't rule the day. Where an Outerlander can bind with an elf king, and where an elf king can save the heart of someone who thought...who thought—"

Lorial squeezes her legs when her words falter, and she takes a deep breath before continuing.

"Where a king can save the heart of a woman so darkened by the lies—by the venom—of those who believe that the only way to elevate themselves is to tear us down. We are all elves. We are all worthy. We are Outerlanders! And we fight for our place in this world. In this kingdom.

We fight for Restoval! For the man who said enough is enough. Who said this one—this elfling you all fear simply because she's not one of you—this one is mine. May our actions tonight honor the man who gave his life to give me a voice. Who gave his life to change Lostariel for all of us!"

Lorial's breath catches, and his heart trips over itself as a deafening roar rises around them.

Mother wipes away a tear, and Lorial swings Nestraya off his shoulders and into his arms.

"You've slain your demons, my love," he whispers as he clutches her to his chest. "You are who you are. And you are just what Father always knew you could be. The hope of Lostariel."

"Together. Together, we are what Pera envisioned. And together, we will reclaim your throne and send Hothniel where he belongs."

42

A FORMIDABLE FORCE

As planned, Nestraya marches in the middle of the warrior bands. Hopefully, their numbers will blunt the detection of her magic. Lorial attempted to cloak her as well, but he needs more practice to pull it off, and they don't have time for that right now.

Besides, their warriors need to see at least one of them marching at their sides.

The longer Hothniel believes the Outerlanders answer to him, the easier this will be, though.

The sun dances in the growing daylight as they make their way south. Nestraya keeps her life magic attuned for signs of newcomers, but so far, none have approached that she's sensed over the warriors surrounding them. No runners have reported to her, either.

Deridyn and Quilian lead their bands while Corivos and the other Seconds stay farther back, where they're less likely to be noticed. Corivos, especially.

When the elves ahead of them slow, Nestraya cranes her neck to see what's going on, to no avail. If only she wasn't so easily detected, she'd be closer to the front lines and not back here waiting for Quilian and Deridyn to report.

"My queen." An elf woman approaches and lowers her head before Nestraya. "Second Deridyn wishes me to tell you we've encountered Hothniel's scouts, and so far, everything goes according to plan."

"Understood."

Lorial's invisible hand tightens around Nestraya's, and she breathes out slowly.

This is it.

Soon, the bands press forward again. The sense of humans in the distance fills Nestraya moments before the sound of musket fire reaches her ears, and her stomach churns.

The fighting with the humans has resumed.

She tugs Lorial's arm closer. "Don't even think about—"

"I'm not. I have a sore shoulder to remind me to listen to you. Perhaps you could refrain from yanking on it, my love."

She stills. "It hurts? You should have said something. Perhaps Healer Cadowyn—"

"Perhaps later. It's a dull ache. We have more important things to worry about right now."

He's right.

Reluctantly, she pushes her concern to the back of her mind, and they move forward again.

As they near the battlefield, the acrid odor of gunpowder mixes with the musty scent of the forest and the coppery sweet smell of blood. It's enough to turn Nestraya's stomach and unfurl her anger.

"File in!" A voice calls over the weary cries of fighting elf warriors and humans as musket fire echoes around them.

It's Hothniel's own third, relaying Hothniel's orders, no doubt.

"There. Behind that giant cedar," Lorial says, and Nestraya stretches to spot Hothniel giving orders from the safety of the trees with a wall of high borns around him.

Far from the musket fire.

"These murderous humans killed your king Restoval, and yesterday, they murdered Restoval's son in cold blood!" Hothniel himself cries, though his words are hard to make out over the noise. "We cannot rest until we've sent these humans a message! Avenge our kings!"

"Avenge, indeed," Nestraya mutters as she pushes down her eager plant magic. It would be so easy to wrap a vine around the man's neck.

But that would sow chaos and give them away, and her efforts would surely be stymied before she ended the man.

He'll receive his dues soon enough.

To their credit, the Outerlanders act appropriately dismayed at Hothniel's news. And despite his words of solidarity against a common enemy, Hothniel sneers as the Outerlanders pass. No doubt he can sense their stone wielders.

Poor man. Not as special as he pretends to be.

"Cry me a river," she mutters, "so I may drown you in it."

"What?" Lorial whispers.

"Nothing. Are you ready for this?"

"You seem to think I am."

She nods, on high alert as they march forward, soon angling between the high borns and the other low-born warriors.

Hothniel has no idea he just willingly cut himself off from the bulk of his army. Nestraya's lips curl at the thought.

The musket fire slows at the appearance of reinforcements. The humans are the wildcard in this equation. Hopefully, they'll see the value in licking their wounds for a time while Nestraya sorts out who the elf and human renegades are that goad both sides to war.

She has little doubt who they're working for.

"Everyone, follow your orders," Nestraya says quietly to the surrounding elves, and her words spread like ripples through the Outerlander lines.

The efficiency with which they communicate is astounding.

"Now," she whispers to Lorial, and he lobs a fireball high into the air.

On cue, half of the Outerlanders turn as one to face Hothniel while the other half hold steady behind the low-born ranks facing the humans, who seem unsure what to do.

"What are they doing?" Hothniel hisses.

"You can do this," Nestraya whispers to Lorial.

A moment later, Lorial drops his cloak, and his air magic fills Nestraya's senses—that comforting ocean breeze that makes her heart beat just a little faster.

Hothniel's eyes swing toward Lorial and Nestraya, and the disbelief on his face is priceless.

"You were saying, Hothniel?" Lorial calls out.

"My king. You live."

"I do. Tell your warriors to stand down. We wish to negotiate a ceasefire with the humans."

"I believe you tried that yesterday. They shot you."

"I brought my own warriors with me this time," Lorial calls out. "You will find them a formidable force to be reckoned with. I offer amnesty to any elf who wishes to return to the command of my First Nestraya!"

Most of the high borns scoff in amusement, as Nestraya assumed they would.

"How about this offer," Hothniel returns. "Bring me the weak elfling posturing as king and his fae-slops pet, and you will be greatly rewarded!"

No one among the Outerlanders moves.

"You understand little about us, Hothniel!" Nestraya cries. "Outerlanders never betray their own—a loyalty you know nothing about!"

Hothniel ignores her completely. "Your so-called king is weak! He plays at games he doesn't understand, getting himself shot in his idiocy. Is that the king you would follow?"

"You earned that," Nestraya mutters.

"I haven't forgotten."

Nestraya eyes the human ranks. It seems Prince Gerault has called a temporary ceasefire while his troops observe the scene unfolding before them.

Perhaps she misjudged him and he's not any more eager to prove himself on the battlefield than Lorial is.

She surveys the warriors around them. The low-born elves look broken. Weary. And far fewer in number than they should be.

"Lift me," she whispers.

"And make you a target? Not on your life."

He's probably right. With a huff, she cups her hands around her mouth as she faces the low-born warriors. "You don't have to do this! March into musket fire as if you don't have a choice? You have a choice. Your king is giving you one! Take it! Please! End this slaughter! You see what Hothniel is doing, don't you? He's murdering the strongest among the low borns because he's afraid of you. Of us. Like Polanis, he sacrifices you to make himself strong. Why would you choose that? Why—"

A musket shot rings out, but...it's not coming from the human side. The human prince cries something, but Nestraya can't understand his words. She needs to work on her Nunian.

"He said, 'Don't shoot,'" Lorial translates for her, but it's too late as magic and muskets resume their dirge of death and destruction.

"Time for the next plan," Nestraya hisses.

Which was really the only plan. It would never have been that easy.

Lorial's eyes turn solemn as he exhales slowly.

And then the air begins to move.

43

FOR RESTOVAL

Tendrils of Lorial's magic flow through him, seeping from him like extensions of himself. Air currents shoot out like nerves, sensing the landscape. The people.

But it's not the people he's searching for. It's the wind itself.

Up, he pushes with his magic. Along the trunks of trees. Over branches. Along leaves and needles to the morning sky above, blue as the eyes of the Lothlesi people who live under the mountains.

Closing his own eyes, he calls to the sky. The wind. And it answers, drawing toward him as he infuses the air with heat from his fire magic.

"Ready?" Nestraya asks.

"Don't overexert yourself," he says between gritted teeth.

Without responding, she pours water vapor into his air currents, replenishing her store with water from the canteens and waterskins the elves around them hand her.

The sky darkens, and the fighting slows.

Then a deafening crack rends the air as the clear autumn day retreats in a cloud of thunder.

"I knew you could do it," Nestraya murmurs.

"What is this magic?" one of the humans cries in Nunian as the musket fire slows.

"Retreat!" the human prince yells.

Lorial opens his eyes and stares at Hothniel, who has the decency to look shocked at this turn of events.

"I am Lorial, King of Lostariel! And you will answer for your crimes, Hothniel!"

Most of the high borns have dropped back slightly.

"Hold your ground!" Hothniel cries. "He hides behind his magic and his fae-slops pet among his sea of elven shields. Is this the man you want leading you?"

The hypocrisy is galling.

"I hide behind no one!" With a shift of his magic, he lifts himself into the air.

Whispers erupt around them, and Nestraya hisses his name and something about a musket, but Lorial doesn't take his eyes off Hothniel.

Hothniel's lip curls. "Take him down!"

A shot rings out, and Lorial's magic falters.

The musket was from the elf side?

"Lorial!" Nestraya screams.

But the shot doesn't hit him.

It hits the barrier of air and fire magic he shoved in front of himself when he rose into the air.

Then it falls harmlessly to the ground.

Wide eyes stare at him from every side.

"Again, I offer you amnesty!" Lorial calls out. "Lay down your bows and quiet your magic. As you can see, your king is not weak! And neither is your queen!"

Mustering even more magic, he lifts Nestraya to his side.

"Speak, my love. Win over the low borns," he whispers over his shoulder, where she hovers behind him, their backs together.

The shock and disgust on the high borns' faces burn at Lorial, but he refrains from letting loose on them with his fire magic.

For now.

"My people!" Nestraya cries. "A new Lostariel hovers on the horizon. My father, may he find rest, believed in it. This future is for all of us, from the lowest born on the streets of Celesta to the highest born in Starhaven! And I straddle both worlds as I stand at my binding partner's back, ready to help him usher in a new era. One where your elflings will not be sent to their deaths by a king-killing monster like Hothniel! In our Lostariel, there is room for all."

Lorial glances back at the low-born elves, who eye Nestraya uncertainly, as if they're afraid to hope her words might be true.

The high borns, on the other hand, wear looks of appalled derision. Several of them have already slunk away to lick their wounds.

They'll have to be rooted out and dealt with, but Nestraya's goal today was to slice off the cobra's head.

"We fight for our king!" someone yells from behind Lorial. "We fight for our queen!"

"Take him down!" Hothniel cries with the hoarseness of desperation.

A few high borns muster their magic, but the Outerlanders don't give them a chance as all manner of magic flies from their ranks.

Stones. Lots of stones.

Lorial flinches at the sight.

"Hold steady, my love," Nestraya whispers behind him.

Hothniel makes no effort to deflect the rocks from anyone but himself.

Without warning, a hooded figure in furs steps forward from among the Outerlander ranks.

"Nestraya," Lorial hisses, and he swings her around to face the high borns, or what's left of them.

"Someone's gone rogue," she says.

"Should I intervene?"

Before he can do anything, the Outerlander lifts her hands, and a lobby of fireballs launches at Hothniel, latching onto his long hair and licking at the length. A cry of agony parts his lips as he yells for a water wielder and frantically attempts to smother the flames. No one answers his call.

Then the elf throws back her hood. "That is for Restoval!"

Mother?

Nestraya flails against Lorial's magic. "Mera! Lorial, put me down!"

Lorial lowers them both to the ground, and Nestraya takes off before he can catch up to her.

Mother lights another volley as a boulder crashes toward her, and Lorial lets go of everything else and pushes with his air currents to stop the rock from hitting her. Without warning, it thuds to the ground at Mother's feet as if the magic just stopped.

Relief fills Lorial as he staggers and drops his own magic. She's fine. She's all right.

But where's Nestraya?

He searches the battlefield as he pushes through the ranks of Outerlanders. There she is. Her eyes glow green with the intensity of her anger and her magic as she twists vines around Hothniel's arms and legs, his torso and his scorched neck.

"This is for taking my pera from me, not once but twice, you sick sack of—" Her voice is drowned out by Hothniel's shrieking and the cracking of his bones as her vines tighten. "May you never know rest, you bastard!"

Her vines yank his head, snapping his neck, and he goes limp, his head lolling unnaturally to the side as a vacant expression fills his face.

Pushing past the bile rising in his throat, Lorial rushes toward Nestraya, pulling her back as the few high borns who haven't fled or been stoned to death beg for mercy.

"It's over. It's over, my love," Lorial says as she hangs against him.

She's weak, but which magic did she drain?

"Are you hungry or thirsty? Hungry or thirsty, Nestraya?"

She shakes her head.

And then he sees it. Lodged in her side, just below her ribs...is a blade made of stone.

"Cadowyn!" Lorial cries hoarsely as his voice attempts to betray him. Gingerly, he lowers Nestraya to the ground. "Cadowyn!"

Nestraya looks up at him with a pained expression. "I'm the one who did something stupid this time." Scarlet stains her lower lip, and the image of Father dying in his arms flashes across his eyes.

"No, no, no. You hold on. I can't live without you, remember?"

"I'm trying," she says around the blood filling her mouth.

Cadowyn drops to the ground beside them. "I'm here. What—" His lips press into a thin line.

Her heart grows weak. Lorial can feel it.

"Do something!" he cries.

Cadowyn sets to work as Lorial murmurs every plea to the fates and the essences of his forebears that he can think of.

Mother hovers beside him, too, though when she reached them, Lorial couldn't say.

A moment later, Rafelis is there. "How can I help?"

"Lead him in the words of the heartbinding," Cadowyn says. "An infusion of his magic might strengthen her enough to give me time to heal her."

Rafelis begins to speak, but Lorial cuts him off, murmuring the words etched on his heart as Rafelis pours his life magic between them to once again seal the heartbinding.

"My soul is a well unto yours. May you find refreshment in me. My light will fill your darkness, and when my light wanes, yours will guide me. My heart to yours. Your soul to mine. Our bodies as one until the beating of our hearts fades."

He takes a deep breath and exhales slowly as tears flow unchecked down his face. Mustering his strength, he pushes through the final words.

"From this moment on, our two hearts beat as one. I bind myself to you until my end of days."

Then everything goes dark once more.

44

HOW THE STORY GOES

Nestraya gasps as she opens her eyes to the starry night sky.

The heartlanding?

Without warning, Lorial pulls her to his bare chest, squeezing the air from her lungs. "You are not allowed to die. Do you hear me? You're mine." He rocks back and forth with her clutched in his arms as she tries to get her bearings.

Hothniel. He stabbed her with a stone dagger right before she killed him. With her anger clouding her senses, she didn't see it coming until it was too late.

"I'm sorry," she says.

Lorial holds her away from him as he grips her bare shoulders above the same leather bodice she wore the first time they arrived here. "No, Nestraya. No! You will live."

Will she? Will they?

"How did we get here?" she asks softly.

"Rafelis helped me rework the magic of the heartbinding. Healer Cadowyn said it might give him time to heal you."

She reads the anguish in his eyes, the wetness welling up there.

"Might?" she whispers.

He pulls her to his chest again, and she crawls into his lap and wraps her arms around him.

For a while, they sit there together while Lorial chokes on sobs and shuddering breaths.

What can she say? What can she do?

Eventually, his weeping slows and stops, and she rests her forehead against his. "I'm sorry," she whispers. "I just—"

"I know. I know. You were brave and strong. You slayed the demon."

Nestraya blinks, and a single tear slips down her cheek. "I've never been as strong as I am with you, my love."

"And I've never felt free as I do with you."

Gently, she smooths back long silver tendrils of his hair, gazing into his beautiful gray eyes. How they shone when he mastered the storm. He became everything she knew he could be.

She's seen him. Lorial, the man. Her *estrasse*. Her love. Heard his words of encouragement and healing. Smelled him at his best and his worst and everything in between. Tasted the saltiness of his kisses. The sparks as he pressed his lips to hers.

There's only one thing left to experience.

His touch.

If these are their last moments together...

With a tenderness reserved only for him, she finds his lips, and his breath catches.

"I wish for a bed," she whispers against him. "And a gentle, misty rain."

The heartlanding is quick to grant her requests, and Lorial pulls away to gaze into her eyes.

"I want to get carried away with you, my love," she whispers. "Please?"

Swallowing, he nods, grazing her lips as the misty dampness settles around them.

Soft, easy kisses of affection and devotion pass between them, and Nestraya wraps her arms around his neck once more. Then he lifts her and gently lays her on the bed before crawling up beside her and finding her lips again.

The urgency of their situation hovers over them like a dark cloud, but he doesn't rush, and neither does she. Every kiss. Every touch.

Slow. Tender. Full of all the days and years they were supposed to have together. Too precious to hurry.

The drizzle dampens his fire magic, but not his heat as warmth radiates from him, his hands on her skin chasing away the chill. His lips leave warmth in their wake as he trails kisses across her body, his humid breath caressing her flesh.

Lost in a world that includes only the two of them, all Nestraya's thoughts of the real world drift away on the wind.

It was always him. How could it ever have been anyone else?

"Nestraya," he murmurs. "My Nestraya."

"Let's get carried away, my love. I want to be yours in every way."

He groans at her words, heat threading through every part of him that presses against her, keeping them both warm as she clings to him.

And it's awkward and beautiful and glorious in its perfect imperfection. This lover's dance they should have had centuries to master together.

But it doesn't matter. Nothing else matters but his touch. His love. His passion. This slow-burning fire that fills her and builds within her as she abandons all the fears, all the walls keeping them apart. Letting go of everything but the sensation of his touch.

Safe in his arms. His heat. His love.

His.

Nestraya wakes under a mound of blankets cocooning her and Lorial as his lingering heat warms them both. It's morning again in the heartlanding. The drizzle stopped after their passion was spent last night. Lorial must have requested the blankets when she fell into a blissful sleep tangled up with him.

A bird trills nearby, and Nestraya nestles closer to Lorial. To his warmth.

When he wraps his arm around her, she sighs contentedly. If only this moment could last forever.

"Are you warm enough?" he asks, his voice thick with sleep.

"As long as I stay close to you."

He wraps his other arm around her beneath the blankets. "We're still here. That must be a good sign."

"Time is different here," she murmurs, though it probably doesn't matter if he gets his hopes up. They'll either wake or they'll sleep the eternal sleep, and if clinging to hope will help him endure this, she'll grant him that mercy. "I think you're right," she adds. "It's a good sign."

At least, it's not a bad one.

"Your feet are cold," he whispers, and she laughs.

"Shall I move them?"

"Don't even suggest it. I have dreamed of waking with you in my arms like this."

"Have you really?" She traces her fingers along his chest. "For how long?"

"Far too long."

"I would have been horrified had I known."

"You seemed pretty horrified to find yourself bound with me mere days ago," he teases. Then he sobers. "I hope you're not horrified anymore."

"I'm pretty sure horrified doesn't describe what I was feeling last night."

Far from it.

"That's a relief. With the way you swore like a drunken warrior, I wasn't sure."

She smacks his chest. "I did not!"

"I believe your exact words were, 'Oh my whistling f—'"

She covers his mouth as his eyes alight with mirth.

"I...may have said something like that," she admits. "I think I've spent too much time in the barracks."

He pulls her hand away from his mouth. "I agree. You'll have to sleep with me from now on."

Her smile falters, and he runs his hand over his face and sighs.

"Let's pretend everything is going to be all right," she says softly. "Enjoy our time here together, whether we wake or not. As Mera says, let's not borrow trouble."

His throat bobs as he nods. Is he about to fall apart again? If he does, she'll be here to pick up the pieces.

"My light will fill your darkness," she whispers.

He tightens his arms around her again. "Your light is the only thing keeping me going."

Perhaps a distraction would help.

"How about a warm bath and then breakfast?"

He stills beside her, his muscles tensing. "When you say bath—"

"I'll need you to keep the water warm."

He turns his head to see her face better. "Just the water?"

"Yes. Just the water."

"Oh." The look of disappointment on his face is so comical she can't help laughing, and a grin slips across his mouth. "Are you mocking me again, my queen?"

"Never."

Then his lips find hers in a gentle kiss. "I don't believe that for a minute."

The day passes, slowly at times, more quickly at others. They eat and laugh and make love as the sun journeys toward the horizon.

If this is to be their last day, Nestraya wouldn't change the utter perfection of it, though the longer they linger, the more hope swells within her own heart.

As stars appear in the night sky, Lorial points at the brightest light dotting the inky blackness and the one beside it. "That one's Nestraya, and that one is Lorial." He keeps his voice soft. Low. Silky like the sheets he ran over her bare flesh earlier.

She shivers at the thought.

"Lorial and Nestraya," he says. "They belong together forever. You can't separate them. Is that how the story goes?"

"Yes, my love. That's exactly how the story goes."

Then, once again, the light vanishes, and a sea of dull pain is left in its wake.

45

AFTERMATH

"They're waking."

The relief in Rafelis's voice draws Lorial back to the Wildthorne Woods.

"Nestraya," he whispers.

"No, don't sit up," Rafelis says. "Give the dizziness time to pass."

No wonder the trees are swaying.

"Nestraya," he says again.

Mother's voice arises from nearby. "She lives. It was close. I thought…" In an uncharacteristic show of emotion, a sob lodges in Mother's throat. "I feared I would lose you both."

Lorial reaches toward her to grasp her hand. "How is she?"

A soft moan sounds, and Lorial turns his head. Nestraya lies under a pile of furs, a grimace on her beautiful face.

But she lives.

"It's all right, my elfling," Mother murmurs as she caresses Nestraya's brow. "I'm here."

"Mera? Where's—" Her words cut off in a hiss of pain.

Forget the dizziness. Lorial rolls to his knees, closing his eyes against the whirling around him as he crawls to her side. "I'm here, my love."

She relaxes at the sound of his voice.

"Up-update on the b-battle?" she asks.

Before Lorial can express his thoughts on her question, Mother speaks again. "Just rest, my elfling. Corivos and Quilian have everything well in hand."

"Is it...over?" Nestraya asks.

"Yes," Rafelis says. "It's over. You need to rest, my queen."

"Lorial?" Nestraya whispers as she blinks up at him.

"I'm right here, and I'm not leaving."

She shakes her head. "You're the king now. Go. I'll be fine."

"You can't be serious. I'm not—"

"I didn't almost die regaining your throne so you could sit here, you oaf of a man." A faint smile ghosts her face before she grimaces again, and he stares at her. When he glances at Mother and Rafelis, they're both barely holding back their own smiles.

"I'll sit with her, my king," Rafelis offers. "She's past the danger now. I promise."

"Go," Nestraya says.

Reluctantly, Lorial presses a kiss to her forehead before rising. As he gazes at the battlefield around him, his stomach turns.

So much loss of life. Families whose loved ones will never return. And for what?

Anger fills him as his eyes alight on Hothniel's broken shell. Someone draped a jacket over his upper body, but the brutal effects of Nestraya's plant magic are obvious in the unnatural bend of his legs.

Other high-born warrior elves lie in pools of blood—some of them the sons and daughters of the elves serving on Lorial's Council of Elders.

What is he supposed to tell them now? What is he supposed to do?

Nestraya was right. This will not be easy. They may have won a battle, but the real war has only begun.

Turning from the high borns, he can barely bring himself to gaze out over the lines of low-born elf bodies his loyal warriors carry away from the battlefield as healers, warrior class or otherwise, kneel over the fallen elves who haven't yet succumbed to their wounds.

At least the humans haven't returned. Yet. Lorial's magic may be enough to keep them at bay for now, but it's only a matter of time before the inventive humans develop some new technology even Lorial will struggle to fight against.

They need lasting peace. Negotiated peace.

That's a problem for tomorrow, though. Today, Lostariel needs his focus.

Corivos stands near the sidelines, directing several low-born elves from Lorial's elite warrior band, and Lorial pushes his feet forward.

Relief slips across Corivos's face when he spots Lorial walking toward him. "How is she?"

"Cranky."

Corivos nods. "Good. I have scouts at the border, so we'll know if the humans return. Quilian and Deridyn are heading up the...clean-up efforts." Corivos sighs, and Lorial claps him on the shoulder.

"Thank you. For everything."

"I could say the same."

Lorial gazes off toward the woods where the high borns who left their posts ran. "Were you able to identify any of the warriors who abandoned the fighting?"

"I've separately interviewed a number of our low-born warriors. I have a few names to cross-reference against the fallen high borns in addition to the elves I recognized myself. Nestraya can tell you more than I can. She mingled with high borns more than I did."

Lorial nods.

"I sent out a few warriors to try tracking them," Corivos continues, "but they didn't find anyone. If those high borns are smart, they're long gone by now. It'll be a challenge to root them out."

"If anyone can manage, you can, Corivos. Of that, I have no doubt."

"I appreciate your confidence." He stifles a yawn.

"I don't suppose I can convince you to rest?"

Corivos grins. "Will you threaten to demote me?"

"Not a chance. I need you too much. I can't vouch for my queen, though. Perhaps steer clear of her for now."

Corivos chuckles, and soon Lorial leaves him to his business directing the other elves.

"My king."

Lorial turns toward Deridyn's voice. "What is it?"

"I just spoke with our queen, and she said to speak to you. What do you wish us to do with the humans left behind?"

Lorial frowns. "Are they alive?"

"Some of them. Most who live are injured."

Lorial exhales through pursed lips. Perhaps some goodwill might improve their relationship with the humans.

"Treat their dead with respect and heal those that need healing. See if we can get some wagons to transport the bodies across the border. As soon as possible, I want their people returned to them unharmed."

Deridyn eyes him for a few moments, and Lorial fidgets under the older man's gaze.

"Is that a bad idea?"

It takes Deridyn a few moments to respond. "I knew Cerian Thariosi well, my king. He would be proud to number you among his House. I'll see to it personally that the humans are treated with respect."

The man departs, and Lorial watches him go. Then, with a sigh, he walks toward the thick of things and approaches Quilian.

"My king. Forgive me for abandoning my post a moment ago. I saw you up and about, and I wanted to check on my qu—"

Lorial holds up a hand. "We are family, Quilian. Call me Lorial. How can I help?"

Quilian gapes at him for a moment before finding his head. "Yes. Right. Are you certain? You're the king. No one expects you to—"

Lorial holds up a hand again. "If you approve, I would like to send a message that even a king is not above helping where help is needed."

"You hardly need my approval, but you have it. Perhaps with the humans? That would send the strongest message, I think. To both sides. I overheard you're planning to send them back to their prince."

"I am. You think this is wise? Deridyn seemed to approve."

"To think the King of Lostariel is asking me for advice." Quilian chuckles and shakes his head.

"Your brother's son is asking. How about that?" Lorial looks hesitantly at him, awaiting his response.

After a moment, Quilian nods. "He would gladly call you family, Lorial. As do I. As for the humans, the last thing we need is war with our southern neighbors. Lostariel is in turmoil. Anything to generate goodwill should be grasped at while we rebuild. If you keep the wounded humans as prisoners, their people will return stronger than ever."

Lorial nods. "That's what I thought. Thank you."

They part ways, and Lorial threads a path across the gully separating the human and elf lines. Warriors bow their heads as he passes, a surprising level of awe on many of their faces.

Clearly, they see him differently now than they did mere days ago, though whether it's because of his magic or his choice of a binding partner or some combination of both is impossible to say. Probably the latter.

The fallen warriors are hard to look at. Could he have done more to save them? It's a question that will haunt him for the rest of his life.

As he approaches the humans, some eye him warily as if they're afraid of him. Probably with good reason.

He stops in front of Deridyn. "How can I help?"

Deridyn doesn't question him. He just nods. "We have a wagon coming. My warriors have been lining the dead up over there. Perhaps you can use your magic to load them for transport? Show these frightened humans you're not the monster they seem to fear you are?"

Lorial nods. He can do that easily enough, though it's hard to think about.

"Which able human ranks highest?" Lorial asks, but before Deridyn can respond, a man with a sling steps forward. He appears older like Quilian, but reckoning human years is not a skill Lorial has mastered.

"I'm Major Farnsworth. What do you mean to do with us?" the man asks in Nunian.

"You understand Elvish?" Lorial says carefully in the human tongue.

"Some. I don't speak it well. Your Nunian is better than my Elvish."

Not surprising. Elvish is difficult for non-native speakers to master. Not that Lorial has ever needed to speak much Nunian. It's a good thing it's him and not Nestraya. For all her strengths, language learning is not one of them.

"We will be returning you and your people to Nunia as soon as possible," Lorial says.

"In exchange for what?"

"Peace, I hope."

The man looks surprised, but then his eyes darken. "That's all Prince Gerault has ever wanted. With all due respect, your raiders started this."

"Yes. On behalf of Lostariel, I apologize. Tell your prince it is a problem I mean to deal with as quickly as possible."

The man eyes him skeptically but says nothing more, and soon, Lorial sets about helping load the fallen humans to return to their kin.

46

STARDUST

Nestraya groans. "I am fine, Lorial. Stop hovering."

"You almost died. I will hover. Now eat. It will help."

He's so infuriating at times.

With a huff, she takes the tin of nuts he procured somewhere and shoves a handful in her mouth as she glares at him.

"Shall I find a leaf to caress your skin?" He grins at her, and she throws a nut at his face.

"My plant magic is fine. I'm just ready to help. You've been keeping busy all day while I sit here doing nothing."

"Did Healer Cadowyn clear you to get up?"

"He's been too busy healing everyone else. As he should be. But I've checked my wound with my own magic, and—"

Lorial frowns. "So it's not your plant magic. It's your life magic. How much did you expend healing yourself?"

They stare at each other for a moment before she turns away. It wasn't that much.

"Lean forward," he says, and she looks at him curiously.

"Why?"

"Because I'm going to help you."

Carefully keeping the furs in place, she does as he says, and he slides between her and the large cedar she was leaning against. Then he unfastens the bindings on his jacket, exposing the muscles of his chest. "What are you wearing under these furs?"

"Not much. They seem to have cut my leathers off me."

He gently pushes the furs aside, exposing her back to the cool evening air before pulling her against his chest.

That does feel good.

"You won't set anything on fire, will you?" she asks, only partially teasing.

He laughs, and the sound vibrates against her back. "I seem to have adequate control at the moment." Wrapping his arms around her over the furs covering what's left of her small clothes, he leans his cheek against her temple. "Why did you send Deridyn to me earlier? You could have told him what to do with the humans."

"They respected you more because it was your idea. There was no doubt in my mind what you would decide."

He kisses her ear before settling in again. "What are we going to do?"

She sighs. "I don't know. We need to deal with the high borns who defied you, though."

"If we can find them. I hope with Hothniel gone, the border raids will stop. We have a temporary truce with the humans, but if elves keep attacking human cities, that will be short-lived."

"Perhaps you should consult the Tree of Memories when we return."

"That's a good idea."

She traces a pattern on his leathers over his thigh. "There's also the issue of an heir to consider."

"Careful. I might burn down the forest."

She laughs, but she stops teasing him with her touch.

"I'm not sure now is the best time," he says more seriously. "We have a lot of work to do. I need you by my side. And these are dangerous times. We both almost died. Twice. Do we really want to bring an elfling into the midst of all this turmoil?"

She sighs. "You need an heir, Lorial. Especially because we almost died."

"We don't need to decide right this minute. How are you feeling?"

She nestles against him and closes her eyes. "Better."

"Just sleep, my love. For an hour or two. When you wake, we'll have one of the healers examine you." He presses his lips to her ear again as memories of the way he caressed them and the rest of her in the heartlanding fill her thoughts. Weariness wins out, though, and soon the noises around her fade as she gives in to sleep.

"Nestraya, love. Wake up."

She blinks her eyes open in the dark woods lit by lanterns. It looks as though several warrior bands are getting ready to head out. Back to Darlei, probably.

"How long was I asleep?" Her throat is thick from her nap.

"A few hours. Healer Cadowyn examined your wound while you slept and cleared you to return to Windhaven with the low-born bands. The Outerlanders will stay and finish up while they guard the border just in case. I've left Deridyn in charge here. Quilian will lead the low borns under Corivos until you're ready to return to duty."

She nods against him as her stiff muscles beg to be stretched and used.

A stamping horse nearby draws her eyes, and then she does a double-take. It's not a horse.

"A unicorn? I thought the fae"—she clears her throat—"the Lothlesi are the only people to tame the unicorns."

"They are. This one was your first mother's. A gift to her from the Lothlesi people upon your birth. Deridyn has cared for it since your mother died. He brought it as a gift for his princess."

Nestraya gulps as she studies the pale gray creature. "I thought all unicorns were white."

Lorial shrugs. "Deridyn said something about it changing color the closer it got to Darlei. It used to be black."

"It takes on the color its owner's heart loves most," Quilian says from nearby, and Nestraya turns to him.

"My first mother's favorite color was black?"

Quilian laughs. "No. Elowyn loved blue. Her heart loved black. Just as yours loves silver. I'll let you sort it out."

Nestraya frowns as he ambles back to the warrior bands.

"Silver?" she says. "Why in the Wildthorne Woods would my heart love silver enough to change a unicorn's color?"

Behind her, Lorial shakes with laughter, and she smacks his leg.

"Stop laughing! What am I missing?"

"You tell me, Nestraya. Why would your mother love black?" He gently tugs on her braid. "Ebony and emeralds."

She closes her eyes and shakes her head at his mirth. "Don't get a big head, my king."

"Why would I do that? Because a unicorn knows how much you love my hair?"

"We're done with this conversation. Enjoy being twins with a unicorn."

He laughs again.

"Do you know what its name is?" she asks, ignoring his amusement.

"According to Deridyn, her name is Stardust. As soon as you're ready, we're going to ride her home. I've been told she'll carry us both easily."

Stardust drops her head and whinnies. She is beautiful.

"Mother brought you this." Lorial holds up a simple linen shirt. "I'll help you, all right?"

"I'm pretty sure I can dress myself."

"With everyone watching? Go right ahead."

She glances around. "Perhaps you could hold up one of these furs."

He shrugs. "Only if you wish me to. My queen."

She rolls her eyes. "Just do it."

With a grin, he extricates himself from behind her and helps her stand, and then, while he shields her, she quickly slips the shirt over her head.

She's a little dizzy, but she keeps that to herself. No need to give Lorial cause to make her sit back down.

At least he'll be on the unicorn, too, so she won't have to worry about falling off.

Slowly, she approaches Stardust, her palm outstretched. To her surprise, the unicorn nuzzles it as if reuniting with an old friend. The vaguest memory surfaces, and Nestraya tilts her head thoughtfully. "I know you. I learned to ride on you."

Stardust rubs her nose against Nestraya's neck, and Nestraya gently wraps her arms around the magical beast, trying to grasp at the memory, but it's gone.

"She knows you, too," Lorial says softly. "Let's get you in the saddle, all right?"

Before Nestraya can respond, his air magic wraps around her and lifts her off her feet.

Perhaps she's not hiding anything from him.

As she looks down at him from atop Stardust, he draws her hand to his lips.

Perhaps she doesn't want to hide from him. Not anymore.

It's a long ride back to Darlei, and they don't stop to rest partway as they did the other day. But Stardust is a gentle, strong mount, and she has no trouble carrying both Nestraya and Lorial such a distance through the woods.

Nestraya glances back at the wagons following behind them, full of the bodies of beloved sons, daughters, and binding partners who will never hold their loved ones again.

Tired and sore as Nestraya is, she sighs. "It's our job to bring sad tidings to the kin left behind."

Lorial's arm tightens around her. "Corivos has gathered their names and the names of their kin for us. I can do this alone if you wish to go home and rest."

"I'm First Nestraya, Queen of Lostariel. My place is by your side."

Together, they ride into Darlei. Elves line the streets, especially in the low-born parts of town. Many high-born homes are eerily quiet, though a few binding partners and mothers stand pale in their dressing gowns on the streets.

So many families torn apart.

"What do I tell them?" Lorial whispers as they come to a stop near the gathering crowd.

"To the low borns, the truth. That their loved ones died bravely for their king. And their new queen. And while it's a small comfort, their sacrifices herald a change in Lostariel. Their elflings will have a better future because of it."

"Most of these elves betrayed me."

"They didn't know what they were doing. They fought to protect the people they love. That's all their kin need know."

Exhaling slowly, Lorial nods, and Nestraya reaches for his hand.

"We'll do it together, my love."

47

SLEEP WELL, MY LOVE

By the time they trudge through Windhaven toward their private chambers, sunlight dances on the eastern horizon. Nestraya's wound aches, though Healer Cadowyn gave her his approval to resume her regular activities aside from sparring.

And other more intimate pastimes.

Not that she's thinking about intimacy right now. She just wants her bed. Grime and dried blood cover her, and the korathite on her face is probably a smeared mess. Occasional faint whiffs of vomit hit her nose, turning her stomach. A bath sounds glorious, but bed sounds better.

As she stumbles toward her chamber door, Lorial watches with an uncertain expression on his korathite-smudged face.

Whistling wind. She's bound now.

Before she can marshal her thoughts enough to say or do anything but stand there, Lorial reaches around her to open her door. "Let's get you cleaned up and in your bed."

She doesn't have the energy to do more than nod.

When he leads her to her private water closet, she doesn't protest. It would take too much effort.

He tugs the cord to call for water, and soon the water wielder on duty in the central water supply room for Windhaven sends enough warm water through the wooden pipes to fill the tub.

She usually just summons it with her own magic, but she's too exhausted to do anything of the sort and doesn't complain.

She also doesn't complain when Lorial strips off what's left of her clothes. His hands grow warm as they graze her skin, but he doesn't say anything, and neither does she.

Then she's in the glorious water.

Once again, he was right. She needed this. She'll sleep so much better after bathing.

He doesn't let her linger this time, though, drawing her from the water and handing her a fluffy towel while he searches her drawers for a sleeping gown.

"The second one down," she says softly, and he soon brings her one of the high-waisted, sleeveless black dresses she sleeps in when she's home. She pulls it over her head, and it falls just past her knees, the soft silk draping gracefully over her.

When she looks up, Lorial is staring at her, but he clears his throat and looks away.

She's too tired to care how awkward this feels. It's not as if they didn't experience each other completely in the heartlanding.

When she sways, he lifts her and carries her to the bed.

She's about to insist she's fine, but something prompts her to thank him instead. After lowering her to the familiar sheets, which he's already turned back, he tucks the blankets around her and presses a soft kiss to her lips. "Sleep well, my love."

When Nestraya wakes in her own bed, Lorial's arm drapes over her. He slept in here? She assumed he would go to his own chamber after he settled her this morning.

He clearly didn't.

She also expected to meet him in the heartlanding, but perhaps the magic felt they were doing fine bonding in the real world.

The sun illuminates the room around the lightweight drapes covering the windows, and Nestraya stretches her toes as she tries to get her bearings. It must be afternoon, judging by the angle of the sunlight pouring through the window.

Beside her, Lorial groans, his hand grasping a fistful of the silk at her waist.

"You stayed," she says as his eyelids flutter open. The korathite has been wiped clean from his face—he must have washed up after she did.

He stretches and rubs at his eyes. "Is that all right?"

"Yes. It's just strange having you in here."

His hand relaxes against her waist, and that boyish grin of his returns. "So I'm welcome in your bed?"

When his palm warms, she smiles at him. "As long as you don't set it on fire."

Immediately, he removes his hand, his grin fading, but she pulls it back.

"You don't have to hide when you're with me. I'll tell you if it's too hot. How's your shoulder?"

"Stiff and achy."

"Here." She presses her hand over his scar and gives him a small infusion of her healing magic. "How's that?"

He sighs. "Much better. Thank you."

Gently, she traces her fingers over the puckered skin. "We both have scars now."

"Reminders that we're stronger together?"

"I like that." She trails her touch along his neck to the tip of his ear, and his eyes slide shut as his fist closes around her gown again.

"I will set you on fire if you keep doing that."

Memories of their time in the heartlanding flood her, filling her with a gnawing ache, and when he leans down to kiss her, she slides her fingers into his hair and holds him close. His hand lies against her hip with its comforting heat.

Then he groans and pulls away. "I really am going to set you on fire. And I heard what Healer Cadowyn told you."

She sighs in frustration. "We also need to discuss the matter of an elfling."

They lie beside each other, staring at the ceiling, and he reaches for her hand. "We should go talk to the tree."

He's right. They don't have time to lie in bed all day.

He swings his legs to the floor, and she watches him get up—looks her fill at the flex of his muscles as he moves.

How did she not see him before?

When he offers her a hand, she takes it and lets him pull her to her feet.

He runs his finger under the strap of her sleeping gown and smiles. "I like this."

Her face grows warm under the intensity of his gaze as he looks at her, and she swallows. "I'll keep that in mind, my love."

Once more, they stand beside the ancient willow tree containing the memories of Lostariel's kings. It's a much quieter expedition this time. No guards hover nearby since the old ones abandoned Lorial along with most of the warrior elves that day in the woods, and no elves stand ready to mourn the passing of their king.

The sacredness of the place remains, though.

"Go ahead," Nestraya whispers as she takes Lorial's arm.

He doesn't move as he looks thoughtfully at the tree.

"What's wrong?" she asks.

"Nothing. I'm just curious about something." Gently, he removes her hand from his arm and steps away. "You try it."

"What? I'm not—"

"Just try."

There's no reason not to humor him, but the fact that he thinks she should try makes her question his sanity as she reaches for the hanging branches.

When they part for her, she gasps and pulls her hand away. "What just happened?"

"You happened, my love. Did you know that when this tree was enchanted, *estrassa* wasn't just a term of endearment? It carried legal and magical weight. An *estrassa* elfling was considered in every way equivalent to a biological elfling. Corivos told me so the other day."

"How does he know these things?"

Lorial laughs. "I have no idea. The important part, though, my love, is that from the tree's point of view, you have the same legal claim to the Westarian throne as I do."

"That's ridiculous. Queen consort. I'm the queen consort."

He gestures to the willow. "Tell that to the sacred tree."

She looks back at the branches where they remain magically parted for her. "This stays between the two of us. And the tree."

He nods. "If you insist. You know what that means, though?"

"What?"

"The Tree of Memories should talk to you as well."

A lump forms in her throat as she considers his words. "I could talk to Pera?"

"It's not quite like—" Lorial's words cut off, and he purses his lips. "We're not in the heartlanding. I can't tell you here."

"It's just his memories, isn't it?" she asks softly, and Lorial nods.

"I still think you should say what you need to say, my love," he whispers.

After taking a deep breath, she returns her gaze to the tree. Reaching for his hand, she steps into the circle of the Tree of Memories with him by her side as the branches close behind them.

The mist isn't as thick this time, though the bioluminescent flowers still dance to their own silent music. Hand-in-hand, Nestraya and Lorial walk toward the glowing trunk the way they did less than a week ago.

It seems as if years have passed since that night.

"Try talking to it," Lorial whispers to her.

She hesitates. This feels...like something not meant for her. As though she's a thief in the night trying to claim that which isn't hers.

"It won't hurt to try," Lorial says.

He's right, of course.

Her hand trembles as she extends it toward the light and waits for something to happen.

48

STRONGER TOGETHER

*N*estraya.

She gasps and almost pulls her hand back.
How he loved you.
She chokes on a sob. "Pera?"
Restoval's essence is with us, our young princess.
"I'm not a—"
You are estrassa *to a king.*
The tree says it so matter-of-factly that Nestraya almost laughs.
You would have been granted Restoval's throne had you been the one to carry his essence to us.
"What?"
This surprises you?
"What claim do I have on the throne of Lostariel?"
A claim on the king's heart.
"The law doesn't work that way anymore."
The magic does. In fact, we sense new magic in you. Forgive us for our mistake, our young queen. This development pleases your father's essence.
"Pera?"
He's here. Say what you need to say, our young queen.

"I'm sorry," she whispers. "I love you, Pera. I always have. I'm sorry I pushed you away."

Dear one, he knows all this. Do not let your regrets burden you.

He knew. He knew she loved him all along. A sob shakes her, and her hand falls.

Lorial's arms are there, wrapping around her and pulling her to his chest. "Slay your final demon, my love. He knew." He holds her until her crying slows. "Let's do this together. All right? We're stronger together."

She nods and wipes her face before extending her hand once again as Lorial twines his fingers with hers in the light.

Both together. This is a first, our young king and queen.

"We come seeking your wisdom." Lorial explains everything that's happened since they last visited the tree.

These are difficult things you've faced and overcome. Polanis wishes to express his disgust with you. We have silenced him.

Nestraya turns wide eyes to Lorial, but he just smiles.

"What should we do?" Lorial asks. "About the high-born traitors and their families?"

What did you do about the low-born traitors, our young king?

Lorial opens his mouth and then closes it again.

And the humans?

"I offered them amnesty."

Why?

"Because it was the right thing to do for Lostariel."

And for the traitors who stayed to fight you?

"Most no longer live."

So what message have you sent to all of Lostariel?

"Mercy," Nestraya whispers. "Or annihilation. The choice is theirs."

Indeed. Just remember, mercy and trust do not necessarily go hand in hand.

"So offer mercy, but watch our backs and root out treasonous activity?" Lorial asks.

"And do nothing stupid," Nestraya adds.

Your queen is wise, our young king. You would do well to listen to her. That is the wisdom for the ages.

Lorial laughs. "This I have gathered. Thank you, sacred tree."

"What of the humans?" Nestraya asks.

That future is bright because you will make it so, our young queen. We are weary now. Let us rest.

The light fades, and they lower their hands.

"That was surreal," she whispers. "Do you think we can talk about it?"

Lorial grins. "You mean about the fact that it only gave me the throne because I asked first? It was pretty obvious what you were discussing."

Laughter bubbles up inside her. "If only I had known!"

He tugs her close and circles his thumbs on her lower back. His hands are warm but not burning.

Yet.

His lopsided grin makes her belly flutter, and he leans toward her ear. "You're older than I am. I think I stole your throne."

"Usurper. Shall I challenge you for it?"

"I vote we share it. I'll just pretend it's mine so no one asks questions."

She laughs again before lacing her fingers behind his neck. "Deal. You should have asked Zelovon how to manage your fire."

His brows knit. "I'm not sure that's the sort of question the tree was designed for."

"It concerns the line of succession. Seems appropriate. I promised you an elfling, after all."

He pulls away and shakes his hands out while she struggles not to laugh.

"Maybe you're right," he mutters, glancing at the tree.

She takes his hands and cools them herself. "I don't want to wait. We aren't guaranteed tomorrow, Lorial. Didn't we learn that already? Who knows what this day may bring? And we have a message to send to all of Lostariel."

Her magic can barely keep up with his heat.

His brow knits. "I might need to talk to Mother, after all. Because I have no idea how long this tree takes to refresh its magic, and I have plans for you as soon as Healer Cadowyn clears you for—what did he call it? 'Other more intimate pastimes'?"

"Come on. We'll talk to her together."

His eyes turn serious as he gazes at her. "Stronger together, my love?"

"Yes, Lorial. Stronger together." Then, without letting go of his hands, she lifts her chin and presses her lips to his.

EPILOGUE
Ten Years Later

"Corivos told me. He knows everything."

Lorial looks down at the ebony-haired elfling walking beside him and laughs. "Does he?"

Tharios nods. "The heartbinding was even used to save an elfling's life before it was born. Or they tried, at least." His smile fades. "The life wielder's magic wasn't strong enough to hold the partial connection for very long."

Lorial frowns. "Corivos told you this?"

Tharios shrinks under his gaze. "I may have read that myself."

Lorial shakes his head and scoops the boy onto his shoulders. "Let's go find your mother. I need to tell her what the tree said."

"You know you can't tell her, Pera."

Right. It will have to wait until they meet in the heartlanding. He warms at the thought.

As they approach Windhaven, he jostles Tharios down his back so the boy doesn't hit his head on the doorframe.

"Where do you think Mera went?" Lorial asks.

"Probably her study. Corivos had news for her."

Lorial glances over his shoulder. "I think it's you that knows everything."

Tharios grins, and Lorial's heart warms at the glimpses of Nestraya that alight in their son's face, though Tharios has Lorial's eyes. Maybe the next one will have emerald eyes.

Someday. She promised him elflings, after all.

"She's definitely in her study," Tharios says.

"You can sense her?"

Tharios nods. "Barely. It's hard with you here."

Lorial laughs. "You sound like your mother."

Soon, they reach the door to Nestraya's study. Technically, it belongs to Corivos, but she never vacated it after they made Corivos First in her place, and Corivos didn't dare ask.

He's probably afraid she'll demote him if he does.

Lorial swings Tharios to the floor and pushes the door open. "Knock knock."

Nestraya's face brightens when she sees Tharios, but not before Lorial reads the frustration in her eyes.

"Back already? Did the flowers dance for you, my little love?"

Tharios nods happily as he climbs on the desk. "They sway in the wind, but there is no wind in the sacred tree. It must be magic."

Nestraya smiles at Lorial over their son's head before bopping Tharios's nose with her finger. "It sounds like you have it all figured out."

He nods solemnly.

"Why don't we go find Grandmera?" Lorial scoops Tharios up again. "I'll be right back," he mouths to Nestraya, and she nods.

A few minutes later, he returns alone.

"What darkens your light, my love?" he asks softly as he leans back against her desk, facing her.

Nestraya sighs. "There was another raid last week. I thought we flushed all the raiders out after the last skirmish."

"Elf raiders or human this time?"

"Elf. They wreaked havoc in Feressa again."

"We'll have to provide restitution."

Nestraya nods. "King Gerault requests a summit to discuss the matter."

Lorial breathes out through pursed lips. "At least he's not marching toward Darlei this time."

"I wouldn't blame him if he did. This is ridiculous. It's been ten years. The humans are losing patience. They took care of the human mercenaries Hothniel hired years ago. Now the only raids by humans are in response to elven aggression."

"Corivos said Gerault's queen lost another youngling within the womb last month. He's probably not eager to leave her right now."

"My heart goes out to them. So much loss and no heirs."

She gets a far-off look in her eyes, and Lorial draws her hand to his lips. "Thinking about your first mother?"

A smile ghosts across her face. "You know me too well. If only we could help them somehow. I'm not sure even our magic can keep a youngling alive in the womb, though."

Lorial stills. "What did you say?"

"Which part?"

"The part about magic. Tharios was just telling me someone attempted to use a heartbinding to keep an elfling alive within the womb."

"A heartbinding?" Nestraya leans back in her chair. "Fascinating. How does he know these things?"

Lorial grins. "He spends too much time around Corivos."

That draws out Nestraya's smile. "Did it work?"

Lorial shakes his head. "The life wielder's magic wasn't strong enough to maintain the heartbinding for long."

"It wouldn't work like a normal heartbinding. A youngling's heart can't consent. It would be a temporary holding of the initial stages of the magic, I imagine. Just enough to maintain the physical link until the youngling grew up. Think how much magic that would take." Nestraya shakes her head. "I'm amazed someone would even try."

"They must have been desperate."

Nestraya looks at him thoughtfully, and a sick feeling forms in the pit of his stomach.

"No," he says. "Don't even consider it."

"You brought it up. I should speak with Healer Cadowyn. See what he thinks."

She stands and starts for the door, but he reaches for her with his air magic.

"Really, Lorial?"

"Just come back for a minute."

He lets her go, and she steps between his knees.

"You realize what you're suggesting, right?" he asks. "Decades of you draining your life magic, and that's assuming it works. And the youngling would need a heart to bind to."

"So we provide one. You want peace? What better way to find it? Look what our own heartbinding has done for our people. An alliance between our elfling and their youngling? Lorial, this could be the perfect solution. And then we won't need to worry about who our elfling will bind with someday. People may have begrudgingly accepted us, but many are still wary of Tharios."

Lorial's hackles rise. "Which makes absolutely no sense."

"No." She sighs. "But what would our lives be without him? If we could give that to the human king and queen—"

"Decades, Nestraya. It would require decades from you. You couldn't spar or fight or do anything other than exist and keep up your magic stores."

"What's twenty years to an elf? Besides, we'd still have the heartlanding." She trails her finger along the fastenings of his leather vest, and his hands warm. He needs to let some of this heat off soon. At least Tharios didn't inherit his fire magic.

"Why are you so eager to do this?" he asks. "If it's even possible?"

She doesn't respond at first. Eventually, though, she meets his gaze. "The Tree of Memories told us our future with the humans would be a bright one because of me. Remember? Perhaps this is what it meant. What if Pera saw me doing this in one of his visions?"

"It won't solve all our problems, though. The raids won't just stop."

"You've spoken of creating a barrier between us and them to give us time to finish rooting out the raiders. Will twenty years be long enough?"

Lorial groans. "It had better be. Maybe my magic won't get so restless all the time with a barrier to take the edge off."

She leans her forehead against his shoulder and laughs. "You and your endless magic stores. I can feel your heat through my leathers."

"I know. I need to deal with it soon. It's been a few days since I worked it out."

She drapes her arms over his shoulders and looks into his eyes again. "Let's put Tharios to bed early."

His right hand starts to tingle, and he shakes it off. "I definitely need to let off some heat."

"While you do that, I'm going to talk to Healer Cadowyn."

"Nestraya—"

"Just talk. See if it's possible. What harm is there in exploring our options?"

He sighs. "None."

"If I kiss you, will I need to replace the rug again?"

He laughs. "You might."

She shrugs. "It's probably worth it." Then she presses her lips to his, all sweetness and berries and waterfalls.

His Nestraya.

Her Lorial.

Lorial and Nestraya.

They belong together forever. You can't separate them.

That's how the story goes.

The story doesn't end here! Follow the next generation in Elven Heartbound, *the Kindle Vella sensation that started it all! (Keep reading to learn more!) Thank you so much for going on this journey with me. I never imagined when I created a little tale about a human princess and her elven prince that the story would catapult to the top of the charts on Kindle Vella and inspire more companion books than I have time to write. For now, I will leave you with this: you are who you are, and who you are is enough. I'll see you in the heartlanding! -Elizabeth xoxo*

ELVEN HEARTBOUND

A Serial Novel

Born of elven magic. Bound to an elven prince. All her life, Arisanna has been destined to wed the son of the elf king, and now the elves have come to collect. Nothing, however, goes as expected when the elves arrive to claim her. Despite their misunderstandings, Arisanna agrees to wed the aloof elf prince with whom she's been heartbound since before her birth. Is the prince as hard as he seems? Or is there more to him than meets the eye?

Elven Heartbound is a serial novel on Amazon's Kindle Vella platform, and it picks up twenty-three years after the end of Lorial & Nestraya. The first three chapters are always free! To find out more, visit www.elizabethash.com/elven-heartbound or visit Kindle Vella to start reading now!

MY TIME OR YOURS

King's Road Book One

Save a kingdom? Or sacrifice everything to save a man who could never be hers?

In a world where magic is all but extinguished, Bria and Rogue have one chance to change everything. Using the last vestiges of magic, they travel a hundred years into the past with one goal: change a crucial moment in history.

If they succeed, they could bring back magic, restore kingdoms, and prevent one hundred years of war.

But the risk to the man Bria loses her heart to—a man who belongs to the past, whose future is already written—is too great. When the time comes, will she put his life at risk to save kingdoms? Or will she sacrifice everything to save him?

And will he ever forgive her if she does?

The King's Road series:

One man's journey to fulfill his mother's dying wish transforms into an epic adventure across time as the Westwood family comes together to right the wrongs of the past and ensure a better future for everyone. Full of swoony romance, sword fights, magic, family, forgiveness, redemption, and plot twists galore, the King's Road series will have you hanging on until the very end. Find out more at www.elizabethash.com/kings-road-series. Start the journey today in e-book or paperback on Amazon or in serial format on Kindle Vella.

A Dance of Sand and Magic

A King's Road Serial Novel

This handsome prince I barely know wants to marry me, but his magicless world is so different from my own. Does he want me for a weapon or for his wife? I worry he may fear me when he finds out how powerful I truly am. And will the ancient traditions his father esteems come between us if I agree to become Jamar's future queen? But will my heart ever be the same if I let him go?

A Dance of Sand and Magic is a serial novel on Amazon's Kindle Vella platform. It takes place in the King's Road world a century before My Time or Yours begins. The first three chapters are always free! Find out more at www.elizabethash.com/a-dance-of-sand-and-magic or visit Kindle Vella to start reading now!

DID SOMEONE SAY BONUS CONTENT?

Want to receive bonus content and updates about all your favorite Elizabeth Ash characters right in your inbox? Visit elizabethash.com/newsletter to sign up today!

THANK YOU!

I never planned to write this book, but when I met Lorial and Nestraya in my *Elven Heartbound* serial, I knew their story needed to be told. And it turned into so much more than I ever imagined. Squeezing a full-length novel into my busy schedule led to many moments of pure craziness, though! It wouldn't have been possible without the help and support of some of the important people in my life.

First and foremost, my husband. You've shouldered so many extra chores and kept us fed while I've walked around in a daze, dreaming of characters and plot and writing and editing and doing everything else that goes into publishing a novel. Thank you for always supporting my dream and for not complaining too much when you got romance instead of a battle scene!

My beautiful girls. Every story I write contains a little bit of you. As I repeat the refrain over and over throughout *Lorial & Nestraya* and *Elven Heartbound* that you are enough, it's always with you in mind. I desperately hope that you hold on to the knowledge that you are exactly who you were always meant to be, and who you are is enough. I love you to the moon and back, and that will never change.

My parents. You are my rocks. I couldn't do this without all of your support. From loving on my girls to planning birthday parties and remembering all the little details I always seem to forget, you are my heroes, and I love you desperately.

My writing friends who keep me sane. Or dive into insanity with me on those IG chats that last long into the night as we discuss anything and everything related to our stories and this crazy writing journey we're all traveling. These friendships have been the best part of becoming an author!

And last, but certainly not least, my Lord and Savior, without whom I am nothing. All praise to You.

About the Author

Elizabeth Ash writes fantasy romance and romantic fantasy fiction with a smattering of time travel, oodles of humor, and lots of romance that doesn't end when a couple says, "I do." Plus elves. Lots of elves.

When she's not busy writing, she loves reading, playing tabletop games, eating nachos, and walking around with her own life soundtrack playing on repeat through her ever-present earbuds.

Elizabeth lives with her husband and two children in the middle of the woods in the Pacific Northwest, where she keeps a wary eye out for any sign of Sasquatch.

elizabethash.com
elizabeth@elizabethash.com
Follow on:
Facebook.com/elizabethashbooks
Instagram.com/elizabethash_books
Amazon.com/author/elizabethash

Made in United States
Troutdale, OR
03/29/2024